A president of OUDS, Simon Brett spent nine years as a producer with BBC Radio Light Entertainment, before leaving to become Entertainment Producer with LWT. He now writes full time and is the author of seventeen Charles Paris novels as well as the Mrs Pargeter series; he is also the creator of the BBC radio series *After Henry* and *Dear Diary*, as well as the bestselling *Little Sod* books. Simon Brett lives in Arundel, Sussex, with his wife.

By the same author

CAST, IN ORDER OF DISAPPEARANCE
SO MUCH BLOOD
STAR TRAP
AN AMATEUR CORPSE
A COMEDIAN DIES
THE DEAD SIDE OF THE MIKE
SITUATION TRAGEDY
MURDER UNPROMPTED
MURDER IN THE TITLE
NOT DEAD, ONLY RESTING
A BOX OF TRICKS
(stories)
DEAD GIVEAWAY
WHAT BLOODY MAN IS THAT?
A SERIES OF MURDERS
CORPORATE BODIES
A RECONSTRUCTED CORPSE
SICKEN AND SO DIE
DEAD ROOM FARCE

CRIME WRITERS
AND OTHER ANIMALS

Simon Brett

ORION

An Orion paperback
First published in Great Britain by Victor Gollancz in 1998
This paperback edition published in 1999 by Orion Books Ltd,
Orion House, 5 Upper St Martin's Lane, London WC2H 9EA

ISBN: 0 75282 731 6

Printed and bound in Great Britain by
Clays Ltd, St Ives plc

'Happy Christmas, Darling – and Goodbye!' first appeared in the
Daily Mail, 1994; 'Best Behaviour' first appeared in the CWA
anthology *Whydunit*, Severn House, 1997; 'The Man Who Got the
Dirt' first appeared in *The Man Who . . .* , edited by H. R. F.
Keating, Macmillan, 1992; 'A Little Learning' first appeared in *A
Classic English Crime*, edited by Tim Heald, Pavilion Books, 1990;
'Political Corrections' first appeared in *A Classic Christmas Crime*,
edited by Tim Heald, Pavilion Books, 1995; 'Letter to his Son' first
appeared in *Winter's Crimes 18*, edited by Hilary Hale, Macmillan,
1986; 'False Scent' first appeared in *Midwinter Mysteries I*, edited
by Hilary Hale, Scribners (UK), 1991; 'The Battered Cherub' first
appeared in *Winter's Crimes 21*, edited by Hilary Hale, Macmillan,
1989; 'Ways to Kill a Cat' first appeared in *Malice Domestic 6*,
edited by Beth Foxwell, Pocket Books, 1997; 'A Good Thing' first
appeared in *Ellery Queen's Mystery Magazine*, 1996.

CONTENTS

HAPPY CHRISTMAS, DARLING –
AND GOODBYE! 7

BEST BEHAVIOUR 33

THE MAN WHO GOT THE DIRT 46

A LITTLE LEARNING 72

POLITICAL CORRECTIONS 84

LETTER TO HIS SON 114

FALSE SCENT 134

THE BATTERED CHERUB 161

WAYS TO KILL A CAT 186

A GOOD THING 214

HAPPY CHRISTMAS, DARLING – AND GOODBYE!

'We're going to kill him,' Natalie announced.

Trevor looked shocked. 'Kill George? But—'

'Well, come on, he's never going to divorce me. How else can you and I be together – for ever?'

'Things're OK like they are now ... aren't they?' Trevor suggested tentatively. 'We see each other every day as it is.'

But his objection was quickly blasted away. 'It's not just being together that matters. We need George's money.'

Trevor bridled. 'I'm sorry I don't make more. They keep saying the recession in building's over, but I don't see any signs of it. In a year or two perhaps things'll pick up, and I'll be able to keep you in the manner to which you've become accustomed.'

Natalie's hand was instantly stroking his thigh, soothing away the childlike hurt in his voice. 'I'm not criticizing you, darling. You're everything I've ever wanted in a man.'

He was. Ten years younger than her, with the easy strength of a manual worker. Dark curly hair, brown eyes. Sometimes Natalie couldn't believe her luck.

Trevor was pretty happy with what he saw, too. He liked older women. He knew the blondeness of her hair was assisted, but that, and the fine tracery of lines which spread around her eyes when she smiled, only added to her appeal.

'All I want from George,' Natalie continued, 'is his money. God knows, I deserve some payoff for all those years I've put up with being married to that sexless wimp. And I want *us* to be able to spoil ourselves a bit. I hate having to think about scrimping and saving all the time.'

'But there must be another way. Does he have to be killed?'

'Oh yes.' Natalie nodded decisively. 'He has to be killed. Down here at the cottage. Over Christmas.'

It was not an unusual triangle. So far as Natalie Marshall was concerned, her marriage had been dead in the water for a long time. When they'd first met, George had bowled her over with the force of his devotion, and in the numbness which followed the suicide of her first husband Robert, Natalie had been easily persuaded to accept George's proposal of marriage. After the wedding, however, she had discovered that although her new husband's protestations of love continued unabated, they found little physical expression. George Marshall was just not very interested in sex. In marrying Natalie, he had achieved the possession he coveted, but his desire for her seemed to be fulfilled by the fact of ownership alone.

So Natalie, frustrated, bored and forty, had fallen like a stone for Trevor Roache when the younger man came to refurbish the bathroom of the Marshalls' country cottage in West Sussex. Conveniently, he was their next-door neighbour, and indeed their only near neighbour. Conveniently, his wife had just walked out on him after ten years of marriage. Less conveniently, she'd left him with two children of eight and six. Still, you couldn't have everything, and Natalie was extremely satisfied with what she did have. After fifteen years of her husband's minimal interest in sex, Trevor's uncomplicated and dependable lust was like a breath of fresh air.

She made no attempt to hide the affair. She knew she had found the man she'd spent her life searching for, and presented George with the facts the evening of the day that she and Trevor had first gone to bed together. Her husband was, as ever, infuriatingly reasonable about it. He still loved Natalie, he announced, but he would not stand in the way of her happiness.

Since selling the family engineering firm at a large profit, George no longer worked, and he already spent much of his time in their London flat. What he did when he was up there Natalie neither knew nor cared. She never worried that her husband might be unfaithful to her. No woman was going to want anyone as short and bald and boring and passionless as fifty-eight-year-old George Marshall.

When he was informed of his wife's affair he announced without rancour that he'd stay in London and not come back to the cottage until 'this thing's burnt itself out'.

For Natalie, who found each new encounter with Trevor only added fuel to the flames of her passion, this was the ideal solution. She had the pretty flint-faced cottage to herself, George had left her the Volvo, and her lover's house was only fifty yards away. Nor did Trevor's children get in the way of their affair; they held little interest for him, and he farmed them out whenever possible to school friends whose parents took pity on his single state. No, in many ways Natalie's situation offered her everything she could have dreamed of.

Except for money. Not that George exactly kept her short. He still looked after the domestic bills and gave her a generous housekeeping allowance, but the awareness of that huge fortune of his that she wasn't sharing niggled away at Natalie like a rotten tooth.

For a while she nursed hopes of getting a divorce and, with it, a substantial financial settlement from her husband.

Though George was entirely blameless in the situation, Natalie knew what could be achieved by the right sort of expensive lawyer. She wrote to her husband more than once, itemizing the benefits of making their separation permanent and official. But George, usually so mild and malleable, proved stubbornly resistant to the idea of divorce.

His response at first just irritated, but gradually came to infuriate her. She felt a mounting sense of injustice. If he'd wanted her, it might have been different. As it was, George's attitude was pure dog in the manger. He had no use for her himself, but he didn't want anyone else to have her. He still thought of his wife as his property, and George Marshall was very possessive of his property.

It was out of Natalie's sense of injustice that the idea of killing her husband was born. At first just a casual, almost whimsical, fantasy, it quickly hardened into a positive intention. George's death would solve all her problems. It would be much better than divorce; if they were still married when he died, his jubilant widow would collect the lot.

Natalie Marshall began to plan her husband's murder.

On Christmas Eve she rang the flat at a time when she knew George would be out. Regular as clockwork – and about as interesting – in his habits, he always went out at two in the afternoon for what he insisted on calling his 'constitutional'. In Sussex it was a walk through the woods, in London through the park; in both cases he arrived back exactly forty minutes after his departure.

Natalie knew there was only one message that would bring George down to the cottage, and that was the one she left on the answering machine. She manufactured quite a convincing sob in her voice as she spoke the words.

'George, darling, it's me, calling at two-fifteen. You were right. My affair with Trevor's come to an end. And he's . . .

taking it very badly. I'm ... I'm really worried about what he might do, George. Look, after what's happened between us, I know I've no right to ask you this ... but is there any chance you could come down ... today? And if you do come ... a purely domestic detail, but the ventilation tube on the tumble drier's broken ... could you try and get a replacement? I'm sorry about these last few months, but ... please come down. I'll try to make everything up to you – and give you a happy Christmas, darling.'

She felt confident she'd judged the effect just right. The sudden switch to the domestic detail of the tumble drier was a bit abrupt, but it had been necessary. And George's love of DIY was so strong she felt sure he'd respond to the appeal.

When she'd left her message, she switched on the answering machine at the cottage and sat by the phone, listening impassively when her husband rang back at two forty-five. The boring ordinariness of his voice, as ever, set her teeth on edge.

'Hello, Natalie darling, it's me. I can't tell you how delighted I was to hear your message. I've just got to get some stuff together – I'll pick up the tumble-drier part, don't worry – and I'll be with you as soon as possible. I should be able to catch the four-twenty train. I'll get a cab from the station and be with you about six-thirty. Darling, this is the most amazing surprise I'm ever likely to have.'

Don't you believe it, darling – you've got an even more amazing one coming, thought Natalie with a grim little smile, and then went off to type a letter on George's word processor.

George Marshall looked thoughtful after he had put the phone down. Then he did what was necessary to the answering machine and started to get together the things he would need for a Christmas visit to his wife.

Neatly filed in his desk were all the letters that Natalie had written to him since they separated. He riffled through them, his eyes snagging on hurtful phrases: '. . . and I never want to see you again . . .'; '. . . so far as I'm concerned, anything there ever was between us has long gone . . .'; '. . . why can't you just accept that the whole thing's over . . .'

George Marshall made a careful selection from the letters and put them in his pocket. He packed a few clothes for himself, and put in a pair of Natalie's stiletto-heeled shoes which she'd left in the flat after some long-forgotten London function.

He got a cab to a nearby shopping centre. It was crowded with panicked last-minute present-buyers. Carols washed over the public areas. Weary Santas rang hearty handbells. Groups of giggling secretaries and raucous young men meandered in the boozy aftermath of office parties.

George knew exactly where to go for the tumble-drier ventilation hose, and knew exactly which model was required. All kinds of machinery fascinated him. He then went on to a supermarket where he loaded up with a packet of mince pies, a pot of brandy butter, a bottle of champagne and one of brandy. Finally, he entered a lingerie shop and purchased a sexy silk basque, suspender and stocking set. He hailed another cab and reached Victoria Station in time to catch the four-twenty train.

There was a Father Christmas costume hanging in the hall of Trevor's cottage when Natalie called round at four-thirty. 'Kids always insist I do the full number when I fill their stockings,' he explained. 'Have to dress up for them. It's daft – I swear they're never awake to see me when I'm in the kit. Still, the little pains take it all very seriously – leave out a glass of brandy and a mince pie for Santa, carrot for the reindeer. They like their silly rituals.'

'Where are they now?' asked Natalie.

'Round at a friend's. Being brought back nineish.'

'Did you find that sleeping draught?'

'Uh-huh.' He produced a bottle. 'My wife used to give it to the blighters when they were teething. Didn't have much effect on them after a while, they built up an immunity, but it's powerful stuff. I tried a spoonful once when I had toothache and it knocked me out for, like, twelve hours.'

'Good,' said Natalie.

As she reached out for the bottle, Trevor took her hand and drew her close to him. She saw the familiar spark of lust in his brown eyes.

'Later,' she said, planting a little kiss on his nose. 'We'll have earned it later.'

When she got back to her cottage, Natalie once again dialled the number of the London flat. As soon as she heard George's voice on the answering machine, she used the remote control to play back any messages that might have been left. There were none. Good, she thought, that meant he'd wiped hers.

She put the phone down, waited a moment, then pressed the last number redial button. At the tone she left another message on the machine.

'George, this is Natalie. I'm begging you, please don't come to the cottage. I know you say you're in a terrible state, but your coming down here is not going to help either of us. Our marriage is over, you know it, and no melodramatic gestures from you are going to make any difference to that. I love Trevor, and you're just going to have to accept that fact. Please see reason and stay in London over Christmas. Goodbye.'

The children's sleeping draught had a sickly fruity flavour, but the brandy's powerful taste smothered it. Natalie mixed the proportions carefully in the brandy bottle and then got out the ingredients to make brandy butter. George had a sweet tooth; he could never resist brandy butter.

Her husband was almost gleeful when he got out at the familiar station and felt the sting of frost on his face. There were few passengers, not the commuter hordes that would have been travelling most other weekdays. But now most working people seemed to assume Christmas Eve was an automatic part of their holiday entitlement. George did not approve of that kind of thing. He'd grafted hard all his working life and had earned his current leisure and prosperity. He was determined to enjoy them both to the full.

In high spirits he got into a waiting cab and gave its driver the familiar address. Could be just like old times, thought George Marshall.

At six-fifteen, Natalie went up to the bathroom and washed her face with soapy water. Deliberately she kept her eyes open. The soap stung like mad, but left a satisfactory redness around her lids. She dampened a handkerchief and tucked it in her sleeve, then dishevelled her hair a little. The face reflected in the bathroom mirror looked suitably traumatized. When she heard the doorbell ring downstairs, she added a dash of contrition to her expression.

George stood on the doorstep, blinking through his spectacles. The coloured Christmas lights she'd draped over the porch reflected off his bald head. He looked even shorter than Natalie remembered. And she'd forgotten how much she hated the sight of him.

'I didn't use my keys. Didn't want to startle you.'

'That was very thoughtful.'

Natalie was still for a moment, swallowing down the distaste for what she had to do. Then, as if impulsively, with a little strangled sob in her voice, she reached forward to enfold her husband's plump shoulders. 'Oh, George, can you ever forgive me?'

'Yes, of course,' he replied, as if he were soothing an over-excited pet. 'Of course I can.'

He looked up to where a sprig of silver-ribboned mistletoe hung from the porch light. 'Well, there's an invitation,' he chuckled, as his mouth nuzzled towards hers. 'Happy Christmas, darling.'

Natalie steeled herself for the touch of his lips. She had forgotten how repellent and slug-like they were, but managed to simulate some enthusiasm in her response. Then she drew back and looked at her husband, her face a mask of suffering and apology.

'Happy Christmas, darling,' said Natalie Marshall. 'Come in and let me get you a brandy.'

Except for the detail that Natalie had decided to murder her husband, it was almost as if George Marshall had never been away. As soon as he arrived at the cottage that Christmas Eve, he instantly took over domestically, scurrying straight into the kitchen with his carrier bag of supermarket goodies to rustle up a snack for the two of them. It was with difficulty that Natalie dissuaded him from immediately fitting the new ventilation hose on to the tumble drier. George Marshall was back in his own home and back into his role as boring homemaker. Every moment she spent in his company, Natalie hated him more and became more aware of the differences between her husband and her lover, Trevor.

Still, I don't have to put up with it for long, she comforted herself. By this time tomorrow, George will be dead, I'll be in line to inherit all his money and there'll be nothing in the way of Trevor's and my happiness.

She followed George into the kitchen and indicated the bottle of brandy on the dresser. Her intention had been to fill her husband up with the drugged fluid as quickly as possible, but George's dutiful domesticity made this impossible. He said he'd settle down with a drink once he'd knocked up their little snack. Natalie must be feeling dreadful after what'd happened. She should just put her feet up, and he'd sort out everything in the kitchen. He ushered his wife back into the sitting room, sat her in an armchair, placed another log on the fire and put a glass of champagne into her hand.

Natalie sipped her drink and bided her time. The delay did not worry her unduly. She still felt confident her plans would work. There was no danger that she herself might inadvertently get drugged. Natalie never drank brandy – it was George's favourite tipple – and her constant dieting, even more important now her body had Trevor to admire it, ruled out the possibility of her touching the brandy butter.

She switched on the television and surfed quickly through the channels, but nothing caught her attention. Jovial game-show hosts in Santa suits did not fit with her current mood and preoccupations. The traditional red costume and beard did give her an idea, though. She and Trevor enjoyed dressing up for sex. Maybe that night she'd make love to Father Christmas. The thought gave her a warm anticipatory glow.

George soon came bustling in with a loaded tray. Boringly predictable, he'd done scrambled egg on toast for them. More satisfactorily, from Natalie's point of view, he'd also brought in a plate of mince pies and a large dish of brandy butter. The doctored bottle of brandy and a balloon glass were also on the tray.

'Oh, got something for you,' George remembered just before he sat down. He disappeared into the hall for a moment, then returned carrying his briefcase.

'What is it?' asked Natalie, her curiosity aroused.

George winked mysteriously. 'Something you'll like very much. Show you after supper.'

Then, finally, he uncorked the brandy bottle and poured a generous measure into the balloon. He raised it to his wife. 'To us, Natalie. To us.'

She lifted her champagne glass to his, though she could not bring herself to echo his words.

While he ate, George talked, unworried by the spray of crumbs from his mouth. Natalie had forgotten how disgusting she'd always found this habit of his. Still, that was just another detail which would very soon cease to be a problem for her.

'So what happened with Trevor?' her husband asked, a fleck of yellow egg beading the corner of his mouth.

'It came to an end,' Natalie lied. 'I just realized it wasn't working. I fell out of love with him, I suppose, and then it seemed incredible that I had ever loved him. When I came to my senses, I hated myself for what I had done to you. I knew the whole episode had been a ghastly mistake, so I told Trevor it was over.'

'Ah.' George nodded sagely.

'And you're fully at liberty to say what you like. God knows, you have the right.'

'What do you expect me to say?'

'I don't know. I suppose "I told you so" would be appropriate.'

George Marshall reached across and took his wife's hand. The touch of his flesh felt to her like a thawing chicken breast. 'I'm not going to say anything like that,' he confided. 'I'm so delighted to have you back that nothing else matters.'

Natalie managed a weak smile of gratitude.

'How did Trevor take it?' asked George.

She grimaced.

'You said on your phone message you were worried about what he might do. Do you mean you're afraid he might turn violent towards you?'

Natalie had prepared her answer to this question carefully. If George thought she was in danger, he might be capable of going round to confront Trevor. The last thing her plans required at that moment was heroics from her husband.

'Not violent towards me, no. I'm more worried he might turn his violence against himself.' The thought of what she was saying almost made her laugh. Trevor was so uncomplicated, so full of animal vigour, that the idea of his entertaining even a moment's thought of suicide became ridiculous. Natalie began to enjoy embroidering the lie. 'He was terribly cut up about the whole business . . . you know, with his wife having walked out so recently. I suppose he kind of thought I was his salvation. Certainly, the affair went much deeper with him than it did with me.'

'So you're genuinely afraid he might try to kill himself?'

Natalie shrugged. 'I hope not. I hope the thought of his two little kids'll stop him, but . . . yes, I have worried about it. He's very unstable,' she concluded, secretly gleeful at the incongruity of her words.

'Dear, oh dear,' said George. Then, to his wife's intense satisfaction, he poured another healthy top-up into his brandy glass. To her even greater satisfaction, he picked up a mince pie, lifted its pastry lid and piled the interior with brandy butter.

Speaking through flakes of puff pastry, George continued, 'Don't you worry about a thing, darling. From what I remember of Trevor, I'd think he was an extremely unlikely candidate for suicide. As you say, he's got the kids to think of, apart from anything else. And, even if he did do something stupid, you shouldn't blame yourself. Suicide is the ultimate act of selfishness. No one else is ever to blame. It involves only the person who commits the act,' he concluded pompously.

'Well, I hope you're right . . .' said Natalie, playing out her anxiety a little longer, and noting with satisfaction the sight of her husband decapitating a second mince pie and ladling in the brandy butter.

'Ooh, now, your present . . .' George reminded himself. He crammed the whole pie into his mouth and picked up his briefcase. Holding it on his lap with the lid shielding its contents from his wife, he reached teasingly inside. 'I don't think you'll ever guess what I've bought you . . .'

Natalie certainly never would have done. She looked with dumb amazement at the silk lingerie set George proudly produced. Trevor enjoyed that sort of thing; she took pleasure in dressing up for their erotic encounters; but George had never shown interest in anything but the most traditional sex – and not a great deal in that.

'Do you like them?' her husband prompted.

'Well, yes, but . . . why did you buy them for me?'

George winked roguishly. 'I read an article in this magazine about how couples who've been married for a long time can . . . as it were . . . recharge their interest in each other.'

Oh my God, thought Natalie, I'm not sure I can cope with this. But then, mercifully, on cue, George yawned.

She waited until he was snoring heavily. To be extra sure, she spoke to him and shook his plump form, but there was no response. Reassured, she went to the phone and told Trevor she needed his help.

Briefly she had contemplated doing the job alone. Though he was chubby, George's lack of height meant that she could have carried him or dragged him without too much difficulty. But second thoughts decided her that she must enlist Trevor. It wasn't so much his physical strength she needed as the fact of his involvement. The murder would be their secret, a shared sacrament that would bind them even closer together. In the hopefully unthinkable eventuality of Trevor losing interest in her, Natalie could use the crime to blackmail him back into line.

Trevor was jumpy when he came round at her summons. He had raised no objections when she had spelled out her plans to him, but the reality of what they were about to do made him nervous. Natalie, on the other hand, was icily efficient and in control.

'Do we take him out straight away?' asked Trevor tentatively.

She shook her head. 'I'm just going to go through his pockets first. See there's nothing that might spoil the picture we're trying to create.'

There was nothing that spoiled the picture. Indeed, as she pointed out to Trevor, there was something that improved the picture considerably. 'These are letters I wrote to him. Look.' She pointed to the words. '"... So far as I'm concerned, anything there ever was between us has long gone ..."; "why can't you just accept the whole thing's over ..." – this is great – couldn't be better.'

'Why're the letters torn?' asked Trevor.

'God knows. He probably started to get rid of them, but then couldn't bring himself to *lose any souvenir of me.*' She made the last five words heavy with irony, then quickly reverted to the businesslike. 'Right, the tumble-drier hose is in a plastic bag in the hall. You fix that and then come back for him – OK? Got some gloves, have you?'

Trevor nodded, pulled a pair of gardening gloves from his pocket and put them on as he left the room.

He was back within five minutes and bent to hoist up George's snoring body. 'No, we'll do it together,' said Natalie, also putting on gloves and picking up a rubber-covered torch. 'You take one arm, I'll take the other.'

George half woke and mumbled something incoherent as the lovers lifted him out of his chair. His legs even helped them in a loose-limbed shuffle as they guided him out into the frosty darkness. But he didn't regain consciousness.

Trevor had left the door of the detached garage open. The Volvo was in place. With surprising ease, they manhandled George into the driver's seat, where he slumped sideways against the headrest. He grunted a little as he settled, but still did not wake.

Natalie handed the torch to Trevor. 'I'll just go and get the note and the bottles,' she whispered.

While she was gone, Trevor ran the torch beam along the passenger side of the car to check his handiwork. One end of the tumble-drier hose was firmly attached with insulating tape to the exhaust pipe. The other end led into the car, clamped in place by the nearly closed passenger-side front window.

Natalie returned and reached unsentimentally across her husband's body to place the near-empty bottles of brandy and sleeping draught on the seat beside him. Then she drew a folded sheet of paper from her pocket.

'What does it say?' asked Trevor.

She opened the letter and held it up to the torch beam for Trevor to read.

TO WHOEVER FINDS ME – and I hope it's you, Natalie. And I hope what you find will really hurt you, when you see what your cruelty has driven me to. I love you. I've always loved you, and the thought of you with someone else is more than I can bear. I'm killing myself the same way that your first husband did – and that's deliberate. It's meant to hurt you – to make you realize what an unfeeling bitch you are. I hope the rest of your life is really miserable. I'm glad to be out of it.

Trevor looked up as he finished reading. 'Pity it's not signed.'

'I thought of pretending it was an insurance document or

something and getting him to sign, but it wasn't worth the risk. And the police'd spot it if I tried to forge his signature.'

Trevor nodded. He looked suddenly awkward, young and frightened. 'So ... now ... do we ... ?'

'Yes,' Natalie replied firmly. She reached a gloved hand into her pocket and took out George's bunch of keys. Briskly, she put one into the ignition and turned it. The engine fired first time.

'How long're you going to wait till you discover him?' asked Trevor.

'Till the morning.' Natalie slammed the car door, led Trevor out of the garage and closed its doors behind them.

He was trembling in the cold air as Natalie put her arms around him. 'When did you say the kids get back?'

'Nine,' he gulped. 'Round nine.'

'Good.'

'I'll have to be back then. They'll be very excited. Got to do my full Santa routine.'

'Eat the mince pie and drink the brandy they leave out for him?'

'That's it.'

'What about the carrot for the reindeer – you don't eat that too, do you?'

'Bin it. Have to be careful it's nowhere they might find it, mind. Spoil the whole boring charade, that would.'

Though his words were light, Trevor was still quivering with shock. Natalie pressed her body against him, and felt his infallible lust begin to replace the fear. 'Come to bed. I've got some sexy new undies to show you.' She chuckled throatily as she remembered something. 'But first – go and put on your Father Christmas costume.'

The dressing-up and the bond of their shared guilt brought their sexual pleasure to new heights. When Trevor slipped away at ten to nine, Natalie glowed with fulfilment, and with the knowledge that nothing could now stand in the way of their happiness. She slept surprisingly peacefully and deeply.

At eight o'clock the next morning, anyone who happened to be passing would have seen Natalie Marshall go out of her front door and cross to the garage as if to get the car out. They would have heard her catch her breath as she opened the garage doors, seen her dart in with a hand over her mouth to switch off the Volvo's engine. They would have heard a scream as she identified her husband's slumped body, and seen her rush in panic back into the house.

In fact, there was no one there to witness these events, but Natalie knew how important it was to go through the whole scenario correctly. And she knew how important it was to get the right note of shock and hurt into her voice when she rang the police to tell them that her husband was dead.

Detective Inspector Jeavons looked across at the woman sobbing on the sofa in the cottage's expensively furnished sitting room. 'And had he ever spoken about taking his own life?'

Natalie Marshall, giving the performance of her life, nodded in anguish. 'Yes, I'm afraid he had. Particularly recently. Oh God, I feel so terrible about it.'

'It's only to be expected, Mrs Marshall. Must be an awful shock for you.'

'He meant it to hurt me, you know. Doing it right on my doorstep, right here.'

'I wouldn't know about that,' said the Inspector, stodgily. He paused. 'When you went into the garage this morning, Mrs Marshall, you didn't make any attempt to revive your husband . . . ?'

'No. He was obviously dead. And I couldn't stay in there – the whole place was full of fumes. Goodness knows how long he'd had the car running.'

'I assume you didn't hear it being switched on or anything?'

She shook her head decisively. 'You can't hear what's happening in the garage from inside the house. It could have been any time.'

'Well, the police surgeon'll be examining the body now. And my other colleagues'll be checking out the garage. We'll know more details soon.' The Inspector selected his next words with delicacy. 'Do you feel able to tell me why your husband might have wanted to kill himself?'

'Jealousy, I'm afraid – and despair. Our relationship was over. I'd fallen in love with someone else. He just couldn't come to terms with that.'

'No.' The Inspector nodded sympathetically and was about to say something else when he heard the front door open. 'Ah, be the forensic people, I imagine.'

They both looked towards the sitting-room door. It opened, and, with a breezy 'Happy Christmas, darling!', in walked George Marshall.

All the colour drained from his wife's face. The rawness around her eyes, once again created by applications of soapy water, showed stark red in the white mask. 'George . . .' she murmured in disbelief. 'George . . .'

Her husband looked quizzically at their visitor. 'Don't believe I've had the pleasure . . .'

The policeman reached out a formal hand. 'Detective Inspector Jeavons.'

'Oh yes? Some problem? Been a burglary locally, has there? I don't know, you'd think they'd have the decency to spare people over Christmas,' George burbled on, 'but then nobody seems to have any values in this country any more. In the old days—'

'Excuse me,' the Inspector interposed, 'but who are you?'

'What, you don't know? Sorry, I'm George Marshall.'

'This lady's husband?'

'Yes, that's right.' The little man looked puzzled by the detective's incredulous reaction. 'What's the matter?'

'Mrs Marshall telephoned us this morning saying that you'd committed suicide in your garage.'

It was George's turn to look incredulous. '*What?*'

'Your wife said you'd attached a tumble-drier hose to the exhaust of your car and switched on the ignition.'

'Good heavens! She must have been getting confused. That's how her first husband killed himself.'

'Oh, really?' said Inspector Jeavons, with a hint of a raised eyebrow.

'But why on earth am I supposed to have committed suicide?' asked George in amazement.

'Mrs Marshall said that you were in despair over her having taken another lover.'

'Well, I was pretty cut up about it, yes, at the start, but that's all forgotten now. Natalie and I are back together again. *And how* – after last night!' He managed to imbue his last words with unambiguous salaciousness, which he then amplified. 'Goodness, did she make me welcome – exotic lingerie, stiletto heels, the full number. It certainly felt like Christmas for me! Christmas and my birthday rolled into one!'

He chuckled, then, for the first time since he'd come into the room, looked directly at his wife. He could see how quickly Natalie's mind was working, as she tried to produce the right reaction to her new circumstances. Any denial of what George was saying was likely to raise awkward questions from Inspector Jeavons about what had really happened the night before. For the time being, shocked silence remained her best policy.

'So you are saying, Mr Marshall, that you spent last night here with your wife?'

'Yes. Sleeping in the same bed. Well, not sleeping *all* the time,' George added, with another vocal nudge.

Inspector Jeavons turned a stern gaze on Natalie. 'So, Mrs Marshall, have you been wasting police time? Did you make up this story of finding a body in your garage?'

She opened her mouth as if to reply, but then hesitated, uncertain which way to jump.

'So you haven't seen the supposed body, Inspector?' asked George.

'No, I came straight in here to talk to Mrs Marshall. My colleagues went to examine the garage.'

'You'd've thought they'd've come straight back out again if they hadn't found anything in there ... wouldn't you?' George observed casually.

It took a moment for the implications of his words to sink in, and the point registered more quickly with Natalie than with the Inspector.

'Oh no!' she screamed, rising to her feet. 'Oh, my God, no!'

And, moving like a thing possessed, she rushed out of the cottage to the garage.

The police had taken Trevor's body out of the car and laid it on a sheet of plastic on the cement floor. Incongruously, he was dressed in his Father Christmas suit. His dead face was hideously congested and contorted.

Natalie threw herself down on the ground, taking the stiff, cold body in her arms. Sobs shuddered through her frame. 'The bastard!' she muttered. 'The heartless, cruel bastard!'

The Scene of Crime team continued their investigations outside the cottage. A WPC comforted Natalie Marshall with sweet tea and sympathy in the kitchen, while in the sitting room Inspector Jeavons questioned her husband for background information about Trevor Roache's death. George didn't need any prompting; he was anxious to be as helpful as he could.

'Trevor was Natalie's lover, yes. He was the one we split up over. I suppose knowing we were back together again and that he had no more chance with Natalie must have made him do this dreadful thing.'

'Did he strike you as a potentially suicidal type?'

'I didn't know him well – only met him a couple of times when he came here to do building work for us – but Natalie was clearly worried that he might do something like this.'

'What makes you say that, Mr Marshall?'

'She said as much in a message she left on my answering machine yesterday morning.'

'Oh? Presumably that message would have been erased by now?'

'Well . . .' George Marshall looked sheepish. 'In normal circumstances it would have been, yes, but the fact is . . . As you know, our marriage wasn't going very well, and I did actually get to the point of consulting a solicitor about the possibility of divorce. He advised me to try and get some recordings of conversations with Natalie about Trevor and . . . well, her phone message more or less fitted the bill, so I – it seems ridiculous now Natalie and I are back together again – but I did actually take the tape out of the answering machine and put in a new one.'

'You wouldn't by any chance have that tape with you, Mr Marshall?'

'Well, as it happens . . .' George reached down to his briefcase and produced the tape and a small cassette player.

The Inspector listened to Natalie's message impassively, though his eyebrow twitched at the words, '*My affair with Trevor's come to an end. And he's . . . taking it very badly. I'm ... I'm really worried about what he might do, George.'*

When the message had ended, George Marshall said rather diffidently, 'Actually, there is another tape ...'

'Oh?'

'Well, when Natalie summoned me down here last night, I thought we were in for some kind of confrontation, so I followed my solicitor's advice and ... using this cassette player hidden in my briefcase ... actually recorded a bit of our conversation ...'

'You'd better play it,' said Inspector Jeavons quietly.

Again the detective tried not to show any reaction, but was unable to suppress a flicker of interest when George's voice asked, *'So you're genuinely afraid he might try to kill himself?'*, to which Natalie replied, *'I hope not. I hope the thought of his two little kids'll stop him, but ... yes, I have worried about it. He's very unstable.'*

'So ...' the Inspector said when the recording ended, 'it does begin to look as if the victim was predisposed to suicide ... particularly when your evidence is taken in conjunction with the letters we found in his pocket ...'

He held out a transparent folder through which scraps of torn letters were visible. As if he'd never seen them before, George read the words, *'... so far as I'm concerned, anything there ever was between us has long gone ...'*

'That is your wife's handwriting, is it, Mr Marshall?'

George sighed. 'Yes, I'm afraid it is. Hard not to feel a bit sorry for Mr Roache, isn't it?'

'He also left a note.' The Inspector produced another transparent folder, through which could be seen a printed sheet which began, *'TO WHOEVER FINDS ME – and I hope it's you, Natalie ...'* At the bottom of the page was scrawled in biro the name 'Trevor'.

'Of course, we'll have to check the signature's genuine, but

I don't have many worries on that score. No, Mr Marshall, I'd say we've got an open-and-shut case of suicide here.'

But during the afternoon a few details emerged which made the case look less open and shut. The signature on the suicide note was found to match no existing samples of Trevor Roache's handwriting; it began to look increasingly like a rather crude forgery.

Then there was the mud, grass and cement dust found adhering to the back of the dead man's Father Christmas costume. These traces suggested that, rather than walking voluntarily to the garage and to his death, Trevor Roache had quite possibly been dragged there while unconscious.

What had rendered him insensible was quickly found. His children, before being taken into the care of their grandparents, confirmed that they had left out a glass of brandy and a mince pie for Father Christmas. No, they had not put any brandy butter in the mince pie. And yet the dead man's stomach was found to contain traces of brandy butter, heavily laced with a sleeping draught. The police found some corresponding brandy butter, also drugged, in a supermarket pot in Natalie Marshall's fridge.

Marks on the frosty ground between Trevor's cottage and the Marshalls' garage doors supported the hypothesis that his body had been dragged across the intervening ground.

Most damning of all were the deep heel prints left by the person who had dragged him. They had been made by the sharp points of stiletto heels.

The police hadn't got quite enough to arrest her on the spot, but it was no surprise when they asked Natalie Marshall to accompany them to the station for further questioning. Before she was taken away, she was allowed a brief moment alone with her husband. They stood in the garden, out of earshot of the police, in the dusk of Christmas Day, the frosty air prickling at their cheeks and fairy lights twinkling overhead.

'You bastard!' Natalie hissed. 'You won't get away with this.'

George blinked mildly through his spectacles. 'Oh, I think I will. You can't tell them what really happened without incriminating yourself for attempting to murder me.'

'Attempted murder would get a lighter sentence than murder.'

'Sure. Well, that's a decision you'll have to make for yourself. Anyway, if you're already thinking of plea-bargaining, it looks like you've accepted what's going to happen to you . . . darling.' He smiled an infuriating smile.

'God, I hate you!' Natalie seethed. 'I'll tell the police how much I hate you.'

'They'll think you're just saying that to divert suspicion. They have my word for it that we're reconciled . . .' he chuckled, '. . . and had wonderful sex last night to celebrate the fact.'

'How did you do it, George?'

Her husband shrugged modestly. 'I knew what you were planning. I brought brandy and brandy butter with me, and, while I was getting our scrambled egg last night, substituted mine for yours, putting most of your drugged stuff into the supermarket pot in the fridge. So I was eating ordinary brandy butter and drinking ordinary brandy.'

'And what I destroyed last night was the supermarket stuff?'

George nodded cheerfully. 'That's right. Then I just pretended to pass out and stayed that way, while you fetched Trevor and manhandled me into the garage. I knew it'd take a while before the fumes in the car built up to noxious levels, so I stayed for five minutes after you'd closed the garage doors, then let myself out.

'All I had to do after that was wait till Trevor went back to his cottage and follow him. Through the window I watched him with his kids, saw them putting out the mince pie and brandy by the fireplace for Father Christmas. When he went up to put the kids to bed, I nipped in, replaced the brandy with some of your drugged stuff and put a huge dollop of doctored brandy butter in the mince pie.

'Thereafter it was just a matter of waiting and watching. Eventually Trevor ate and drank the stuff. Pretty soon after that, he fell asleep, out cold in his armchair. I'd brought a pair of your stilettos with me for the purpose, and wore them as I dragged him across to the garage. The rest you know.'

'Not all of it,' Natalie objected. 'I still swear it was your body I found in the car this morning.'

'Oh yes. When I heard you getting up, I moved Trevor's body out – bit tricky that, he was already stiff with rigor mortis – but I managed. I tucked him under the front of the Volvo and got into the driver's seat myself. I knew you wouldn't look too closely once you'd identified me. Then, as soon as you'd gone, I got out and put Trevor's body back in place.'

The light of hatred burned in Natalie's eyes as she stared at her husband. 'But how? How did you know what I was planning?'

George smiled complacently. 'Wasn't difficult. You've never had that much imagination, Natalie. As soon as I heard you mention the tumble-drier hose on the answering machine, I knew exactly what your murder method would be.' In response to her quizzical look, he went on, 'Because it was exactly how your first husband died, wasn't it? Even down to the detail of using a tumble-drier hose.' George Marshall let out another gleeful chuckle. 'I should know. I was the one who fixed that.'

All colour drained from his wife's cheeks. 'You? You killed Robert? You mean, it wasn't suicide?'

'No, of course it wasn't. You'd never have married me while he was alive, and I very much wanted you to marry me. Generally speaking, Natalie,' he concluded smugly, 'I get the things I want.'

'But . . .' Now there was a pleading look in his wife's eyes. 'Don't you still want me, George?'

'Oh no,' he replied. 'Not any more. Not since you took up with Trevor. I found that very hurtful, you know, and I was determined to punish you for what you'd done to me. Now I've had my proper revenge, I'll give you that divorce you so wanted, darling. No percentage for me being married to someone who's in prison, is there?'

It was at that moment Inspector Jeavons came forward to lead Natalie Marshall to the waiting car.

From his sitting-room window, George Marshall watched the police convoy disappearing down the lane. He dialled his mistress's number. And when she answered, he said, 'Happy Christmas, darling.'

BEST BEHAVIOUR

I know how to behave. I do. That's one thing my papa taught me. It's really the most important thing he left me with – knowing the right way to behave.

And I never thought it was cruel. He had my best interests at heart. I know he did. If there was any cruelty involved, then he was only being cruel to be kind. He often used that expression. 'Edmund,' he'd say, 'I'm only being cruel to be kind.' And I respected that. Even though the things he did sometimes hurt, I could still respect his reasons for doing them.

It's a matter of justice, you see. Being fair to people. Not just being fair to yourself – that could so easily become selfishness – but being fair to everyone else you come into contact with. 'We're social beings,' Papa would say. 'Humankind're social beings, and one's success as a member of humankind is demonstrated by how well one relates to other human beings. You have to behave, Edmund. Never knowingly do harm to another member of the human race.'

Those were the values Papa dinned into me from a very early age and, from the time I could understand what he was talking about, I very quickly came to respect what he stood for.

He was entirely consistent, you see. His rules were clear. He never punished me for something that I didn't know at the time – or at least understood pretty soon afterwards – was wrong. 'Bad behaviour must never go unpunished,' Papa used to say. 'Otherwise it's bound to lead to worse behaviour.'

Papa didn't have any truck with the view that, equally, good behaviour should be rewarded. 'Good behaviour should be instinctive. Good behaviour brings its own reward. Though, in fact, for you, Edmund, good behaviour is not good enough. Any son of mine must always be on his *best* behaviour.'

So that's what I always aspired to. And, most of the time, achieved. When I fell short of Papa's high standards – no, of *my* high standards ('It's within *you*, Edmund,' he always used to say. 'It should be instinctive within yourself.') – then I knew punishment was inevitable. But it was perfectly fair. I knew the rules. I'd broken them. I had failed as a member of humankind.

Papa himself avoided doing unwitting harm to other members of the human race by not having a lot to do with them. We didn't see many other people as I was growing up. There was just Papa, Mama and me. 'We don't need other people,' Papa used to say. 'We're self-sufficient. We are fortunate – unlike a lot of the poor bastards out there – to be a secure, loving family unit.'

And he was right – we were fortunate. Money was never a problem – we always had enough to eat, we lived in a nice house, I was sent to a private school. It was all very nice.

And I'm proud to say, Mama and Papa never had any of the problems with me that you read about other families having with growing children. They were never going to see my name in the papers ... not, that is, until this current business. And now they're both dead, so it's not as if any amount of cruel lies in the tabloids can cause them any anxiety. Not now. Not any more.

My father's teaching stood me in good stead, though, you know. I didn't backslide after he died. No, the training Papa had given me was so good that Mama never had to raise her voice to me. I was permanently on my best behaviour.

But I don't want to sound like I'm a goody-goody, not to give that impression, no. I do have my ... I was about to say 'vices', but I think 'vice' is probably too strong a word. 'Vice' means doing things to other people, body things, things with your secret bits. And I've never felt the urge to do any of that, don't understand why people make such a fuss about it. No, for what I do, 'indulgences' is the word I prefer. Yes, I do have indulgences.

There are only two, really. Two big ones. They're hot buttered toast with golden syrup on, and Children's BBC. And, well, actually, now I come to think of it, there is sort of a third. My parents always hated the idea of my name being shortened, but now I tell people to call me not 'Edmund', but 'Eddie'.

All right, you could say I'm reacting, greedily taking the things I wasn't allowed when I was a child, but I don't think mine're too bad, as indulgences go. Other people do much worse things.

And by Papa's rules ... you know, about not doing harm to another member of humankind ... well, I can't honestly think that my indulgences harm anyone. No matter how much Children's BBC I watch and video, no matter how much hot buttered toast with golden syrup I eat, nobody else gets hurt by it.

Mind you, the golden syrup does make me fat. I was always big – used to get rather unkind things said about my size when I was at school – but since Mama died, I have got a lot bigger. She used to keep an eye on how much golden syrup I ate, used to say, 'Hold back, Edmund, enough is enough, you know,' but since she died ... well, there's no one to stop me. But, like I said, nobody gets hurt by it.

I'm lucky. I know I'm lucky. My parents left me enough money so that I won't ever have to work. Probably that's just as well, because the few interviews I did have for jobs didn't turn out very well. I think my size put people off, partly, and then they did seem to ask very difficult questions. I admit there are a lot of things I don't know about, and the subjects on which I am good . . . like Children's BBC . . . well, they didn't ask about them. The experience rather put me off applying for other jobs.

But I'm lucky, too, in that I have friends. Not that many, but there are some children round where I live and I get on well with them. They know about Children's BBC, you see, so we've got things to talk about. I often meet them in the park, near the children's playground. I'm too big to go on any of the swings or anything . . . I'd probably break them if I did, I'm such a big lump . . . but it's a good place to meet the children.

I get on better with them when they're on their own. I buy sweets for them. Never go out without a couple of bags of jelly babies in my pockets. The children like those. (So do I, actually!) But I only give them sweets when they're on their own. Their parents don't seem to like the children talking to me. Sometimes they say rather cruel things. Things that wouldn't pass muster under Papa's rules. I'm another member of humankind, and the things they say *do* do harm to me. What's more, I think they do it knowingly.

Still, in the park I quite often see children on their own, so it's not all bad. I tell them to call me 'Eddie'. I like it when I hear their little voices call me 'Eddie'. Of course, the children get bigger and seem to lose interest in talking about Children's BBC with me. But there's always another lot of little ones growing up.

I've got so many children's programmes videoed that I

sometimes think I should ask some of the children to come back home with me to have a good watch and lashings of hot buttered toast with golden syrup. But I haven't done that yet. I don't know why, but something tells me it's a bad idea.

And now, after some of the questions I've been asked in the last few months, I know my instinct was right. It would have been a very bad idea.

My problems . . . yes, I suppose I have to call them problems . . . began in relation to a little girl called Bethany Jones. I didn't know her second name when I met her. She just told me she was called 'Bethany'. But recently her name's been so much in the newspapers and on television that everyone in the country knows she's called Bethany Jones.

I met her in the park, like the other children. She was six – just been six, just had her sixth birthday party, she was very proud of that. She lived quite near the park, over the other side from my house. Her parents didn't like her going to the children's playground on her own, but she was so close she used to sneak out when they weren't looking.

That's when I'd met her. And we'd talk about Children's BBC. She didn't call me 'Eddie'. She used to call me 'Fat Boy', which I suppose could have been cruel, but I didn't mind it from Bethany. She didn't mean any harm. That's what they said in the papers. Her mother said, 'Bethany never did any harm to anyone.'

I didn't know what had happened to Bethany before the police arrived. I don't read a paper or watch the news – well, except for *Newsround* on Children's BBC. And that's on at five, and she wasn't found till four-thirty, so they'd have been hard pushed to get it on that day's programme. Anyway, *Newsround* wouldn't have covered a story like Bethany Jones's. It was too unpleasant for a children's audience.

The police arrived very quickly. Children's BBC had just

ended, at five thirty-five as usual, and *Neighbours* was starting. Sometimes I watch *Neighbours* and sometimes I don't. It's not proper Children's BBC, though I know a lot of children watch it. As for me, I'll watch it if I like the story. If there's too much kissing and that sort of thing, I'll switch it off. I don't like stories with kissing in them. I never saw Papa and Mama kiss, and the thought of people doing it sort of like in public, on the television . . . well, I don't think it's very nice.

The day the police arrived, there wasn't a kissing story in *Neighbours* and I was watching it. And videoing it, obviously. I video everything I watch. I had to switch off the television when the police came in. But I left the video running.

The first thing the police asked me was if I knew Bethany and I said, yes, of course I did. And they said they had been talking to some of the other children and was I the 'Eddie' who used to give them jelly babies, and I said, yes, I was.

There was one of them, the policemen, who seemed to be in charge. He was not wearing a uniform and he was very forceful. Detective Inspector Bracken he was called. Not the sort of person you'd argue with. He reminded me of Papa, and in the same way that I'd never have contradicted Papa, I found it difficult to stand up to this man and say he was wrong, even when the suggestions he was making were absolutely untrue. It seemed rather rude for me to disagree with him.

'And did you ever give jelly babies to Bethany?' Detective Inspector Bracken demanded.

'Yes,' I said. 'Of course I did. I like Bethany. She's one of my friends.'

'So she was one of your friends, was she?'

'*Is* one of my friends,' I said. '*Is* one of my friends.'

Detective Inspector Bracken looked at me thoughtfully. But

his expression wasn't just thoughtful. There was something else in it too, something that almost looked like distaste. He kept on looking at me.

I suddenly remembered that the police were guests in my house and I hadn't even offered them anything. ('Black mark, Edmund,' Papa would have said. 'Black mark on the hospitality front.') 'Could I get you some tea or something?' I asked. 'Something to eat, perhaps? I often have buttered toast with golden syrup round this time. Maybe you'd like—?'

'No, thank you,' said Detective Inspector Bracken. And he kept on looking straight at me. I found it embarrassing. I tried not to look him in the face.

'So . . .' he said, after what seemed a long silence, '. . . have you always had this urge to hang round little girls?'

He was getting the wrong end of the stick. I had to explain it to him. 'It's not just little girls,' I said. 'It's little boys, too.'

'Is it?' he said. 'Really?' And somehow he didn't say it in a kind way. Then he went on, 'Can you tell us what's happened to Bethany Jones?'

'Happened to her? Why should I be able to tell you that?'

'I just thought you might be able to.' Detective Inspector Bracken was looking at me in the way Papa used to, when I'd done something wrong and he was just waiting for me to own up to it. I always did own up; Papa knew he only had to wait. But with Detective Inspector Bracken it was different. There was nothing for me to own up to.

'Save us the trouble of doing it,' he went on after a silence. 'Save us the trouble of telling you what's happened to Bethany Jones.'

And then he did tell me what had happened to her. It was horrid. I don't like things like that. It's like kissing, and people's secret bits . . . I don't like it.

Apparently she'd been attacked in the park. She'd been dragged off into the bushes near the children's playground.

Then she'd been 'sexually assaulted'. And then she'd been beaten on the head with a stone until she was dead.

'Bethany – dead?' I said in disbelief. 'But I was talking to her only yesterday.'

'Yesterday,' Detective Inspector Bracken repeated. 'Were you? And what about today?'

'No, I didn't see her today.'

'Where were you, Mr Bowman,' asked Detective Inspector Bracken, 'between three-thirty and four-thirty this afternoon?'

I smiled at the question. Anyone who knew me at all – and granted there weren't that many people who did know me – but anyone who knew anything about me would know the answer to that. I was where I am every weekday afternoon at that time.

'I was here,' I replied. 'Here watching Children's BBC. I always am. Go on, I can prove it. You ask me any questions you like about this afternoon's Children's BBC. I bet I can give you the right answers.'

Detective Inspector Bracken smiled wryly, and looked across at my video recorder. 'Yes, I'm sure you can, Mr Bowman. Pretty unusual habit for a grown man, I'd have thought, videoing children's television programmes . . .'

'Oh, but I like to have a full record,' I told him. 'I feel awful if I think I've missed a single minute of Children's BBC.'

'I see,' he said. But he didn't look at me as if he did see. Soon after that, he said he wanted me to accompany him and the others to the police station, if I 'didn't mind'. No, I said, I didn't mind. I knew it didn't do to be difficult with forceful people like Detective Inspector Bracken. Best behaviour, Edmund, best behaviour.

They kept explaining things to me. They kept stopping and checking that I understood what was going on. Then, after

I was charged, they got a lawyer for me, and she kept explaining things too. And yes, I did understand. I understood the words and I understood what they meant. What I didn't understand was how they could manage to get it all so wrong.

I think a lot of the trouble was Detective Inspector Bracken. His manner, the way he put things, was so like Papa's that . . . well, I still found it very difficult to argue with him. He'd say something which was complete nonsense and I'd . . . well, I'd try to point out, sort of, why what he was saying wasn't true, but somehow my words didn't come out right.

I felt very trapped. I wanted to get back to my house, put on a video of some old *Tom and Jerry* cartoons or something like that, and let it wash all the horrid thoughts and images out of my mind. But they wouldn't let me do that.

I felt very lonely too. Although there were always people around – indeed, they wouldn't leave me on my own for a second – none of them were friendly. They all looked at me as if I was carrying some awful infectious disease. I wanted someone there who'd just talk to me in a relaxed, simple way. I'd've loved to have one of the children from the park there to talk to. At one moment when I was particularly stressed, I said that to Detective Inspector Bracken. He gave me a very strange look.

The lawyer they got me – there was no way I could have got one for myself, I've never had any cause to need a lawyer – was, I'm sure, fine, but she didn't seem very interested in my case. Maybe it was just a job of work for her. She didn't seem concerned about putting my side of things. But maybe that wasn't what she was there for. Certainly she didn't stand up to Detective Inspector Bracken much. He was so strong, so dominant, so like Papa.

It was the same at the trial. There was this woman barrister who defended me. I've nothing against women. I like women.

But I don't think of them as strong. Probably that comes from having grown up with my parents. It was always Papa who was in charge. Mama was a kind of shadowy figure in the background. So I never really expected the judge and the jury to take much notice of my barrister.

Also I don't think she took the right approach for my defence. She kept saying it wasn't just Bethany Jones who was a victim. I was a victim too. Then she said things that were a bit hurtful. She said just because I was odd, it didn't automatically make me a criminal. She said, yes, I was a sad, rather pathetic figure, somebody who didn't fit society's norms. But that didn't make me a murderer.

I'm not sure that was the right way to go about it. Calling me 'odd' and 'sad' and 'pathetic' made me seem as if I *was* all those things. I thought she was playing into the hands of the other barrister. He was a man, much more forceful in his manner. He was like Papa, or Detective Inspector Bracken. He spoke in a way that didn't brook argument. I'm not surprised that the jury believed what he said rather than the arguments my barrister put forward. If I'd known nothing about the case and I'd been sitting in that jury box, I'd have done the same.

But of course I did know something about the case. I knew I'd never touched Bethany Jones, never touched any of the children. At the time those dreadful things happened to her, I was in my house watching Children's BBC.

There was another thing I knew, too. I knew my secret bits didn't work like men's are supposed to. I knew my body wasn't capable of doing the things that had been done to her body. But I didn't like to mention that. It was a bit embarrassing. Maybe, if I'd had a male barrister . . . But to talk to a woman – any woman – about that kind of thing . . . well, I couldn't ever have done that.

It wasn't nice before the trial, or while the trial was going on. I was kept in this prison. 'On remand', they called it. They didn't have any golden syrup in the prison. I asked for it, but you couldn't get it. And you weren't allowed to watch Children's BBC.

Also, the other prisoners were horrid to me. They all seemed to take it for granted that I'd done all those things to Bethany Jones. There was more than one occasion when only the intervention of the prison officers stopped something rather unpleasant happening.

After the trial was over, though, and that horrid wrong verdict had been given, the prison officers' attitude seemed to have changed. I was taken back to prison – the remand prison, that is; I was going to another one to serve my sentence – in a van with barred windows. Inside the prison, the guards were leading me back to my cell. I still had handcuffs on, and we were going through one of the corridors, when suddenly this man stood in front of us, blocking our progress.

I'd seen him round the prison before. He wasn't a nice man, very rough. He didn't speak nicely, didn't have good vowels. He was the kind of man Papa would have told me not to mix with. 'They're not our sort of people,' he'd have said. 'You steer clear of them, Edmund.'

And it was good advice. If I could have steered clear of him, I would have done. But there was nowhere to go. It was a narrow corridor. The prison officers who were leading me along just drew back as the man launched himself at me. He hit me in the stomach first. 'Take that, you filthy fat pervert!' he said.

And when I fell down and tried to scramble away from him along the wall, he started kicking me. All over. My stomach, my arms, my legs, even my secret bits. With the handcuffs on, I couldn't protect myself. He kicked my face as well. Two of my teeth were broken. I could taste the blood and feel their jagged edges.

Then he stopped and laughed. 'That's just a taster,' he said. 'A taster of what they'll do to you when you get in the real nick. They don't like nonces in the real nick.'

After he'd finished kicking me, the prison officers came and moved him away. But they'd been there all the time, watching. They could have come to my rescue more quickly, I'm sure they could. I hope the prison officers in 'the real nick' are a bit more efficient.

They took me to 'the real nick' in another van with barred windows. When I was leaving the remand prison, they asked if I wanted a blanket over my head. Why would I want a blanket over my head? I'd had few enough chances to see the outside world in the last couple of months. I wanted to see everything I could out of the van's windows.

The trouble is, what I did see, when the van emerged from the gates, was a crowd of people. There were photographers, and a lot of women too, women probably about the same age as Bethany Jones's mother. But they weren't like women should be. They weren't quiet and well behaved like Mama always was. No, they were shouting and screaming. As the van went slowly through the crowd, they started banging on the sides. Some of them threw things and spat. I saw one face quite close to mine through the window. It was contorted with hatred. It wasn't nice.

The drumming sound they made against the walls of the van stayed with me. It kind of reverberated in my head. And now I've arrived at the new prison, I can hear it again. I've met the governor, I've been through all the entry procedures, and now I'm being led to my cell. The drumming sound comes from all the other prisoners, banging things against the doors of their cells.

I can hear things shouted too. Not nice things. I can hear that word 'nonce' that the man in the remand prison used. I wonder what it means.

Still, I'm sure it'll be all right. They may find the person who really did those horrid things to Bethany Jones, and set me free. Or they may reduce the length of my sentence. I've heard they do that for some prisoners. They reduce the sentence 'for good behaviour'. And I'm going to continue to do what Papa told me. All the time I'm here, I'm going to be on my absolute best behaviour.

I wonder what it'll be like here. I know there are only certain times when you're allowed to watch television in prison. Maybe Children's BBC will be one of those times.

I hope they have golden syrup in this prison.

THE MAN WHO GOT THE DIRT

To have killed Bartlett Mears from motives of jealousy would have been a small-minded, petty crime; but fortunately Carlton Rutherford had a much more respectable, wholly practical, reason for eliminating his old rival.

Murder had not been involved in his original plans for settling old scores, but Carlton Rutherford felt not the tiniest twinge of regret when he realized it would be necessary. In a sense, it would tie together a lot of ends otherwise doomed to eternal looseness.

The rivalry between the two writers had lasted nearly forty years, and though Bartlett Mears, had he been questioned on the subject, would have dismissed it with a characteristic shrug, for Carlton Rutherford the wound had never healed, and its scab required daily repicking.

Both had written their first novels at the end of the fifties. By then Kingsley Amis, John Osborne and others, burglarizing the shrine of pre-war British values and shattering its first hollow images, had declared the open season for iconoclasm.

Carlton Rutherford, at that period climbing the North Face of a doctorate on George Gissing at the University of Newcastle, had used his spare time to good effect and written his first novel, *Neither One Thing Nor The Other*.

This was a work of searingly fashionable nihilism, the story of Bob Grantham, a working-class genius, son of a postman in Salford, who struggled, against the odds of misunderstanding parents and virginity-hugging girls, all the way up to university. The book contrived to pillory traditional educational values, and at the same time potentially to alienate everyone with whom the author had come into contact in the twenty-five years he had been alive.

And therein lay its problem. Bob Grantham was so patently the *alter ego* – in fact, not even the *alter ego*, just the *ego* – of Carlton Rutherford that all of the book's other characters became readily identifiable.

Dashiel Loukes, the lean and hungry literary agent to whom (randomly from a reference book in a Newcastle library) the manuscript had been sent, confided to its author over a boozy lunch at Bertorelli's in Charlotte Street, that, though he was 'excited, but very excited' about the book, he was 'just a tidge worried' about the libel risk. And thought a little bit of rewriting might be prudent.

That had been in 1958. Though simplified by the death of both Carlton Rutherford's parents in a charabanc crash soon after his meeting with Loukes (you cannot libel the dead), the rewriting had proved unexpectedly difficult and time-consuming.

Eventually, a year later, at another Bertorelli's lunch, the author presented the agent with a revised manuscript, announcing that he had contrived to disguise all of the living characters save for that of Sandra, the toffee-nosed solicitor's daughter who had proved so tragically insensitive to the exceptional genius of Bob Grantham and so provincially unwilling to be the recipient of his extremely tenacious virginity.

Dashiel Loukes, thin and acute as a greyhound, had asked how closely this character resembled its original, and dragged from Carlton Rutherford the unwilling admission that, except for the detail of having had her eyes changed from blue to

47

brown, Sandra was identical in every particular to Sylvia, a toffee-nosed solicitor's daughter who had proved tragically insensitive to the exceptional genius of Carlton Rutherford and provincially unwilling to be the recipient of his extremely tenacious virginity (still, though Carlton did not mention the fact, intact in 1959).

The agent, aware that in *Neither One Thing Nor The Other* he had a fashionable and marketable commodity, suggested an extreme solution to the problem. The author should send a copy of his manuscript to Sylvia/Sandra and ask her to give a written undertaking that she would not take any action if the book were published. They had nothing to lose; it was worth a try.

Sylvia/Sandra was not for nothing the daughter of a solicitor. Now married to another solicitor, she was appalled by the manuscript and announced her firm intention to put an immediate injunction on the work if it was ever scheduled for publication.

Another gloomy Bertorelli's lunch, and Carlton Rutherford returned to another year's rewriting. In his new version, the Sylvia/Sandra character was virtually erased from the text. The dynamics of the novel were somewhat weakened by this alteration, but at least *Neither One Thing Nor The Other* could now be published without fear of litigation.

But a new shadow stretched over the 1961 Bertorelli's lunch at which Carlton Rutherford handed over his newly sanitized manuscript to Dashiel Loukes. The Sunday papers that week had been full of rave reviews for *Chips On The Elbow*, a first novel by a hitherto-unknown author, Bartlett Mears.

This was a work of searingly fashionable nihilism, the story of Ted Retford, a working-class genius, son of a milkman in Stockport, who struggled, against the odds of misunderstanding parents and virginity-hugging girls, all the way up to university. The book contrived to pillory traditional educational values, but what distinguished it from the novels of the other voguish 'angry young men' was that it told the story with a sense of humour.

According to the *Sunday Times*, 'It is spiced with a refreshing wit, and, whereas other contemporary novelists have used their tongues to lash outdated institutions, Mr Mears keeps his firmly – and wisely – in his cheek. *Chips On The Elbow* contrives to express its own distinctive anger while at the same time deflating the pretensions of the other "angry young men". In Bartlett Mears the arrival of a major new literary talent must be celebrated.'

The ensuing events were predictable. When, in 1962, *Neither One Thing Nor The Other* was finally published, its launch caused only minor ripples on the surface of literary life. The *Observer* referred to 'yet another whining catalogue of the ways in which the working class misunderstands the hypersensitive artist in its midst', and the *Spectator* even spoke of 'a self-regarding diatribe in the manner – but without the wit – of Bartlett Mears'.

All this was gall and wormwood to Carlton Rutherford – particularly because he knew he had finished his novel before Bartlett Mears had even started his.

Another spur to fury was the discovery, from the deluge of newspaper profiles, radio and television interviews of the new genius, that Bartlett Mears was not even the genuine article. He was not the son of a milkman in Stockport, but of a bank manager in Guildford. He had been educated at a minor public school and – of all places – Oxford University.

Chips On The Elbow had not been written in the light of bitter experience, but as a patronizing satire by a Southerner on the kind of life that Carlton Rutherford had led.

Given such a start, it was perhaps not surprising that the relationship between the two writers should end in murder.

*   *   *

The reception of their first books set the pattern for the future. Carlton Rutherford, having made a borehole into it in *Neither One Thing Nor The Other*, continued to mine the rich seam of his own childhood hardship and consequent feelings of alienation. The heroes of his subsequent novels were not all *called* Bob Grantham, but they all *were* Bob Grantham. Or, to put it another way, they all *were* Carlton Rutherford.

However, the vogue for gritty Northern realism passed. Other authors moved on to new subjects. Only Carlton Rutherford continued to produce the same tales of unrecognized genius. And, in an ironically self-fulfilling prophecy, his genius was recognized less and less with each succeeding book.

The novels, laborious to write, became even more laborious to read. Those reviewers who had found promise in *Neither One Thing Nor The Other* found it thereafter in decreasing measure, and eventually applied their ultimate destructive sanction – by not reviewing Carlton Rutherford's books at all.

Dashiel Loukes, initially such a champion of his author's cause, also proved a fair-weather friend. Through the sixties the agent grew fatter and more sleek, as he gathered under his banner an ever-increasing troop of ever-more-popular novelists. His early commitment to what he had described to Carlton Rutherford as 'really sensitive literary fiction' gave way in his priorities to the pursuit of the dollar.

Publishing changed, going through yet another of those recurrent attempts to shake off its image as the last refuge of a gentleman and prove it really *is* a hard-nosed commercial business. This involved, among other economy measures, the shedding of a large number of middle-list 'literary novelists'.

The British film industry began to disappear. The vogue

for films of the type that might have offered Carlton Rutherford hope, *Saturday Night and Sunday Morning* or *A Kind of Loving*, gave way to breathlessly trendy reflections of Swinging London, which in turn gave way to nothing.

Dashiel Loukes, fatter but still as sharp, trimmed his sails accordingly. He began to specialize in cold-war thrillers, which offered possibilities of lucrative American film deals.

Carlton Rutherford became more and more a dinosaur in the agent's stable of fleet-footed winners.

The crisis came in 1967. Dashiel Loukes was unable to find any publisher willing to take on the latest novel, in which Bob Grantham (by now named Sid Doncaster and working as a novelist) had another disastrously unconsummated love affair and suffered from writer's block.

For Carlton Rutherford, though it still continued to strain constipatedly off the typewriter, the writing was on the wall.

His agent broke the news in a pub one evening after work. Carlton Rutherford no longer justified the expense of a lunch. Indeed, had the author not insisted on a face-to-face meeting, Dashiel Loukes would have made the perfunctory severance by telephone.

(As things turned out, though, the encounter was not without its uses for the agent. He was at the time in the throes of a very heavy affair with an editor from Hamish Hamilton. Telling his wife he had to meet 'that dreary old bellyacher Carlton Rutherford' gave him the perfect alibi. So long as he kept the actual meeting brief – which he ensured that he did – Dashiel Loukes efficiently managed to carve out two hours of uninterrupted bliss between the editor's satin sheets in Notting Hill.)

Such categorical obliteration of his hopes might have turned a less resilient author away from the literary life for good, but it did not have that effect on Carlton Rutherford. Partly, he was made of sterner stuff; and partly, his doctorate on George Gissing having been abandoned some years before, there was nothing else he could do.

So Carlton Rutherford set about constructing something which a surprisingly large number of other literary folk have managed – a career as a writer that does not involve the publication of books. He gave lectures on the theory and practice of writing. He attended seminars and symposia on writing. He joined writers' committees. He wrote reviews of an increasingly waspish nature, deploring the decline of British letters since ... well, since his own books had been regarded as publishable.

And, of course, he taught creative writing courses.

In spite of all these activities, he still found time to go on writing his own novels, which charted further the conspiracy of an unfeeling and philistine world against Bob Grantham.

And he lived in daily anticipation of a change in the fickle tastes of the literary marketplace. The revived career of Barbara Pym in the late seventies prompted hopes for a similar rediscovery of Carlton Rutherford. When these were unrealized, he began increasingly to rely on thoughts of posthumous acclaim like that accorded to Gerard Manley Hopkins.

And when such thoughts proved inadequate to check his spleen, Carlton Rutherford comforted himself with fantasies of revenge on the man who had blighted his entire career. Bartlett Mears.

It might have been easier for him if Carlton Rutherford could have been unaware of his rival's activities, but the career of Bartlett Mears continued to maintain the high profile initiated by the success of *Chips On The Elbow*.

Mears, unlike Rutherford, had not allowed himself to be trapped into rewriting the same book time and again. Each of his publications was different from the last, each one attacked a new target, and in each the author's wit was more venomous. The books themselves did not get better – indeed, they undeniably got worse – but they did get reviewed.

And they got talked about. Bartlett Mears had an instinct for subject matter that would prompt controversy. His books gave rise to passionate love and passionate hatred in equal measure, but they always gave rise to some reaction. Each new publication was derided as evidence of a sad falling-off in the author's former talents, as each one made its inexorable way into the bestseller lists.

It was impossible to be unaware of Bartlett Mears.

He became a media pundit, never far from the centre of literary debate. His opinion was sought on every innovation. His reactions were frequently ill-considered and bad-tempered – sometimes even infantile – but they were always quotable. His favourite weapon was inadequately informed blanket condemnation. He genuinely did not care what people thought about him, and as a result, whether with relish or disgust, people thought about him a great deal.

The profile of Bartlett Mears' domestic life was equally high. *Private Eye* would have been lost without him.

A few well-publicized affairs with glamorous literati preceded a very public divorce from his pre-celebrity wife. More well-publicized affairs preceded his very public courtship of, and marriage to, the dauntingly attractive and intelligent novelist and critic Mariana Lestrange, another potent magnet for gossip columnists and press photographers.

The stormy course of this marriage, its public rows, separations and ultimate collapse in a spitting crackle of recrimination were known well outside the literary world – even in households where nothing was read more taxing than the *Sun*. Bartlett Mears' subsequent vituperative attacks on his ex-wife and general misogyny added further fuel to the blaze of his publicity.

And all this before one even mentioned the drinking.

Bartlett Mears had started his literary life as an *enfant terrible* and stayed *terrible* long after he had relinquished all possible right to be called an *enfant*.

He was a selfish, drunken loudmouth of diminishing talent, with the physical allure of a warthog, the tact of a rhinoceros, the morals of a sewer rat.

And the public loved him for it.

The more he abused them, the more restaurants he was banned from, the more television programmes he appeared on incapable through drink, the more the public loved him.

Try as he might – and after a while he didn't try that hard – Carlton Rutherford could not be unaware of Bartlett Mears and his latest outrage.

Soon, rather than trying to escape references to his rival, the less successful writer was positively seeking them out.

He was well placed to do so. He moved in the same literary world – albeit on its fringes – as Bartlett Mears. The two were frequently in the same room – in restaurants, at book launches, publishers' parties, writers' seminars, newspaper offices – and Carlton Rutherford witnessed many of the famous author's more spectacular misdemeanours.

All of these he chronicled in a notebook, which over the years became a series of notebooks. Soon, in addition, he started building up scrapbooks of newspaper cuttings, and after a while began the practice of soliciting scurrilous gossip about his rival whenever the opportunity arose. So extreme was Bartlett Mears' general behaviour that such opportunities arose frequently. All this adversarial anecdotage was also punctiliously recorded.

Gradually, over thirty years, was built up an exhaustive archive of misbehaviour.

There was no doubt that Carlton Rutherford had got all the dirt on Bartlett Mears.

*　　*　　*

It was early in 1991 that the idea came to him, and he was immediately impressed by its simplicity and wholeness.

He rang Dashiel Loukes the same day. 'There's a project I want to put to you.'

The agent, who thought he had permanently shaken off Carlton Rutherford some twenty years before, was instantly evasive. He was very busy, he had all the authors he could cope with, the current state of publishing was too depressing for him to offer any hope to another saga of North Country misunderstanding.

'Ah, but what I'm talking about now is non-fiction,' Carlton Rutherford announced triumphantly.

'Well, the state of the non-fiction market is not a lot more encouraging at the—'

'Come on, we must meet and talk about the idea. It's a sure-fire commercial proposition.'

Dashiel Loukes tried valiantly to escape, but eventually succumbed to a meeting. He suggested the author should come to his Mayfair office the following Thursday at eleven-thirty, an appointment whose timing proclaimed 'not only am I not offering you lunch, but also I am having lunch with someone considerably more important than you'.

'What I'm suggesting,' Carlton Rutherford pronounced, once he was safely ensconced in the agent's office, 'is a biography of Bartlett Mears.'

Dashiel Loukes looked up, his face purple from its daily marinade in the good wines of the Garrick and the Groucho. Time had treated his business kindly. Three of his espionage authors were now international bestsellers, and his principal daily task was to sit and work out his percentage of their money as, unprompted, it came rolling in.

'An official biography?' he asked.

'No, no,' Carlton Rutherford replied slyly. 'An extremely *un*official biography.'

'Hm . . .'

'You can't deny that Bartlett Mears is the kind of person the public wants to read about.'

'I'm not denying that. It's a matter of *what* they want to read about him. A literary biography of a living author's bound to be a minority sale.'

'I'm not talking about a *literary* biography of Bartlett Mears. I'm talking about a *scurrilous* biography. I've got all the dirt,' Carlton Rutherford concluded smugly.

Dashiel Loukes was thoughtful. 'It's actually not such a bad idea . . .' he conceded.

The author smiled.

'Trouble is . . .'

'What?'

'*You*, Carlton, I'm afraid.'

'What? At the absolute lowest, I'm a perfectly competent writer.'

'I know, but your name's not . . .'

'Not what?'

'Not *sexy*.'

'I don't see what sex has got to do with it,' said Carlton Rutherford, who was always embarrassed by the subject.

'Look, for a project like this – which, as I say, is actually not a bad idea – if I'm going to sell it to a publisher, I'd be on much stronger ground if I was selling it on the name of a well-known journalist or—'

'But you don't want a well-known journalist, you want someone who knows the facts. And I can assure you – I've got all the dirt,' Carlton Rutherford reiterated.

'Hm . . .' The agent looked at his watch. 'Got to be off soon, I'm afraid. Tell you what – I'll have a ring round some publishers this afternoon – see if I get any nibbles – can't say fairer than that, can I?'

The author considered the agent could say a lot fairer than

that, but was in no position to argue. Meekly he left the office and went home to his flat in Upper Norwood to eat a boiled egg and wait for the phone to ring.

It rang at a quarter to five. The mellowness of Dashiel Loukes' voice suggested he had only just returned from lunch. 'Had a ring round, old boy, like I said I would,' he announced bonhomously. 'Got quite a positive reaction to the idea of a book about Bartlett, but sorry, your name didn't win too many coconuts.'

'How do you mean?'

'I mean there's no chance of my getting a commission for this project with your name attached.'

'Oh. But I'm the one who's got the dirt,' Carlton Rutherford insisted.

'Maybe. I'm afraid that didn't seem to carry much weight.'

'So what do you suggest I do?'

'Well, nothing. Nothing you can do, really. Unless, of course, you want to write the whole thing *on spec* . . .' The agent's voice was aghast at the alien nature of his own suggestion. 'I mean, if you did come up with something really scurrilous, I might not have too much problem placing the completed manuscript. But it'd have to be pretty strong stuff . . .'

'Yes . . .'

'And you'd certainly have to talk to Mariana Lestrange. No book on Bartlett's going to be complete without a few shovelfuls of shit from her.'

'Hm. Right . . .' Carlton Rutherford was silent, until an unpleasant thought came into his head. 'Meanwhile, I suppose, your calls will have planted in a few publishers' heads the idea of doing a book about Bartlett Mears . . .'

'Possibly, yes . . .'

'*My* idea of doing a book about Bartlett Mears!'

'Well . . . They could have come up with it on their own . . .'

'No, they couldn't! They'd never have thought of it if I hadn't asked you to—'

'Carlton, Carlton . . .' the agent remonstrated. 'There is no copyright in ideas. Now you know that as well as I do – don't you, old boy . . . ?'

It didn't take Carlton Rutherford long to make his decision. He had no other means of revenge at his disposal. Besides, if he did not publish his findings, nearly thirty years of chronicling the misdemeanours of Bartlett Mears would have been wasted.

And there was a new spur to action. Now that Dashiel Loukes had spread around London publishers the idea of a book on Bartlett Mears, it was only a matter of time before some suitably 'sexy' journalist was commissioned to write one.

Carlton Rutherford reckoned that, because all his research was already done, he had a head start. But only if he got down to the writing straight away. He knew that experienced journalists could – and frequently did – paste-and-scissor together celebrity biographies over a weekend.

He was greatly reassured as soon as he started the actual writing. So exhaustive had been his chronicling of Bartlett Mears' life that he could copy out most of his notebooks verbatim. The book was virtually written; all it needed was a little judicious editing, to take out the only-mildly-scurrilous incidents and bring the thoroughly scurrilous ones closer together.

He worked flat out for three weeks and the draft was done. It was the most searing indictment of a human being he had ever read.

One thing still niggled, though. Dashiel Loukes had been right. No biography of Bartlett Mears would really be complete without an infusion of Mariana Lestrange's distinctive vituperation. Her public set-tos with her former husband were well chronicled; but she was bound to have a store of character-destroying reminiscence of their life together. That was the dash of venom which the biography required.

He got her phone number from a literary editor who gave him occasional reviewing work. She answered the phone with the brusqueness of someone who jealously guards her privacy, but when Carlton Rutherford announced his mission, her manner changed.

Yes, she would be delighted to tell him anything he wanted to know. No fate was bad enough for that bastard Bartlett Mears.

Mariana Lestrange lived in Hampstead. Of course she did. Bartlett Mears still lived in Hampstead, come to that. So did the majority of the glamorous literati with whom he had had affairs before, during and after his second marriage. The supply of them in Hampstead was so constant, he'd rarely felt the need to look elsewhere.

She received the biographer in her imposing sitting room. One of its walls was shelved with British and overseas editions of her novels; another with international awards and citations.

'So,' Mariana Lestrange purred in her famously sexy voice, 'you want all the real dirt on Bartlett Mears . . . ?'

She must have been nearly sixty, but was still very beautiful. Tall, slender, with a surprisingly ample bosom, she wore her artfully blonded hair as a frame to the small face whose nose would have been too large on someone less striking.

Carlton Rutherford felt a little uneasy in her presence. He always reacted that way to women of obvious sexual attraction. The state of his virginity remained precisely as it had been in 1959.

'Yes,' he said nervously. 'Anything you're prepared to tell me. Obviously, I know all the stuff that's been in the papers, but, er, anything more intimate would be ... very welcome ...'

'Hm. Who's publishing your book?' she asked sharply.

'Well, er ... The thing is, that's not quite decided yet ...'

'Ah, I see. You mean it's going to be auctioned.'

Carlton Rutherford did not disabuse her of this error. For a writer of Mariana Lestrange's stature, auctions would be a regular occurrence. She knew nothing of the end of the market where publishers don't fight over books, but have to be cajoled into accepting them, and even then frequently don't.

'Well, where shall we start ...?' Mariana purred on. 'Impotence the first night I agreed to make love to him ...? Or Bartlett peeing over the bed in our honeymoon suite ...? Or the time he hit me so hard he broke my jaw ...?'

'Oh, any of those. All of those. It all sounds wonderful!' Carlton Rutherford responded gleefully. 'Fire away!'

So Mariana Lestrange fired away. She produced a savage catalogue of meanness, drunkenness, sexual malpractice, infidelity, theft and cringing deceit. She enumerated her former husband's disgusting personal habits – his practice of stubbing out cigarette butts in coffee cups, his self-pitying hypochondria, his pill-gulping, his nose-picking, his farting, his belching, his snoring, his halitosis and the revolting state in which he left his underwear.

The resentment born of five years' cohabitation seemed not to have mellowed one iota with the passage of time. Only the tiniest of prompts was required to bring it once again bubbling to the surface.

Carlton Rutherford's pen could hardly move quickly enough across the page to record this cataract of domestic villainies. With each new revelation he hugged himself, gleefully envisaging where it could be inserted into his narrative.

Dashiel Loukes had been right. This was the secret ingredient that the biography needed. There is nothing like total character assassination to send a book rocketing up the bestseller lists.

At times Mariana Lestrange's account sounded so vicious, the antics she described so evil, that Carlton Rutherford almost suspected her novelist's instinct was fictionalizing for his benefit, but if ever he asked a hesitant 'Did he *really* do that?', she snapped back, 'Of course! I know. I lived with the bastard!'

He'd thought he was doing all right before, but after the interview with Mariana Lestrange, he knew he'd *really* got the dirt.

It took him less than a week to thread this new vein of vindictiveness into his text. At the end of that time, Carlton Rutherford checked carefully through his manuscript before delivering it personally to Dashiel Loukes' office. According to the agent's unnervingly pretty assistant, her boss was still out at lunch. Carlton Rutherford thought this slightly odd at five forty-five in the afternoon, but did not question it.

He went back to Upper Norwood to await the reaction to his literary bombshell.

At least this time their meeting merited lunch. Dashiel Loukes took him to the Groucho Club and, bathed in the sunlight of the upstairs dining room, gave his verdict.

'Sorry, old boy. Not a chance in hell of placing it.'

'But come on, it's good. All that detail – fascinating stuff. You can't say I haven't got all the dirt, can you?'

'No. Certainly not. No, it's the most compulsive manuscript I've read for years. I was up half the night reading it – absolutely riveting.'

'Well then . . . ?'

'It's your old problem, Carlton. Just like it was with *Neither One Thing Nor The Other* . . .'

'What do you mean?'

'Libel, old boy, libel. Your manuscript has got something actionable on every page.'

'But it's all true! It's all substantiated. I actually witnessed a lot of it.'

'Surely you didn't witness the incident in the gents' lavatory with Joe Orton . . . ? Or the benedictine-drinking contest with David Niven . . . ? Or that business with Malcolm Muggeridge and the spatula . . . ?'

'No, I wasn't actually there, but it's all true! I got it from Mariana. Anyway, Joe Orton's not going to pop up from the grave to deny it. Nor's David Niven likely to—'

'I agree, old boy. No problems with *them*. They're all safely dead and you can't libel the dead. No, it's Bartlett himself who's likely to make a stink – absolutely guaranteed to make a stink, I'd say.'

'But it all happened! Mariana Lestrange said he even used to boast about a lot of it.'

'Boasting in private about it is very different from sanctioning the printing of this kind of unsubstantiated gossip.'

'Dashiel, how many times do I have to tell you – it's all fully substantiated!'

'Carlton, the bottom line is that I've consulted a top libel lawyer whom I've used many times before. He's read your manuscript and he says it's absolute dynamite.'

'But it's *good*,' the author wailed plaintively.

'I'm not denying it. It's very good. Easily the most readable thing you've ever done.' Carlton Rutherford decided not to rise to this implied slight to the rest of his *oeuvre*, as the agent went on, 'But the fact remains that it's good *dynamite*. No publisher will touch it.'

'But—'

'No, old boy, you have to face the truth. There is no chance of publication for this book while Bartlett Mears is alive!'

From that moment Carlton Rutherford realized that he would have to commit murder.

The idea didn't worry him at all. In fact, the more he thought about it, the more he relished the prospect.

The manner of Bartlett Mears' killing did not really matter, so long as he ended up safely dead. But self-preservation dictated that Carlton Rutherford should use a method which could appear to any investigating authorities as an accident.

He did not have to look far to find it. Details that he knew of his quarry's personal habits – his smoking, his drinking, his addiction to a variety of pills – they all pointed in the same direction.

Bartlett Mears would die in a fire at his home.

It was hard for Carlton Rutherford – or anyone else – to avoid knowing his victim's tall Victorian Hampstead house, so frequently was it featured in colour supplements and television profiles of its owner.

Bartlett Mears took the image of the impractical artist to extremes and was nationally known to live in a state of paper-strewn chaos. Coupling this fact with his heavy drinking and smoking – not to mention his reliance on sleeping pills – what was more likely than that a casually discarded cigarette butt should ignite a pile of papers in his house and cause a life-ending conflagration . . . ?

Carlton Rutherford began surveillance of the murder scene, and soon discovered that Bartlett Mears never walked any-where. If he was going out, a taxi would arrive to take him to his destination; and on his sodden return a late-evening taxi would pour him out on to his doorstep. Then he would presumably take a few more drinks to anaesthetize himself further before falling into bed and – usually – remembering to turn out the light of his first-floor bedroom.

Obviously the fire would have to take place at night. At that time its victim's stupor and the lack of witnesses would give the conflagration a chance to take a good hold before emergency services could be summoned. But a little planning was required to ensure that a really good blaze was quickly achieved.

One day, when Bartlett Mears had been taxied away for a long lunch (all his lunches were long ones), his nemesis – Carlton Rutherford – slipped through the side gate of the house and examined the dustbins in the passage.

He quickly found what he wanted. In common with many other writers, Bartlett Mears was a member of a whole raft of literary organizations like the Society of Authors, PEN and the Writers' Guild. Also in common with many other writers, Bartlett Mears immediately consigned the literature of these organizations – the *Author*, *Pen International*, the *Writers' Newsletter* – unopened and unread into his dustbin. Carlton Rutherford did not have to search long to find a sheaf of solid envelopes all printed with his quarry's name and address.

Once he had secured these, and bought vodka, cigarettes and matches, his preparations were complete. It was just a matter of waiting for the right moment to put his plan into action.

The television gave him his cue. One Tuesday he was watching the end of *Newsnight* and heard the presenter say, 'Tomorrow evening in *Newsnight* we'll be discussing the pros and cons of the Net Book Agreement, and amongst those giving his – no doubt trenchant – views will be the author Bartlett Mears.'

It was typical that the BBC should try to enliven an extremely dull topic by bringing in Bartlett. Whatever the subject, he could always be relied on to say something out-rageous – particularly at such a late hour when his day's drinking would really have started to build up. He was bound after the programme to have a few more drinks in one of the BBC hospitality suites, before rolling into the car that would decant him in Hampstead.

Carlton Rutherford felt almost uncannily calm the follow-ing evening as he sat in his little flat in Upper Norwood, watching *Newsnight*. Bartlett Mears behaved predictably. He was rudely dismissive of other eminent authors, gratuitously offensive to the rather pretty girl conducting the interview, and he used the word 'shit' twice to ensure that the BBC switchboard would be briefly jammed by offended listeners. It was in fact the performance for which he had been booked.

Carlton Rutherford was still calm as he got into his dilapi-dated Austin Allegro and drove easily across London to Hampstead. As he had anticipated, his quarry had refreshed himself for a while with BBC hospitality, and Carlton had been parked opposite the house waiting for a full hour before the chauffeur-driven car arrived.

Bartlett Mears staggered out, with no word of thanks to the driver, and fumbled with his keys for a while before managing to open the front door.

Still icy calm, Carlton Rutherford waited another full hour for Bartlett Mears' nightcaps to be consumed and for the bedroom light to be switched off.

He gave it another half-hour, then got out of the car and sauntered across to the house opposite.

He doused some of the envelopes of literary literature with vodka, and slipped them through the letter box. Then, casu-ally, he lit a cigarette, drew on it a few times to get it thoroughly going, and dropped that through.

He waited.

At first he thought he had failed and was on the point of

starting again, when he was rewarded by a reflected orange glow on the hall ceiling.

Gently, he dropped through more of the envelopes to build up a substantial bonfire.

Then, even more gently, he trickled the contents of the second vodka bottle in through the letter box, careful to restrict its flow so that it would not douse the growing fire, but rather spread across the carpet, warm up slowly and ignite.

He stayed on the doorstep for two more full minutes, until he could feel the heat of his blaze through the wood of the front door; then sauntered back to his Austin Allegro.

He was back in Upper Norwood, in bed and asleep, within the hour.

He slept well, and was wakened by the *Today Programme*'s seven o'clock news on his clock radio.

It was exactly as he had wished. The last item of the bulletin announced the death of the popular author Bartlett Mears, in a fire which had gutted his Hampstead house.

Carlton Rutherford leaped out of his lonely bed, and danced a little jig of triumph which left him flushed and breathless.

It was agony to wait till ten, when he reckoned Dashiel Loukes would have arrived in his office. Back in the sixties, when Carlton Rutherford had been one of the white hopes of the agency, Dashiel would have encouraged the author to ring him at home. But those days were long past, and the agent had moved upmarket through a good few addresses since then. His favoured espionage authors were granted his current home number, but for lesser mortals it remained firmly ex-directory.

Eventually the hands of Carlton Rutherford's clock radio moved round to ten o'clock, and he rang through to Dashiel Loukes' office.

'I'm afraid,' said the dauntingly pretty assistant, 'that Mr Loukes is busy on another call.'

'Well, get him off it!' snapped the author, confident of his sudden value to the agent. 'Tell him it's Carlton Rutherford on the line!'

His confidence had not been misplaced. Dashiel Loukes was through to him immediately, almost fawning in his delight to have made contact with one of his most potentially lucrative authors.

'Carlton, terrific to hear you! Just about to ring you! I assume you're calling about what I think you're calling about . . . ?'

'I would imagine so. Rather changes the situation, doesn't it?'

'That, old boy, is the understatement of the year! Wonderful thing is – there'll now be a whole rash of Bartlett Mears books commissioned, and we've stolen a march on the lot of them, because our manuscript is already finished!'

It was interesting to hear how *your* manuscript had suddenly become *our* manuscript, but Carlton Rutherford was too excited to comment. 'So what's the next step?'

'The next step, old boy, is that I set up the most almighty auction that London has seen for a long time. Bartlett Mears sells in the States too, and he's translated everywhere. We are talking about a really big international book here. It's going to be *the* title at Frankfurt, no question. We are talking big, big bucks. You've really come up with the goods this time, Carlton Rutherford!'

Those were the words that all of his literary life, the author of *Neither One Thing Nor The Other* had longed to hear.

Radio and television were heavy that day with reminiscences, assessments and tributes to Bartlett Mears. Death changes many people's tunes and all of his fellow authors spoke with inordinate affection for 'the old rogue'.

67

Carlton Rutherford hugged himself as he listened. Just wait, he thought deliciously, just wait till my book comes out. That'll really set the record straight.

More details emerged about the accident which had so prematurely robbed the eminent author of his life. The general view seemed to be that, given the chaos in which Bartlett Mears had always lived, the only surprise was that an accident of that sort had not happened before.

The one shocking piece of additional information that emerged was that Bartlett had not been the only victim of the conflagration. He had not been alone in the house at the time of his death.

There had been a woman with him.

Her body had been so charred that immediate identification had not been possible.

By the end of the day, however, news bulletins carried the startling news that the other victim had been Mariana Lestrange.

Carlton Rutherford was surprised by this information, but strangely unmoved. So ... he had murdered two people rather than one. The literary world had lost another of its stars. It was something for which he could not grieve.

He did wonder idly what Mariana had been doing in her ex-husband's house. He favoured a theory that she had been there to sort out some financial detail left over from their marriage, which Bartlett, typically inefficient, had neglected.

The strong rumour around literary circles that the two writers had actually been found in bed together, Carlton Rutherford refused to countenance.

He was not going to admit any thought to his mind that might threaten the sunny feeling of satisfaction that so benignly reigned there.

* * *

The following Sunday, needless to say, the quality papers –
and even much of the gutter press – were full of tributes,
appreciations and assessments of Bartlett Mears.

Carlton Rutherford bought all of them, and read them all
with relish. Again, he was comforted by the knowledge of
how his forthcoming bestseller would upturn all of these
charitable assessments.

It was while he sat there in bliss that the phone rang.

Dashiel Loukes. 'Sorry to bother you on a Sunday . . .'

Carlton Rutherford did not mind at all. No doubt the
agent had received the first 'ball-park figure' from which the
forthcoming book auction would start, and was anxious to
tell his author without delay.

'. . . but something's come up,' the agent continued, in a
voice which suggested he might be the bearer of less pleasing
news.

'Oh? What?' asked Carlton Rutherford, instantly alert.

'Something which I'm afraid may rather put the kibosh on
our scheme, old boy.'

'What!'

'Apparently Bartlett Mears wrote his own memoirs. Did
you know that?'

'No, I didn't. But that needn't worry us. By the time they've
been edited and got ready for publication, my book will have
been out a long time and we'll have cleaned up.'

'No, I'm afraid we won't.'

'Why not?'

'Bartlett Mears' *Memoirs* have been all ready for publication for the last three years. His publishers can have
them on the bookstalls in a couple of months if they want
to.'

'But how? I mean, if they're ready, why haven't they been
published before?'

'They were all set up – pre-publicity about to start –

announcement in the *Bookseller* about to be made – when suddenly they had to be withdrawn.'

'But why?'

'Libel risk, old boy. Most of the people in the book were either dead or unlikely to sue, but there was one who held out. They tried sending her the manuscript to read, but that only made her even more determined to sue.'

'Who was it?' asked Carlton Rutherford weakly, knowing all too well the name that Dashiel Loukes was about to pronounce.

'Mariana Lestrange,' the agent replied. 'But, of course, now she's dead, there's nothing to stop them publishing as soon as they want . . .'

The agent went on for a while, explaining why this news invalidated the chances for their book, but Carlton Rutherford heard no more. He felt a sudden stab of pain in his chest, then his breath seemed to be sucked painfully out of his body until, moments after, blackness descended.

He collapsed, still holding the telephone, and died on the pile of newspaper tributes to his great rival, Bartlett Mears.

The death of Carlton Rutherford did not merit any newspaper obituaries. Memories of any promise contained in *Neither One Thing Nor The Other* had long been swamped by recollections of the subsequent turgid annals of Bob Grantham. There wasn't a lot to say about a novelist who hadn't published a book since the sixties.

The British edition of Bartlett Mears' *Memoirs* was published with great éclat in the autumn of 1992. It shot straight to the top of the *Sunday Times* bestseller list, and stayed there for many weeks. The American and foreign language editions looked set fair to repeat this success.

Part of the appeal of the book was that it was extremely scurrilous. The author made no attempt to whitewash himself, and indeed his account of his own life was infinitely more offensive than anything contained in the forgotten manuscript of Carlton Rutherford. There was lots of dirt, which was why the book proved so phenomenally popular.

The public, as they always do, loved a rogue.

Incidentally, there was no mention in Bartlett Mears' *Memoirs* of Carlton Rutherford. The famous author had been completely unaware even of the existence of his rival.

A LITTLE LEARNING

SIMON BRETT WRITES:

A few years back, I bought an old desk at an auction and, when I got it home, found that the drawers had not been emptied by its previous owner. He, from the papers I found there, I deduced to have been an academic of some kind. In a miscellaneous pile of documents, I came across the following essay. It seems to have been submitted as part of his doctoral thesis by an American postgraduate student named Osbert Mint. Keen that the fruits of his scholarship should be made available to as wide a readership as possible, I have made strenuous efforts to trace Mr Mint. These efforts have proved – regrettably – to be unsuccessful, and the essay is therefore printed here for the first time without its owner's permission.

The Literary Antecedents of Agatha Christie's Hercule Poirot

There is a popular misconception in academic circles that the works of Agatha Christie are simply popular *jeux d'esprit* which have no connection with the mainstream of English literature. This attitude both belittles the quality of the author's work and also underestimates the wide reading and research which went into the creation of her most famous character. Hercule Poirot did not spring fully formed into life on page 34 of his first adventure, *The Mysterious Affair at Styles*. His genesis was part of a much longer creative process and must be seen as the culmination of eleven centuries of English literary history.

Though Agatha Christie was properly reticent about the breadth of her reading, it is clear to the informed student of her works that they reflect a much broader and deeper literary frame of reference than is usually admitted to this particular author. My essay will trace the pattern of references to other literary sources of which the author herself was sometimes no more than subliminally aware.

Though there were clearly classical influences on Agatha Christie's work – most obviously in the collection *The Labours of Hercules* – they are not within the province of this study, particularly since the subject has been expertly covered by other scholars.[1] It is my intention to trace only the English language sources for the creation of Hercule Poirot.

The first unarguable influence on Agatha Christie's writings can be found in one of the Digressions in *Beowulf*. The killing in Hrothgar's meadhall described in the ensuing passage was clearly the origin of the many Country House murders which were to feature in Hercule Poirot's investigations. (The language of the extract has been modernized to render it accessible to the general reader. Those fluent in Anglo-Saxon may prefer to consult the original text.)

Felled on the floor   limp lay the earl,
Blood from the blade   blackening his back,
While all the warriors,   muddled with mead-drinking,
Snored in their slumbers,   lost like the daylight
That darkness has doused.   One of their number,
A murdering bondman –   hated by Hrothgar

(Bringer of boons,   mighty meat-giver)
And by He who made heaven   (granter of goodwill,
Holy helper) –   unfairly faked sleep.
Wakeful eyes worked,   lurking behind lids,
Knowing that another,   whose sword he had stolen,
A goodman not guilty,   a worthy warrior,
Would be caught for the killing –   unless
One much wiser,   a righteous unraveller,
A reader of runes,   a conner of clues,
Might see through the slaying,   righting its wrong,
And finger the fiendish one.

Though it might be fanciful to assert that this passage heralds the arrival of Hercule Poirot on the literary scene, it is clear that the Digression prepares the way for the development of the whodunnit form, and particularly of the private detective, 'the righteous unraveller', whose task it will be to solve the murder.[2]

    Granting that the *Beowulf* reference, though tantalizingly close to unambiguity, cannot be unequivocally accepted as a primary source for Hercule Poirot, the directness of the next reference brooks no denial. It is indeed remarkable – and perhaps a comment on the tunnel vision of many in academic life – that no previous scholars have looked for the Belgian detective's literary antecedents in the most obvious of sources, the Medieval Mystery Play. The very word 'Mystery' could not provide a much heavier clue, and I am bold to assert that Agatha Christie's inspiration to write mysteries featuring Hercule Poirot sprang directly from her reading of the following extract from the Harrogate *Third Shepherd's Play* in the Hull Cycle ('as it hath been divers time acted by the Guild of Chandlers and Gardners upon the Feast of Corpus Christie'):

*   *   *

The three Shepherds wake to find the fourth Shepherd,
Mak, lying still beside them.

1 *Shep.* Now by good Saint Loy – and eke by Saint Beth,
    Why ye lie here, boy, so barren of breath?

2 *Shep.* Aye, why curl up coy, so still on the earth?

3 *Shep.* Oh, gone be our joy – for that stillness be death!
    He is dead!

1 *Shep.* Now deep is my dole, for lost is his life!

2 *Shep.* And taken his soul – how sad be this strife!

3 *Shep.* His purse it be stole. We must go tell his wife.

1 *Shep.* In his back there's a hole! It was made by a knife!
    How he bled!

2 *Shep.* Someone foully hath played, some forsaken swine
    This murder hath made – by evil design!

3 *Shep.* At whose door be it laid? Who's the cause of the
    crime?

1 *Shep.* Let's see whose be the blade? By the rood, it be
    mine!

2 *Shep.* So then thou must be blamed!

1 *Shep.* Nay, by our lakin's grace! I slept right through
    the night!

3 *Shep.* Then why scratched be thy face? Why these signs
    of a fight?

2 *Shep.* Why be blood in this place? On thy sleeve it be
    bright.

1 *Shep.* Now, by Saint Boniface! What ye think be not
    right! I've been framed!
    Oh, would one come, that could prove me guilt-free!

2 *Shep.* Soft, now what be this hum? And this light that
    I see?

An angel appears to them.

3 *Shep.* 'Tis an angel! Be dumb! Nay, drop to thy knee!

Angel Nay, look not so glum! I am come to ye three,
    As the scripture foretells.

> 2 *Shep.* How his bald head doth shine! Like an egg it be
> round!
> 2 *Shep.* His moustache be so fine, I am nigh to a swound!
> 1 *Shep.* Show this guilt be not mine! Let the killer be
> found!
> *Angel* Aye, that villain malign I will catch and confound
> – With my little grey cells!'[3]

The next unarguable literary reference which Agatha Christie must have responded to is found in John Skelton's *Speke, Parrot*. This poem is generally agreed to be made up of material from different dates and there are considerable textual differences between manuscript versions. The most telling one, from the point of view of this study, was found only as recently as 1893 in the Brestimont Collection. It is actually entitled *Speke, Porot* and contains the following significant variants of the first three stanzas:

> My name is Porot, a byrd of paradyse,
>   By nature devysed of a wonderous kynde,
> Daintily dressed, so dylycate and precyse,
>   Blessed with a quyte exceptyonall mynde;
>   So men of all countreys by fortune me fynd,
> And send me greate crymes to investygate:
> Then Porot the culpryt wyl incrymynate.
>
> Cravat curyously clynched, with sylver pyn,
>   Properly parfumed, to make me debonaire;
> A myrrour of glasse, that I may prene therin;
>   Mustaches ful smartly with many a divers care
>   Freshly I dresse, and make blacke my haire.
> Then, Speke, Porot, I pray you, full curtesly they say;
> Porot hath a goodly brain, to ferrit out foul playe.

With my backe bent, my lyttel wanton eye,
    Fancye and fresh as is the emrawde grene,
About my neck a sylke scarfe do I tye.
    My lyttyll leggys, my spats[4] both nete and clene,
    I am essentyale on a murdre scene;
Oh perfecte Porot, the lyttyl clever sluthe,
The clewes wyl trace, and always fynde the truthe.

The evidence in this extract is conclusive, and it can therefore
be definitively stated that Agatha Christie's source for the
character of Hercule Poirot was *Speke, Parrot*.

But the author's debts to English literature do not stop
with John Skelton. In her development of the character of
Poirot, she was clearly influenced by her reading of Sir Philip
Sidney's *Astrophel and Stella*, and particularly of the following sonnet:

CXI
Why I haue ask'd you here

O Fate, O fault, O curse, O crime of bloode!
What caitif could haue caused so foul a showe?
What coward turn'd my smiles to sighes of woe?
What joye-killer haue forced my teares to floode,
And caused Loue's flowres to perishe in the budde?
What trecherie hath brought this man so lowe,
Stabbd deeper e'en than Cupid's darts can goe,
That from his hart the beat no more shall thudde?
Were Stella's eyes the motiue for this crime,
Or stolen rubies, iuorie, pearle and gold?
I might! – nay, will! – if you should graunt me time –
The secret of this heauy case unfold.
To shewe the villain and to make all clere
The reason is why I haue ask'd you here.

There are so many other examples of literature from the Tudor and Stuart period which influenced Agatha Christie that it would be invidious to mention any of them.[5] I will therefore move next to the Augustan Age and another undeniable source-work for the expansion of the character of Hercule Poirot, Alexander Pope's *Essay on Detection*. Almost every line of this surprisingly underrated poem is relevant to the subject in hand, but I will limit myself to the following short extract:

As in the World's, so in Detection's laws,
All force respects the Universal Cause,
Which Logic's enemies do but confuse,
Confounding those who will not heed the clues.
For, from the first, a mighty endless chain
Links clue to crime, and crime to clue again.
One all-connecting, naught-excluding line
Draws Logic's threads within its grand design;
As when a bloodied sword, by Vulcan's skill
Framed to inflict on man the greatest ill,
Be found imbedded in some chilly corse,
Inhuman stabbed with more than human force,
The first thought is to find and clap in jail
The owner of the sword. Of more avail
Might be to check the angle of the blow
And whether struck from left or right to know.
If from the left, you wrongly would indict
The owner of a sword who used his right.
The true Detective to such ploys is wise,
Nor lets the smallest thing evade his eyes.
Though falsely led, his true mind does not stray,
But follows through its thesis all the way,
Nor does forget, but mightily esteems
That One Great Truth: 'All is not what it seems.'

That Agatha Christie's reading was wide-ranging cannot now be denied, but, even so, the source of one of Hercule Poirot's favourite ploys – almost, it could be said, his trademark, the gathering together of the suspects at the climax of one of his investigations – is surprising. It was only after extensive reading through the writings of many authors that I came across the work which undoubtedly gave the author this particular inspiration. Here, from a late volume of *The Scots Musical Museum*, is the poem which clinches my argument. Though published anonymously, it is undoubtedly the work of Robert Burns:[6]

CA' THE BURGIES TAE THE BOGGIN CHORUS.

Ca' the burgies[a] tae the boggin[b].
Whaur the willie-paugh[c] be troggin[d].
Seel[e] a' windies[f] wi' the woggin[g],
    My dearie-oh, my dork[h].
When Macporrit[i] gang a-spoolin[j],
Wi' his ganglins[k] in his troolin[l]
He waur mair a skilfu' doolin[m]
    Wi' a' ca'in'[n] roon his ha'!
And his baughit[o] of the hintree[p]
Was sae bree[q] on ilka wintree[r]
That he niver freemed[s] his fintree[t]
    Till he spoffer'd who doon tha'[u]!
Ca' the burgies tae the boggin, &c.

a Suspects	b Library	c Detective
d Waiting	e Guard	f Exits
g Police Force	h Possibly a reference to Hastings?	
i Poirot?	j Investigating	k Grey cells?

79

l Brain   m Detective   n ?
o Analysis   p Case   q Acute
r Occasion   s Sipped   t Tisane
u Till he had told them whodunnit

I have now supplied sufficient evidence of Agatha Christie's erudition and remarkable range of source-material to silence the most sceptical critic of my thesis. And I think I should definitely be awarded my doctorate as soon as possible.

OSBERT MINT, April 1967

NOTES:

1 Cf. especially Britt-Montes' *The Oresteia: Did Clytem-nestra REALLY Do It?* (Scand. Dagblat, Vol vii, pp. 152–157, 1932) and Bent Istrom's *The Death of Aeschylus: Who Dropped the Tortoise?* (*Christiana Review*, March 1947, pp. 474–523).

2 It has long been a matter of regret amongst *Beowulf* scholars that this particular Digression is not resolved and that the identity of the true murderer is never revealed. Tom St Brien's solution (*Grendel's Mother Did It*, Gunter-rheinischer Festschrift, 1924), though initially persuasive, cannot ultimately be regarded as other than conjectural.

3 Academic opinion has long been divided over the precise meaning of this line, which is seriously obscured in the original manuscript of the play. Professor Ernst Tombi of Geneva University has argued persuasively that the line should read, '*When my little goose calls*', though has unfortunately offered no convincing reason as to why. Enthusiasts of Agatha Christie will be in no doubt that the line should be printed as above.

4 There seems to be no justification for Bo Mitstern's reading of '*spots*' in this context.

5 Scholars who wish to pursue this topic further are recommended to read the seminal works of Sir T. Bemton, *Christopher Marlowe's Mean Streets* and *The Metaphysicals: Who-Donne-It?*

6 Ms N. Briotte's questioning of this attribution on the premise that 'the poem does not contain enough hatred of women to be authentic Burns' can be confidently dismissed as feminist claptrap.

APPENDIX I – THE NAME 'POIROT'

The much-bruited suggestion that Agatha Christie selected the name Poirot randomly is patently ridiculous. Apart from its assonant association with the heavily symbolic 'parrot' (discussed more fully above in reference to Skelton's *Speke Parrot*), the name also reverberates with nuances from the French language. The 'poire' or, in English, 'pear' is an obvious subliminal reference to the distinctive shape of the detective's bald head. That shape is again shadowed in the French word 'poirée', which means 'white beet' and conforms with the frequently mentioned pallor of the detective's complexion.

Though 'poireau', the French word closest in sound to the name Christie chose, with its double meanings of 'leek' and 'wart', appears to have no obvious connection with the detective, the word 'poirier', meaning a 'pear-tree' offers a much more fruitful area for investigation. Its sound provided the first syllable of Poirot's name, '*poir*', and for the second one need look no further than the French word 'perd*reau*', meaning 'a young partridge'. The unusual juxtaposition of these two words can only be a subconscious association in the author's mind with the well-known carol, *The Twelve Days* *of Christmas*, whose repetitive chorus ends, 'And a partridge in a pear-tree.'

The truth of this conjecture would seem to be confirmed by Agatha Christie's choice of titles for the 1938 volume *Hercule Poirot's Christmas* and the 1960 collection *The Adventure of the Christmas Pudding and a Selection of Entrées*.

APPENDIX II – THE NAME 'HASTINGS'

The name of Poirot's occasional assistant is no less carefully chosen than that of Agatha Christie's main protagonist. His nomenclature has a very respectable literary history. Shakespeare hinted at the essence of the character in *Richard III*, Act Three Scene One, when the young Prince of Wales, with a knowledge beyond his years, cries:

'Fie! what a slug is Hastings.'

Goldsmith, at the end of *She Stoops to Conquer* has Hastings say:

'Come, madam, you are now driven to the very last scene of all your contrivances.'

– surely a parallel prefiguring (together with the Burns poem) of all those occasions when Christie's Hastings would be delegated to assemble the suspects for Poirot's latest denouement.

And Hastings' habit of pipe-smoking was clearly taken from Thomas Hood, who in a poem of 1839 wrote:

' 'Twas August – Hastings every day was filling.'

SIMON BRETT WRITES:

Though, as I mentioned, I was unable to make contact with Mr Mint, a letter accompanying his essay did make clear the unfortunate fact that its standard – or perhaps the startling originality of its thinking – did not meet with the examiners' approval. Osbert Mint was not awarded his doctorate. When last heard of – in the early seventies – he had returned to the United States and was apparently working in a fast food restaurant.

POLITICAL CORRECTIONS

There was a large and, to the minds of many observers, unconventional house party assembled for Christmas at Stebbings. The Dowager Duchess of Haslemere had never had any inhibitions about mixing her guests, though the composition of the assembly would have been unthinkable had her husband, the Duke, still been alive.

Apart from her two children, Hubert – who had inherited the title – and his sister Lady Cynthia, none of the Dowager Duchess's guests was quite the goods. There was Adolphus Weinburg, the well-to-do Hebrew financier, whose—

'I'm sorry. We can't have this.'

Tilson Gutteridge did not lift the nicotine-yellowed finger that was following the lines of faded typescript, but raised his eyes to the young woman beside him. She was undeniably pretty, but in a way that didn't appeal. The dark red hair was too geometrically cut, the blue eyes behind the dark-rimmed round glasses were too pale and humourless to accord with his, perhaps old-fashioned, taste.

'What's the problem?' he asked ingenuously.

'This is anti-semitic,' said Juanita Rainbird. 'We can't say "Hebrew financier".'

'Why not? It just means that he's Jewish.'

'We can't say that nowadays. It's discriminatory.'

'But look, that's what Eunice Brock wrote. It was the kind

84

of thing they all wrote in the thirties. You'll find the same in Agatha Christie, Dorothy L. Sayers, the lot of them.'

'We still can't say it. Not in something we're publishing for the first time in the nineteen-nineties.' Her accent became more American as her assertiveness grew.

'But all Eunice Brock's other books have been reprinted as she wrote them.'

'Some of the titles have been changed. Like *The Company of Ishmaels* became *The Company of Fraudsters*.'

'That amendment can hardly have been considered very flattering to the Jews, can it?'

'It has made for an acceptable title,' Juanita Rainbird replied evenly. 'And think how many changes Agatha Christie's *Ten Little Niggers* has been through. First it became *Ten Little Indians*—'

'Then *Ten Little Native Americans* . . . ?' Tilson Gutteridge suggested mischievously.

The editor was unamused. 'No. Now it's known as *Then There Were None* . . . And I'm sure if its manuscript arrived today on the desk of any editor in the country, it would be re-edited for publication.'

'Hm. Shall we press on?'

His finger hadn't moved from the line of text. As his eyes reverted to the typescript, Juanita Rainbird looked at her visitor without enthusiasm. Tilson Gutteridge was a man in his sixties, wearing the shapeless tweeds and knitted tie of another generation. A whiff of cherrywood tobacco, whisky and something else less wholesome hung around him. It was only with difficulty that Juanita had convinced him there were no exceptions to Krieper & Thoday's no-smoking policy and persuaded him to put the noisome pipe back into his bulging pocket.

There was something over-the-top, almost operatic, about the man's appearance. The pebble glasses seemed too thick, the eyebrows too bushy, the ill-fitting false teeth too yellowed. Tilson Gutteridge looked a parodic archetype of a literary figure who had never succeeded and was now long past any possible sell-by date.

Still, Juanita knew she had to humour him. He was yet to reveal how he'd come by the manuscript, but it was undoubtedly a valuable commodity. Krieper & Thoday were still doing very well from the sales stimulated by the continuing Wenceslas Potter television series. The discovery of a new Eunice Brock would be just the sort of publishing coup to endear Juanita Rainbird to her new Australian managing director, Keith Chappick.

The publicity department could get a lot of mileage out of a long-lost manuscript. Regardless of the quality of the book, after some judicious editing it would sell well on curiosity value alone.

And with a bit of luck there wouldn't be any royalties to pay. Eunice Brock had died in 1939. For the fifty years after her death, the royalties on the Wenceslas Potter books had gone to her niece, Dierdre Townley, who had conveniently passed on in 1990, leaving no heirs. Dierdre hadn't made much out of her inheritance. Though the books had remained more or less in print, the real revival of interest in Eunice Brock had started in 1992 with the first Wenceslas Potter television series. That was when the estate had started to be worth something, and by then of course all the profits went direct to Krieper & Thoday.

Increasingly Juanita Rainbird wondered where Tilson Gutteridge had found the manuscript they were perusing, and whether or not he had any rights in it. If he could prove ownership, he'd have to be paid something for the typescript. If he could prove he also owned the copyright, he and his heirs would receive royalties for fifty years after the book's publication.

Juanita knew she must move cautiously, suppress her instinctive curiosity and play the scene at her guest's pace. The information she needed would come in time.

'Could I offer you something to drink . . . ?' she suggested, to thaw the developing atmosphere between them. 'Coffee . . . or something from the fridge . . . ?'

Tilson Gutteridge's eye gleamed. 'Something from the fridge, please.'

She reached to the side of her desk and swung the door open to reveal the fridge's packed interior. 'Orange juice or Perrier?'

The man's face fell. 'I'll have a black coffee, thanks.'

Before she filled a cup for him from the machine, Juanita Rainbird explained severely, 'I should just point out that my getting coffee for you is not an expression of any subservient gender role-play. I would be equally ready to get coffee for a guest of my own sex.'

Tilson Gutteridge looked bewildered. 'Fine,' he murmured.

Juanita Rainbird placed the cup of coffee on the desk in front of him. 'Right, let's get back to the text, shall we?'

His finger moved along under the lines as they both silently read on.

. . . *the well-to-do Hebrew financier* . . .

Without comment, Juanita Rainbird stuck a yellow Post-it sticker in the margin beside these words, and scribbled a pencil note on her clipboard.

. . . *whose hair, black, thick and naturally curly, exuded the fragrance of some violet-scented pomade. He had fleshy, prominent features, his long nose curving down almost in mirror image of his jutting chin* . . .

'That's unacceptable too.'

'She's just saying what the bloke looked like,' Tilson Gutteridge protested wearily.

'Yes, but couched in those terms it becomes a racist slur.'

'Oh, come on, that's how everyone talked in the thirties. For heaven's sake, don't make such a meal of it, darling.'

Juanita's eyes beamed blue fire at her visitor. 'I am sorry, Mr Gutteridge, but I must ask you to refrain from the use of diminishing sexist endearments.'

'Er . . . ?'

She took no notice of his puzzlement, but returned to the typescript.

Another of the Dowager Duchess's guests also aspired to, but failed to meet, the qualification of an English gentleman. Though not of the Semitic brotherhood, he too was an oily cog in the machinery of finance . . .

Juanita Rainbird's pencil, once again offended, raced across her pad.

Ras Gupta was an oriental gentleman who had made a killing from firms about to go smash, scooping up their shares at cat's meat prices . . .

Tilson Gutteridge's finger stopped and he looked up solicitously to Juanita. 'Any worries about complaints from the cat protection lobby?'

The editor pursed her lips. 'Let's just press on, shall we?'

This dark-complexioned aspirant's attempts to pass himself off as the genuine article were let down by the flashiness of the loud attire he favoured, not to mention a native predilection for shoddy jewellery. The ridiculousness of his appearance was accentuated by his dwarfish stature, which qualified him better for a circus ring than the drawing room of a Dowager Duchess.

Juanita Rainbird could restrain herself no longer. 'That'll have to be changed,' she blurted out.

'Why?'

'It's sizeist.'

'Eh?'

'The emphasis on the man's non-average altitudinal endowment could cause offence to readers similarly afflicted.' She realized her mistake and moved quickly to limit the damage. 'That is, I don't use the word "afflicted" in any pejorative sense. In no way do I wish to imply that someone vertically challenged has less validity or viability as a human being than someone of more traditional anatomical configuration.'

'Er . . . ?' Tilson Gutteridge looked at her blankly. 'So what are you saying – Ras Gupta can't be described as short . . . ?'

'No.'

'. . . even though the plot hinges on the fact that he is the only one of the house guests small enough to have crawled out of the scullery window on Christmas night after the Dowager Duchess had been murdered?'

'Well . . .' Juanita Rainbird was momentarily checked. Then her pencil dashed down another note. 'I'm sure we'll be able to find an alternative formula of words to deal with that problem.'

Tilson Gutteridge shrugged and readdressed his attention to the typescript.

Another of the guests at the Stebbings gloried in the name of the Vicomte de Fleurie-Rizeau. An effeminate Gallic lounge lizard, whose fractured English was uttered in an affected lisp and whose movements were almost ladylike in their dainty—

'This won't do,' said Juanita Rainbird. But before she could launch into her homophobia lecture, she caught sight of the watch on her wrist. 'Oh, goodness, I didn't realize it was so late. It's lunchtime.'

Tilson Gutteridge grinned. 'Splendid. Where are we going? Needn't be too lavish. Just an Italian or something. So long as they serve a decent red wine, eh?'

Juanita Rainbird looked at him primly. 'I'm sorry, Mr Gutteridge. That was not an invitation. I'm already committed to sharing a working sandwich with my managing director.'

'Oh well, have to do it another time, won't we?'

'I should also point out that Krieper & Thoday have recently instituted an across-the-board no-lunching policy. The only exception to that rule being the lunching on publication day of authors whose previous works have made the *Sunday Times* bestseller lists.'

'Oh. I thought lunch was one of the main activities of publishers.'

'You have a rather dated image of our industry, I'm afraid, Mr Gutteridge,' said Juanita Rainbird austerely. 'Anyway, it's not as if you're even an author, are you?'

'No,' he agreed. 'So ... what? We'll continue going through the manuscript another time?'

'Yes. Unless you'd like to leave it with me and I'd—'

His hands were instantly out to snatch up the typescript and clutch it protectively to his chest. 'I'm not letting this out of my sight.'

'Well, maybe you'd like to stay here while one of my assistants—' She quickly corrected herself '—one of my *co-workers* photocopies—'

Tilson Gutteridge shook his head firmly. 'This stays with me and is not reproduced until we've sorted out a deal.'

'Yes ...' Juanita Rainbird paused, selecting her next words with care. 'This does of course bring us on to the question of ownership ... more specifically, perhaps, how you came to be in possession of the manuscript ... ?'

The man grinned complacently.

'... and indeed what rights – if any – you might have in the property ... ?'

'Oh, it's mine all right,' he assured her.

'It may be yours in the sense that you physically have the typescript in your possession, but the issue of copyright is a totally different—'

'The copyright is mine too.'

Juanita Rainbird allowed herself a little laugh. 'I don't see how that could be possible, Mr Gutteridge.'

'It's possible,' he told her, 'because I have recently discovered something of my family history.'

'Oh?'

'I have always known myself to be illegitimate. I was adopted as a baby. It was only last month that I found out the identity of my real mother.'

He played the silence for a little more than it was worth.

'My real mother was Eunice Brock.'

Juanita Rainbird said nothing, but her mind was racing.

'So I am not only the owner of the physical manifestation of this manuscript, but also of its copyright.'

The editor did the sums quickly in her head. It wasn't a disaster. So they'd have to pay royalties on the one book; their profits on the rest of the Eunice Brock *œuvre* would remain intact.

'Not only that,' Tilson Gutteridge went on gleefully, 'I am also the copyright holder on the rest of my mother's published work.'

Juanita Rainbird gave a confident smile as, politely but deftly, she dashed his aspirations.

'I'm sorry, Mr Gutteridge, but I'm afraid your mother's published works went out of copyright in 1989.'

'I know that, Juanita sweetie.' He didn't give her time to object to the sexist diminutive as he went on. 'But I'm sure I don't have to tell someone in publishing that, as of summer 1995, the period of copyright is to be extended from fifty to seventy years after an author's death . . .'

Juanita Rainbird gaped.

'. . . so my mother's works are about to come back into copyright, where they will remain until the year 2009.'

*   *   *

Keith Chappick didn't know much about books, but he was good at sacking people, so he was doing very well in publishing. In his native Australia he'd started by sacking people in newspapers, then moved on to sacking people in television. It was as a television executive that he'd arrived in England, and the move to sacking people in publishing had been a logical one. He had been through two other publishing houses before taking up the appointment at Krieper & Thoday. In each one he'd sacked more people and been given a higher-profile job with more money.

The Keith Chappick management style had been quickly imposed on Krieper & Thoday. On his first day he'd sacked the publishing director and two senior editors; thereafter he ruled by simple terror. The staff, secure in nothing save the knowledge that their jobs were permanently on the line, spread themselves ever thinner, taking on more and more work, putting in longer and longer hours. Uncomplaining, they annexed the responsibilities of sacked colleagues, knowing that refusal of any additional burden was a one-way ticket to the dole queue. Within six months of the new managing director's arrival, the same amount of work was being done by a third of the previous staff. Krieper & Thoday's shareholders were delighted.

Complaints about Keith Chappick's idiosyncratic management techniques became as improbable as complaints about workload. No one demurred when the nine o'clock half-hour of Aikido was made mandatory for all staff. They trotted off like lambs to the slaughter of paint-ball combat weekends. Even the no-lunching diktat was accepted without a murmur by people who had hitherto been among the most dedicated contributors to the profits of Orso, Nico Ladenis and the Groucho Club.

Nor would any member of staff contemplate refusing the managing director's summons to 'share a working sandwich' in the half-hour before he went off to lunch at the Connaught.

The invitation – 'subpoena' might be a better word – was literal. The sandwich was singular, and it was shared. That day Juanita Rainbird got half a tuna and cucumber, while Keith Chappick probed her working record for reasons that might allow him to sack her.

Juanita gave him the good news and the bad news. Coming across a new Eunice Brock manuscript was undoubtedly good news; coming across an accompanying copyright holder with a claim to the whole estate undoubtedly bad.

'What proof do we have that he's who he says he is?' asked Keith Chappick once the full story was out.

'None yet, but he's assured me he can produce documentation to authenticate his claim.'

'Hm . . .' The managing director looked thoughtfully out of his top-floor aquarium of an office at the slate-grey winter sky. 'And from what you say, he seems to have an accurate knowledge of copyright law . . . ?'

'An unhealthily accurate knowledge. He reckons, when the extension to seventy years comes in, he'll be due royalties on all Eunice Brock sales since the old girl's niece died.'

'Shit. That's the period when the television series has been on. That's when the books have been really coining it.'

'I know.'

'Could make a nasty big hole in the company's profits – particularly as it'd be retrospective.'

'Yes.'

'Well, there's no way we're going to pay him. We've got to get round it somehow.' He looked blandly at his employee. 'Any ideas?'

This was another typical Keith Chappick management technique. Sacking was really all he did. He didn't regard it as part of his job to have ideas; that's what the staff were there for. Whatever the problem, they had to come up with the solution to it. If they didn't, they got sacked.

'The best thing would be . . .' Juanita Rainbird began cautiously, '. . . if we could prove that his claim was false, that he actually isn't who he says he is . . .'

'Is it known that Eunice Brock did have an illegitimate child?'

'There were strong rumours. That muck-raking biography of her that came out a couple of years back stated it as an acknowledged fact.'

'Hm.' Keith Chappick scratched his chin as he looked out over the London skyline.

'And Tilson Gutteridge'd be about the right age.' Juanita shook her head ruefully. 'The best thing'd be if we could prove someone else was really Eunice Brock's illegitimate child . . . and that that someone was either dead or totally unaware of their true identity.'

'Yes . . .' said the managing director; then, with increasing enthusiasm as the idea took hold, 'Yes. That's what you'd better do, Juanita.'

'What?'

'Find a rival claimant.'

'But supposing there isn't one . . . ?'

Keith Chappick shrugged. 'That's your problem. Incidentally . . . did this old geezer say whether he'd got family . . . you know, heirs of his own . . . ?'

'He's got no one. Not married, no relatives.'

'So, if he were to die . . .' the managing director grinned, letting the idea float for a moment in the air-conditioned air, '. . . our problem would be at an end.'

'Yes.'

Keith Chappick looked briskly at his watch. The audience was over. 'Leave it with you, Juanita. I'm relying on you to get it sorted . . . or . . .'

He didn't need to finish the sentence. The threat had been implicit from the beginning of the interview.

'This is man's work,' averred Wenceslas Potter. *'Don't you bother your pretty little nut about it.'*

'But I want to know who murdered Mummy,' Lady Cynthia insisted. *'It'd be a pretty shabby sort of daughter who wasn't interested.'*

'You're absolutely right!' the detective ejaculated. *'And let it never be said that I could entertain the idea of anyone as pretty as you ever doing anything shabby. But believe me, I have your best interests at heart. I'm afraid the conscienceless cove who did for your mother might strike again.'*

'Oh!' Lady Cynthia's soft hand leapt in alarm to her ruby lips, and beneath the fine silk of her evening gown her bosom heaved. *'How beyond words ghastly if that should happen! Wenceslas,'* she interrogated in a hushed voice, *'are you suggesting that I myself am at risk from this bounder?'*

'Not while I am here to protect you, milady,' he responded with a gallant bow. *'You may be no more than a feeble woman but—'*

'This is horribly sexist,' said Juanita Rainbird, her objections no longer satisfied by the continuous notes she was scribbling.

'Is it?' asked Tilson Gutteridge innocently. 'I actually thought it was rather sexy.'

The editor looked at him with distaste. Tilson Gutteridge seemed to have taken up squatting rights in her office. His tweed jacket was spread untidily across the back of his chair. The braces over his checked shirt were not trendy nineties braces; their perished elastic was reminiscent rather of the truss industry. The tobacco staleness that hung around him seemed to intensify the longer he spent in the room.

Juanita Rainbird wished she had never got into her current situation, having to spend long hours closeted with a man every detail of whose character she loathed. But there was no alternative. She needed to play for time, stretch out the line-by-line copy-editing of Eunice Brock's manuscript until she could see the way out of her dilemma. Because, if she wanted to keep her job, a way out had to be found.

She had made some headway in her investigations. Long hours of research at the Family Records Centre in Farringdon had finally yielded the undeniable fact of a birth certificate. Eunice Brock, under her real name of Phyllis Townley, had given birth to a male child in September 1927. No father's name was recorded.

Unearthing that information, though in one way satisfying, had at the same time been dispiriting, because it strengthened the possibility that Tilson Gutteridge was telling the truth. Proof that Eunice Brock had never had a son would have provided much more comfort.

Finding records of the baby's adoption was proving considerably more difficult, and Juanita Rainbird was beginning to suspect deliberate obfuscation. At the time of her son's birth Eunice Brock was already a published author and something of a celebrity, so it was possible that she had intentionally clouded the waters to prevent any successful probing into her shameful lapse.

Juanita could not at that moment see what the next step of her investigation should be. Her eye strayed to the shelf of hardbacks on the wall and the thought she had been trying half-heartedly to suppress for some days bubbled back to the surface of her mind.

'If he were to die . . .' Keith Chappick had said, '. . . our problem would be at an end.'

As a crime editor, Juanita Rainbird was extremely well

versed in the means of murder. The fantasy methods of crime fiction's Golden Age – injecting air bubbles into veins, high musical notes shattering glass containers of poisonous gases – had given way to greater realism in contemporary examples of the genre. If Juanita ever did decide to murder someone, the works she had edited offered a rich variety of ways to achieve that end.

'So . . . are you suggesting it should be rewritten?'

Tilson Gutteridge's words brought her out of her reverie and back to the typescript. 'Well, I don't like it.'

'That's not the point.'

'All its attitudes are very demeaning and diminishing to women.'

'That's not the point either. And I would draw your attention to the fact that it was written by a woman – my mother, as it happens.'

'Yes, but she was simply conforming to the phallocentric norms of the period. She didn't dare write Lady Cynthia as an assured, assertive woman, so she made her a pathetic little bit of fluff.'

'Actually, it's rather important for the plot that Lady Cynthia's a pathetic little bit of fluff. For God's sake, why shouldn't Eunice Brock write about a stupid woman? Stupid women do exist, you know.'

Tilson Gutteridge looked at Juanita Rainbird very directly as he said this last sentence; there was an edge of insolence in his expression. She turned away, as if suddenly interested in the one Christmas card on her desk. Its message was 'Happy Holidays'. (Juanita had thrown all cards with specifically Christian messages straight into the bin; she did not believe in prescriptive religion and had no wish to offend people of other faiths.)

Once again it was borne in on her what an utterly hateful man Tilson Gutteridge was. At times she didn't think she'd have any problem with her conscience if she did have to end up murdering him.

And, if she couldn't get another lead in her investigation, she probably would have to end up murdering him.

'Shall we press on?' he said rather tetchily, and once again his nicotine-stained finger traced along the lines of typescript.

'*You may be no more than a feeble woman, but with me by your side you'd be safe in a jungle full of man-eating fuzzy-wuzzies.*'

'We can't have that!' Juanita Rainbird objected instinctively.

'Offend vegetarians, will it?' Tilson Gutteridge baited her.

'It will offend people of alternative – though no less viable – pigmentation.'

'Oh, for God's sake! You can't pretend black people aren't black. When I was at school, there was a black chap in my class and his nickname was "Fuzzy-Wuzzy". Everyone called him that. He didn't mind – or at least he never said he minded.'

Juanita prepared to embark on her lecture about how sensibilities had changed, but thought better of it. Instead, she asked casually, 'Where were you at school, actually, Mr Gutteridge?'

'Public school called Whittinghams. South London. You heard of it?'

'No.'

'Not surprising. It closed during the war. Never reopened.'

'Oh, right,' said Juanita Rainbird, carefully salting away the information.

'Now excuse me . . . just got to see a man about a dog.'

Tilson Gutteridge's trips to the Gents were becoming ever more frequent, and each time he used the same odious, arch euphemism. Prostate trouble, Juanita surmised without great interest.

Only when he was out of the room did she realize it was the first time he'd not taken his jacket with him. While this confounded her conjecture that he kept a half-bottle of Scotch in the pocket, it did also open up new investigative possibilities.

She had no conscience about going through Tilson Gutteridge's pockets. Moral qualms prompted by such a minor offence would be pretty specious from someone who was contemplating the option of murder.

The jacket pockets, as she could have predicted, were full of unpleasantness. A handkerchief stained with snot and the nicotine dottle from his pipe. The pipe itself, which would probably be banned in any civilized country on environmental grounds. Some half-sucked peppermints, and other bits of fluff whose precise provenance she did not wish to know.

And an old diary. A 1989 diary, which had clearly been kept because its owner had been too lazy to transfer the telephone numbers in the January of 1990 and of every other year since.

It was to this section that Juanita Rainbird hastily flicked the pages. Few of the addresses and phone numbers had any relevance for her.

The one she did note down, however, belonged to 'BREEN, Horace – Old Whittinghamians Association'.

By the time Tilson Gutteridge returned from the Gents, trying once again to wheedle an Italian lunch 'with a decent bottle of red wine' out of Krieper & Thoday, the diary was innocently back in his jacket pocket.

The voice on the answerphone at Horace Breen's number sounded incredibly old, and when Juanita Rainbird met him at a pub in Dulwich, the reality of the man matched. He must have been well into his eighties, probably once as tall as Tilson Gutteridge, but now bent and shrunken. His face and hands were blotched and freckled; his pale milky eyes peered through thick glasses; and the flat mat of a toupee perched on top of his head seemed to accentuate rather than disguise his age. A shiny pinstriped suit hung off his wire-coat-hanger shoulders. He wore a blue and yellow striped tie, which in his first sentence he identified as 'the Old Whittinghamians'.

He offered the tiresome resistance of his generation to Juanita Rainbird's offer of a drink. 'No, surely it's down to us chaps to buy drinks for the pretty little ladies, not the other way—' But she had no difficulty in cutting through all that. Walking from the door to their table seemed to have consumed his limited stock of energy; the journey to the bar and back would have crippled him.

As she ordered the requested half of bitter and her own habitual Perrier, she looked covertly back at the wizened figure and congratulated herself on her luck. If Horace Breen did hold the key to Tilson Gutteridge's past, she'd been fortunate to catch the old man before he enrolled in that great Old Boys' Club in the sky.

Horace Breen thanked her with excessive gallantry for the drink, taking one sip and then ignoring it for the rest of their conversation.

'I'm delighted to find someone of your generation interested in the history of Whittinghams. You see, I devoted my whole life to the school. I was there as a pupil, then I taught Latin and Greek for many years, and finally acted as bursar. No, splendid to know that a young person is drawn to the history of Whittinghams. Particularly someone in publishing. You say you think there might be a book in it?'

'Yes,' Juanita Rainbird replied, confirming the lie she had used to engineer their meeting.

'Well, I suppose there wouldn't be that many people still around who'd be interested, but I can assure you that those who do survive would appreciate the book enormously.' He let out a wheezy chuckle. 'I wouldn't hold out hopes for a "bestseller",' he separated the word out with racy daring, 'but I think I can guarantee you a *succès d'estime*.'

'Excellent. Now could we—?'

'Of course, the foundation of the school goes back to the seventeenth century. In 1692, Thomas Wooltrap, merchant of the City of London, made an endowment for the education of twelve impoverished young scholars, "that they might enjoy the benefits bestowed by a knowledge of the classical authors." And for the first hundred and seventy years of the school's existence . . .'

Juanita Rainbird had to endure getting on for an hour of this before she could divert the conversation in her desired direction. Why, she wondered bitterly, had it become her fate to spend long hours closeted with boring old men?

All too readily the answer supplied itself. Because she wanted to keep her job. And because, if she didn't solve the Tilson Gutteridge problem, Keith Chappick would have not the tiniest qualm about sacking another editor.

This thought spurred her to interruption. 'When you were bursar, Mr Breen, were you in charge of the collection of fees?'

He looked somewhat taken aback and disappointed by her brusqueness, but replied meekly that such had indeed been his duties.

'And presumably the fees would be paid in a variety of different ways? From a variety of different sources?'

'Yes.'

'I mean, some directly from parents, from grandparents, from family trusts, solicitors and so on . . . ?'

'Indeed.'

'Mr Breen, did it ever happen that a boy's fees were paid secretly?'

'How exactly do you mean – "secretly", Miss Rainbird?'

'I mean, say, in the case of an illegitimate child . . . Did it ever happen that you were asked to be discreet about the actual source of the fees?'

Horace Breen's old-world values were deeply offended. 'If that is the sort of book Krieper & Thoday are planning to publish about Whittinghams, I'm afraid I would feel honour bound to dissociate myself from—'

'No, Mr Breen. My question is relevant, I promise, and nothing to do with muck-raking. Specifically,' she moved speedily on, 'I'm interested in a boy who would have started at the school round 1939, 1940 . . . Do you remember individual pupils?'

This question was a challenge to his professional pride. Drawing himself up – or at least as much as it was possible for someone so shrivelled to draw himself up – he asserted that he remembered every boy in precise detail.

'The one I wanted to ask about was called Gutteridge.'

The old man looked blank.

'Tilson Gutteridge.'

'Tilson Gutteridge?' he echoed.

The total lack of recognition in his voice brought a flutter of hope to Juanita Rainbird. 'Yes,' she confirmed breathlessly.

'I'm sorry. There was no pupil at Whittinghams of that name in all the time I was at the school.'

'Are you sure?'

Once again she'd offended him. 'Of course I'm sure, Miss Rainbird! Was this imagined Gutteridge boy the one on whose legitimacy you were casting doubt?'

'Yes.'

'Well, since he didn't exist, the details of his parentage becomes rather irrelevant, so far as I can see.'

'Mm . . .'

'Of course, in the period we're talking about, illegitimacy was a rather more serious matter than it is in these benighted days. And yes, as you suggested, a parent in such unfortunate circumstances might have obscured the issue of who was actually paying the fees.'

'Did that happen often, Mr Breen?'

'At Whittinghams? Good heavens, no. It certainly wasn't that sort of school. In fact, I can only recall one instance of illegitimacy in all the time I was there.'

'When was that?'

'Round the period we are talking about. During the War. Just before the school so sadly closed. There was one pupil called Crabbett. Crabbett, P. J. Nice lad. Very successful in the school plays – gave a lovely Titania, I recall, and then went on, I gather, to take up the theatre as a profession – one would have hoped for rather better from an Old Whittinghamian. Still, maybe blood will out. He was illegitimate, you see, having been adopted soon after birth, but, er . . .'

His undecided pause was agony for Juanita. 'Oh, well,' he said eventually, 'I suppose it's too long ago now for my telling you to do any harm . . . The boy's fees at Whittinghams were paid by his natural mother.'

'You don't happen to remember what the mother's name was, do you, Mr Breen?'

'Oh yes,' the man said with self-righteous pride. 'I remember everything about Whittinghams.'

Juanita Rainbird gazed at him eagerly through her little round glasses.

'The mother's name was Phyllis Townley.'

'I baint abaht to tell you no lies,' the booking clerk confided. ''Taint my hoccupation to tell lies, no way, guv'nor. I done

hissued eight tickets for the 3.27 to Lancaster – three third singles, two third returns, and three first returns.'

'*So if our birds did catch that train,*' Wenceslas Potter mused, '*they'd have been in time to catch the 4.03 from Preston, joining up at Godlings Halt with the 5.17 fast from Wolverhampton, which should have passed the 3.02 Glasgow Pullman Express going in the other direction in the Fairgrave Cutting at 6.13, though the unscheduled stop to take on water at Hulkiston Yard would have made it 6.21 before—*'

'No objections to this bit?' asked Tilson Gutteridge.

'No.' Juanita Rainbird looked at him curiously. 'Why? There's nothing wrong with it.'

A silence.

'What do you think's wrong with it?'

'Just a bit boring, that's all.'

'Boring's all right. That's not unacceptable.' She hastily qualified this generalization. 'That is – it could be unacceptable if a person were described as "boring". It could be offensive to say that a person is attentiveness-challenging – particularly in a case where you were discussing a person of alternative, but nonetheless viable, ethnicity.'

She spoke the words automatically. Her mind was elsewhere, full of her forthcoming meeting with Peter Crabbett. On the off chance, she'd rung Equity, the British actors' union, to see if they had a 'P. Crabbett' registered as a member, and she had struck gold. They had been unwilling to release his address and phone number until she fabricated the line that she was a Hollywood casting director. With the rare prospect of potential work for one of its members, the union became suddenly more forthcoming.

Pete – he insisted on 'Pete' – Crabbett had sounded mild and amiable on the phone, and readily agreed to meet up with her. By coincidence, he too lived in the Dulwich area, and their rendezvous had been fixed for that evening at the same pub.

Juanita Rainbird's feverish anticipation made the line-by-line editing with Tilson Gutteridge more tedious than ever. Now she knew for certain the man was an impostor, she could hardly wait till she had the solid evidence with which she would be able to denounce him.

Her frustration mounting, Juanita returned to Eunice Brock's manuscript.

'. . . *would have made it 6.21 before the trains passed each other, so it was then that the poisoned dart from the blowpipe must have been projected into the Vicomte de Fleurie-Rizeau's first-class compartment.'*

The booking clerk was lost in admiration. 'Blimey, Mr Potter, guv'nor, you're a whale on detection, and no mistake. How come you can work out difficult hinvestigations so easy while the likes of me's in a real pea-souper of a fog about 'em?'

The aristocratic sleuth laughed lightly. 'Sorry, old chap,' he commiserated. 'Simple matter of breeding.'

Juanita Rainbird ground her teeth.

Pete Crabbett was probably about the same age as Tilson Gutteridge, but whereas Tilson was revolting the actor was all charm. Not aggressive, sexist charm, just a laid-back quiet integrity, and an engaging honesty.

He made no demur about accepting a drink from Juanita. 'Never refuse a free drink,' he said with a rueful grin. 'Never in a position to, I'm afraid.'

'Not much acting work around?'

'Not for me, it seems. Not much writing work either.'

'You're a writer too?'

'Well, I try. Without marked success.'

From the bar Juanita Rainbird looked back at the table,

as she had done the previous week. Pete Crabbett wore jeans and a floppy navy jumper. He had thick grey hair. Not unattractive. The pub was evidently his local; he kept smiling and nodding at people.

In the time since Juanita had met Horace Breen, the bar had been decorated for Christmas. Every surface was tinselled and frosted. For the first time, Juanita began to think she might even enjoy Christmas. The Tilson Gutteridge nightmare was about to end.

Pete Crabbett raised the pint of Guinness gratefully to his lips. 'Wonderful,' he said after a long swallow. 'Now what can I do for you?'

Juanita Rainbird took a prim sip of Perrier before launching into her latest prepared falsehood. 'Well, Mr Crabbett—'

'Pete, please.'

'Pete. As I mentioned on the phone, I'm an editor for Krieper & Thoday, the publishers, and I'm exploring the possibility of commissioning a book on changing attitudes to illegitimacy in the twentieth century.'

'Uhuh.'

'And this is ... I hope you don't mind my asking you about this, Mr Crabbett ... ?'

'No problem.' He grinned ingenuously. 'I knew I was a little bastard from the moment I could understand anything. I don't have any problems with it.'

'Good. In fact, I was put on to you by a Mr Horace Breen ... from Whittinghams School ...'

'Good God, "Sniffer" Breen! I'm surprised to hear the old boy hasn't popped his clogs yet.'

'I don't think it'll be long. He looks pretty decrepit. I actually met him last week in this very pub, and he mentioned that you were one of the few, er ...'

'Bastards?' he offered helpfully.

Juanita Rainbird smiled. It was comforting to find that all men in their sixties were not as repellent as Tilson Gutteridge.

'Exactly ... that you were one of the few, er, bastards at Whittinghams.'

'Hm. I'm actually surprised the school knew.'

'Oh?'

'Well, I was adopted at a very early age. The Crabbetts always treated me as their own.'

'But they didn't pretend to you that you were theirs?'

'No. As I said, I knew I was a bastard. Just lucky they took pity on me.'

'But you did know who your birth mother was ... ?'

'What?' Pete Crabbett grinned again and shook his head.

A surge like an electrical current ran through Juanita Rainbird as he said, 'Good heavens, no. It never really interested me. If she'd showed such a lack of taste as not to want me, why should I want her?'

'So you've never been curious?'

He gave another life-affirming shake of his head. 'Never once.'

'And your adoptive parents – the Crabbetts – paid your fees at Whittinghams?'

He looked a little puzzled by the change of direction. 'Well, I assume so. I wasn't chucked out, so I guess they must have done.'

Oh, it was marvellous. He was so innocent, so ingenuous. It was only with restraint that Juanita Rainbird could stop hugging herself. Everything had turned out better than she'd dared hope.

It was the dream scenario. Tilson Gutteridge could be exposed as an impostor. The genuine claimant to Eunice Brock's estate was totally unaware of his good fortune. He could be kept for ever in blissful ignorance. Krieper &

Thoday could continue to rake in the profits on the Eunice Brock books without paying any royalties. Keith Chappick would be pleased, and Juanita Rainbird would keep her job.

Just one more thing to check, then she could relax and enjoy chatting to this rather amiable actor. 'Tell me, Pete, have you ever met anyone called Tilson Gutteridge?'

He looked surprised. 'Well, yes, I have actually. But what connection do you have with him?'

'He wasn't at school with you, was he?'

'Good heavens, no. I've only met him once.'

'When was that?'

'Three or four months ago, I suppose.'

'How did you meet him?'

'He just came and knocked on my door. Said he was a collector of old books and manuscripts – had I got anything around? Well, there was some stuff in the loft that I'd inherited when my father – that's Mr Crabbett – died. I said he could have a look at it if he liked. He seemed to see something there that interested him, so he made me an offer.'

'How much?'

'Fifty quid. I was dead chuffed, I can tell you.'

I bet Tilson Gutteridge was too, thought Juanita grimly.

'Well, it can't have been worth that much. Just some old typescripts, no doubt way out of copyright.'

Juanita Rainbird once again curbed her excitement. Could he really be as naive as he appeared? 'What do you mean – "out of copyright"?'

'Well, doesn't copyright go on for fifty years after something's written . . . ?' he said vaguely and without much interest.

Better and better. Not only did he not know he had any connection with Eunice Brock, he also had no understanding of copyright law. And he certainly didn't know that the fifty-year limit from an author's death or a posthumous publication was about to be extended to seventy.

'Yes,' said Juanita Rainbird calmly. 'That's right.'

'The unutterable sweep who did this has forgotten every decent thing,' opined Wenceslas Potter, as he gazed down at the body on the floor of the ice-house.

'But how did he do it?' queried Lady Cynthia, from whose cheeks the roses had fled to leave a snowy pallor. 'Mr Weinberg looks as though he has been frozen to death.'

'He has,' the aristocratic sleuth confirmed grimly. 'But, if we had not come in here by chance, nobody would ever have known that.'

'Elucidate, Wenceslas,' Lady Cynthia begged. 'I'm a simpleton when it comes to deduction. My feminine mind does not proceed as speedily as yours.'

Even in the presence of death, the noble detective could not let by an opportunity for a compliment. 'When a lady is as beautiful as you are,' he offered gallantly, 'let her feminine mind move at whatsoever speed it chooses.'

Juanita Rainbird sucked her teeth, but still deferred the inevitable confrontation. She felt nervous, knowing she could not put it off for ever. Downstairs the office Christmas party that Keith Chappick had decreed would be coming to its end, the Perrier by now flowing like water. Soon Juanita would be alone in the building with the odious Tilson Gutteridge.

'No,' Wenceslas Potter continued, 'our murderer did not wish the body to be discovered like this.' He knelt down and sniffed at the Hebrew financier's thick, frozen lips. 'As I thought.'

Lady Cynthia's eyes engaged his interrogatively.

'You see,' the sleuth expatiated, 'our homicidal friend required the sturdy Semite to die of natural causes – so far as the world was concerned. I recognize on Mr Weinberg's

lips the smell of a nerve-deadening drug – almost unknown in Harley Street – whose paralysing properties last exactly an hour and then cease, leaving no trace in the victim's blood-stream. Having immobilized the Israelite with that and dragged him out here, our murderer then filled the man's insensiate, gaping mouth with water which, in the cold of the ice-house, froze solid and clogged the poor fellow's windpipe.'

'How ghastly,' murmured Lady Cynthia. 'How beyond everything ghastly.'

'His intention then was to take the defunct Ishmael to his bedroom where, the paralytic drug having worn off and the water melted, he would have appeared to have died of natural—'

Juanita Rainbird could stand it no longer. 'God, I hate this stuff! It's so unrealistic! It treats the readers like complete idiots. A murder could never happen like that.'

'No?' asked Tilson Gutteridge.

'No. And, since we've stopped, I think the moment has come for me to say what I've been putting off saying to you all day.'

'Oh yes?'

'You're an impostor, Tilson Gutteridge!'

'What?'

'You are not who you claim to be. I have absolute proof of that.' Juanita Rainbird reached suddenly into her desk drawer and pulled out a bound sheaf of typewritten pages. 'It's all in here. My boss has a copy. Your little game is up, Mr Gutteridge.'

Meekly, with apparent puzzlement, the elderly man took the dossier and started to read. He showed no reaction as, with great concentration, he devoured every word. At the end, he placed it down on Juanita's desk.

'So . . . you've found out the truth?'

'Yes.'

'This document proves, beyond any shadow of a doubt, that the rightful heir to Eunice Brock's estate – and to all royalties deriving from it until the new copyright expiry date of 2009 – is Peter Crabbett.'

'Exactly.' Juanita Rainbird looked defiantly at Tilson Gutteridge, glad that at last the pretences were over and she could let her hatred for him show. 'And what do you propose to do about that?'

He moved so quickly, she had no chance to protect herself. In an instant the syringe was out of his jacket pocket and stabbed into her upper arm. The plunger was deftly pressed home.

Juanita Rainbird's eyes widened, and her mouth twitched, but the paralysing drug took effect before any words could emerge.

'Thank God for that,' said Tilson Gutteridge, with feeling. 'For once you'll keep your bloody mouth shut!'

She was still conscious as he opened the fridge. Still conscious, but unable to resist, as he crammed the contents of the ice-tray into her mouth. There was awareness in her eyes as he laid her down with her head on the floor of the fridge. She seemed aware too of his turning the dial to its lowest setting, of his closing the door against her neck, and of the gradual, drop-by-drop way he poured the Perrier to congeal with the ice cubes in her throat.

Then the awareness faded from Juanita Rainbird's eyes.

Tilson Gutteridge waited until the drug – still almost unknown in Harley Street – released its hold and the girl's body slumped in death. Then he sat Juanita Rainbird in the swivel chair behind her desk.

By the time she was found after the Christmas holiday, the building's central heating had melted the obstruction in her throat. Except for a small needle puncture in her upper arm and the symptoms of asphyxiation, there seemed no obvious explanation for Juanita Rainbird's death. Many of her colleagues put it down to overwork. Keith Chappick was happy to go along with this diagnosis; it made the rest of his staff even more paranoid.

The managing director did not mind about the death. Once Juanita had sorted out the Eunice Brock copyright trouble, he'd been intending to sack her anyway. Thwarted in this ambition, on New Year's Eve he sacked the publicity director instead. That cheered him up enormously.

And Keith Chappick remained cheerful, until he got a call from Pete Crabbett's solicitor, staking his client's claim to the estate of Eunice Brock.

In the event the case didn't go to court, but if it had, Juanita Rainbird's meticulously detailed dossier would certainly have ensured that the verdict went in Pete Crabbett's favour. Realizing this and unwilling to add legal costs to the amount they already owed him in back royalties, Krieper & Thoday grudgingly accepted the actor's claim.

With his rights thus established, Pete Crabbett settled down to enjoy his good fortune. He could afford as many pints of Guinness as he wanted now. He even had enough to pay an upmarket nursing home to look after his beloved ninety-year-old natural mother.

And of course he'd long since destroyed the costumes and make-up he'd worn as Tilson Gutteridge and Horace Breen.

He couldn't help feeling rather pleased with himself for how well it'd all worked. The invention of the public school 'Whittinghams' was one of the details that gave him most satisfaction.

And he couldn't really feel much regret for the fact that Phyllis Townley's illegitimate son Terence had been killed in the Blitz.

Peter Crabbett might, at some point, be moved to 'discover' more Eunice Brocks. But he decided, at the risk of anachronism, he'd make any subsequent typescripts a bit more politically correct than the first one. It'd probably save time in the long run.

LETTER TO HIS SON

Parkhurst
16th June, 1986

Dear Boy,

I am sorry to hear the Fourth of June celebrations was a trial. I've used that agency before and they never give me no trouble, but I will certainly withdraw my future custom after this lot, and may indeed have to send the boys round. Honest, Son, I asked them to send along a couple what would really raise you in your fellow-Etonians' esteem when they saw who you got for parents. I had to get Blue Phil to draw quite a lot out of the old deposit account under the M23/M25 intersection, and I just don't reckon I got value for my hard-earned oncers.

OK, the motor was all right. Vintage Lagonda must've raised a few eyebrows. Pity it was hot. Still, you can't have everything. But really . . . To send along Watchstrap Malone and Berwick Street Barbara as your mum and dad is the height of naffness so far as yours truly is concerned. I mean, doesn't no one have any finesse these days? No, it's not good enough. I'm afraid there's going to be a few broken fingers round that agency unless I get a strongly worded apology in folded form.

For a start, why did they send a villain to be *in loco parentis*? (See, I am not wasting my time down the prison library.) Are they under new management? Always when I used them in the past, they sent along actors, people with no form. Using Watchstrap, whose record's as long as one of Barry Manilow's *sounds*, is taking unnecessary risks. OK, he looks the toff, got the plummy voice and all that, but he ISN'T THE GENUINE ARTICLE. Put him in a marquee with an authentic Eton dad and the other geezer's going to see he's not the business within thirty seconds. Remember, in matters of class, THERE'S NO WAY SOMEONE WHO ISN'T CAN EVER PASS HIMSELF OFF AS THE REAL THING (a point which I will return to later in this letter).

And, anyway, if they was going to send a villain, least they could have done was to send a good one. Watchstrap Malone, I'll have you know, got his cognomen (prison library again) from a case anyone would wish to draw a veil over, when he was in charge of hijacking a container-load of what was supposed to be watches from Heathrow. Trouble was, he only misread the invoice, didn't he? Wasn't the watches, just the blooming straps. Huh, not the kind of form suitable to someone who's going to pass themselves off as any son of mine's father.

And as for using Berwick Street Barbara, well, that's just a straight insult to your mother, isn't it? I mean, I know she's got the posh voice and the clothes, but she's not the real thing any more than Watchstrap is. She gets her business from nasty little common erks who think they're stepping up a few classes. But no genuine Hooray Henry'd be fooled by Barbara. Anyway, that lot don't want all the quacking vowels and the headscarves – get enough of that at home. What they're after in that line is some pert little scrubber dragged out of the gutters of Toxteth. But I digress.

Anyway, like I say, it's an insult to your mother and if she ever gets to hear about it, I wouldn't put money on the roof staying on Holloway.

No, I'm sorry, I feel like I've been done, and last time I felt like that, with Micky 'The Cardinal' O'Riordhan, he ended up having a lot more difficulty in kneeling down than what he had had theretofore.

But now, Son, I come on to the more serious part of this letter. I was *not amused* to hear what your division master said about your work. If you've got the idea in your thick skull that being a toff has anything to do with sitting on your backside and doing buggerall, then it's an idea of which you'd better disabuse yourself sharpish.

I haven't put in all the time (inside and out) what I have to pay for your education with a view to you throwing it all away. It's all right for an authentic scion (prison library) of the aristocracy to drop out of the system; the system will cheerfully wait till he's ready to go back in. But someone in your shoes, Sonny, if you drop out, you stay out.

Let me clarify my position. Like all fathers, I want my kids to have things better than I did. Now, I done all right, I'm not complaining. I've got to the top of my particular tree. There's still a good few pubs round the East End what'll go quiet when my name's mentioned and, in purely material terms, with the houses in Tenerife and Jamaica and Friern Barnet (not to mention the stashes under various bits of the country's motorway network), I am, to put it modestly, comfortable.

But – and this is a big but – in spite of my career success, I remain an old-fashioned villain. My methods – and I'm not knocking them, because they work – are, in the ultimate analysis, crude. All right, most people give you what you want if you hit them hard enough, but that system of business has not changed since the beginning of time. Nowadays, there is no question, considerably more sophisticated methods are available to the aspiring professional.

Computers obviously have made a big difference. The advance of microtechnology has made possible that elusive goal, the perfect crime, in which you just help yourself without getting your hands dirty.

For this reason I was *particularly* distressed to hear that you haven't been paying attention in your computer studies classes. Listen, Son, I am paying a great deal to put you through Eton and (I think we can safely assume after the endowment for the new library block) Cambridge, but if at the end of all that you emerge unable to fiddle a computerized bank account, I am going to be less than chuffed. Got it?

However, what I'm doing for you is not just with a view to you getting *au fait* with the new technology. It's more than that.

OK, like I say, I been successful, and yet the fact remains that here I am writing to you from the nick. Because my kind of operation, being a straightforward villain against the system, will never be without its attendant risks. Of which risks the nick is the biggest one.

You know, being in prison does give you time for contemplation, and, while I been here, I done a lot of thinking about the inequalities of the society in which we live.

I mean, say I organize a security-van hijack, using a dozen heavies, with all the risks involved (bruises from the pickaxe handles, whiplash injuries from ramming the vehicle, being shopped by one of my own team, being traced through the serial numbers, to name but a few), what do I get at the end of it? I mean, after it's all been shared out, after I've paid everyone off, bribed a few, sorted out pensions for the ones who got hurt, all that, what do I get? Couple of hundred grand if I'm lucky.

Whereas some smartarse in the City can siphon off that many million in a morning without stirring from his desk (and in many cases without even technically breaking the law).

Then, if I'm caught, even with the most expensive solicitor in London acting for me, I get twelve years in Parkhurst.

And, if he's caught, what does he get? Maybe has to resign from the board. Maybe has to get out the business and retire to his country estate, where he lives on investment income and devotes himself to rural pursuits, shooting, fishing, being a JP, that sort of number.

Now, I ask myself, is that a fair system?

And the answer, of course, doesn't take long to come back. No.

Of course it isn't fair. It never has been. That's why I've always voted Tory. All that socialist rubbish about trying to 'change society' ... huh. It's never going to change. The system is as it is. Which is why, to succeed you got to go *with* the system, rather than *against* it.

Which brings me, of course, to what I'm doing for you.

By the time you get through Eton and Cambridge, Son, the world will be your oyster. Your earning potential will be virtually unlimited.

Now don't get me wrong. I am not suggesting that you should go straight. Heaven forbid. No son of mine's going to throw away five generations of tradition just like that.

No, what I'm suggesting is, yes, you're still a villain, but you're a villain from *inside* the system. I mean, think of the opportunities you'll have. You'll be able to go into the City, the Law ... we could use a bent solicitor in the family ... even, if you got *really* lucky, into Parliament. And let's face it, in any of those professions, you're going to clean up in a way that'll make my pickaxe-and-bovver approach look as old-fashioned as a slide-rule in the days of calculators.

Which is why it is so, so important that you take your education seriously. You have got to come out the genuine article. Never relax. You're not there just to do the academic business, you got to observe your classmates too. Follow their every move. Do as they do. You can get to the top, Son (not just in the country, in the world – all big businesses are going multinational these days), but for you to get there you got to be the real thing. No chinks in your armour – got that? Many highly promising villains have come unstuck by inattention to detail and I'm determined it shouldn't happen to you.

Perhaps I can best clarify what I'm on about by telling you what happened to old Squiffy Yoxborough.

Squiffy was basically a con-merchant. Used to be an actor, specialized in upper-class parts. Hadn't got any real breeding, brought up in Hackney as a matter of fact, but he could do the voice real well and, you know, he'd studied the type. Made a kind of speciality of an upper-class drunk act, pretending to be pissed, you know. Hence the name, Squiffy. But times got hard, the acting parts wasn't there, so he drifted into our business.

First of all, he never did anything big. Main speciality was borrowing the odd fifty at upper-class piss-ups. Henley, Ascot, hunt balls, that kind of number, he'd turn up in the full fig and come the hard-luck story when the guests had been hitting the champers for a while. He sounded even more smashed than them, but of course he knew exactly where all his marbles was.

It was slow money, but fairly regular, and moving with that crowd opened up other possibilities. Nicking the odd bit of jewellery, occasional blackmail, a bit of 'winkling' old ladies out of their flats for property developers, you know what I mean. Basically, just doing the upper-classes' dirty work. There's always been a demand for people to do that, and I dare say there always will be.

Well, inevitably, this led pretty quick to drugs. When

London's full of Hooray Henries wanting to stick stuff up their ancestral noses, there's bound to be a lot of openings for the pushers, and Squiffy took his chances when they come. He was never in the big league, mind, not controlling the business, just a courier and like point-of-sale merchant. But it was better money, and easier than sponging fifties.

Incidentally, Son, since the subject's come up, I don't want there to be any doubt in your mind about my views on drugs. You keep away from them.

Now, I am not a violent man – well, let's say I am not a violent man to my *family*, but if I hear you've been meddling with drugs, either as a user or a pusher, so help me I will somehow get out of this place and find you and give you such a tanning with my belt that you'll need a rubber ring for the rest of your natural. That sort of business attracts a really unpleasant class of criminal what I don't want any son of mine mixing with. Got that?

Anyway, getting back to Squiffy, obviously once he got into drugs, he was going to get deeper in and pretty soon he's involved with some villains who was organizing the smuggling of the stuff through a yacht-charter company. You know the sort of set-up, rich gits rent this boat and crew and swan round the West Indies for a couple of weeks, getting alternately smashed and stoned.

Needless to say, this company would keep their punters on the boat supplied with cocaine; but not only that, they also made a nice little business of taking the stuff back into England and flogging it to all the Sloane Rangers down the Chelsea discothèques.

I suppose it could have been a good little earner if you like that kind of thing, but these plonkers who was doing it hadn't got no sense of organization. The crew were usually as stoned as the punters, so it was only a matter of time before they come unstuck. Only third run they do, they moor in the harbour of this little island in the West Indies and, while they're all on shore getting well bobbled on the ethnic rum, local Bill goes and raids the yacht. Stuff's lying all over the place, like there's been a snow-storm blown through the cabins, and when the crew and punters come back, they all get nicked and shoved in the local slammer to unwind for a bit.

Not a nice place, the jail on this little island. They had to share their cells with a nasty lot of local fauna like cockroaches, snakes and mosquitoes, not to mention assorted incendiaries, gun-runners, rapists and axe-murderers.

Not at all what these merchant bankers and their Benenden-educated crumpet who had chartered the yacht was used to. So, because that's how things work at that level, pretty soon some British consular official gets contacted, and pretty soon a deal gets struck with the local authorities. No hassle, really, it comes down to a thousand quid per prisoner. All charges dropped, and home they go. Happened all the time, apparently. The prisons was one of the island's two most lucrative industries (the other being printing unperforated stamps). A yacht had only to come into the harbour to get raided. Squiffy's lot had just made it easy for the local police; usually the cocaine had to be planted.

Well, obviously, there was a lot of transatlantic telephoning, a lot of distraught daddies (barristers, MPs, what-have-you) cabling money across, but it gets sorted out pretty quick and all the Hoorays are flown back to England with a good story to tell at the next cocktail party.

They're all flown back, that is, except Squiffy.

And it wasn't that he couldn't raise the readies. He'd got a few stashes round about, and the odd blackmail victim who could be relied on to stump up a grand when needed.

No, he stayed because he'd met this bloke in the nick.

Don't get me wrong. I don't mean he fancied him. Nothing Leaning Tower of Pisa about Squiffy.

No, he stayed because he'd met someone he thought could lead to big money.

Bloke's name was Masters. Alex Masters. But, it didn't take Squiffy long to find out, geezer was also known as the Marquess of Gorsley.

Now, I don't know how it is, but some people always land on their feet in the nick. I mean, I do all right. I get all the snout I want and if I feel like a steak or a bottle of whisky there's no problem. But I get that because I have a bit of reputation outside, and I have to work to keep those privileges. I mean, if there wasn't a good half-dozen heavies round the place who owe me the odd favour, I might find it more difficult.

But I tell you, I got nothing compared to what this marquess geezer'd got. Unlimited supplies of rum, so he's permanently smashed, quietly and happily drinking himself to death. All the food he wants, very best of the local cuisine. Nice cell to himself, air conditioning, fridge, video, compact-disc player, interior-sprung bed. Pick of the local talent to share that bed with, all these slim, brown-legged beauties, different one every night, so Squiffy said (though apparently the old marquess was usually too pissed to do much about it).

Now, prisons work the same all over the world, so you take my word that I know what I'm talking about. Only one thing gets those kind of privileges.

Money.

But pretty soon even Squiffy realizes there's something not quite kosher with the set-up. I mean, this Gorsley bloke's not inside for anything particularly criminal. Just some fraud on a holiday villa development scheme. Even if the island's authorities take property fiddling more seriously than cocaine, there's still got to be a price to get him released. I mean, say it's five grand, it's still going to be considerably less than what he's paying per annum for these special privileges.

Besides, when Squiffy raises the subject, it's clear that the old marquess doesn't know a blind thing about this 'buy-out' system. But he does go on about how grateful he is to his old man, the Duke of Glammerton, for shelling out so much per month 'to make the life sentence bearable'.

Now Squiffy's not the greatest intellect since Einstein, but even he's capable of putting two and two together. He checks out this Gorsley geezer's form and discovers the property fraud's not the first bit of bovver he's been in. In fact, the bloke is a walking disaster area, his past littered with bounced cheques, petty theft, convictions for drunkenness, you name it. (I don't, incidentally, mean *real* crimes, the ones that involve skill; I refer to the sort people get into by incompetence.)

Squiffy does a bit more research. He's still got some cocaine stashed away and for that the prison governor's more than ready to spill the odd bean. Turns out the marquess's dad pays up regular, never objects when the price goes up, encourages the governor to keep increasing the supply of rum, states quite categorically he's not interested in pardons, anything like that. Seems he's got a nephew who's a real Mr Goody-Goody. And if the marquess dies in an alcoholic stupor in some obscure foreign jail, it's all very handy. The prissy nephew inherits the title, and the Family Name remains untarnished. Duke's prepared to pay a lot to keep that untarnished.

So it's soon clear to Squiffy that the duke is not only paying a monthly sum to keep his son in the style to which he's accustomed; it's also to keep his son out of the country. In fact, he's paying the island to let the Marquess of Gorsley die quietly in prison.

It's when he realizes this that Squiffy Yoxborough decides he'll stick around for a while.

* * *

Now, except for the aforementioned incendiaries, gun-runners, rapists and axe-murderers ... oh, and the local talent (not that that talked much), the marquess has been a bit starved of civilized conversation, so he's pretty chuffed to be joined by someone who's English and talks with the right sort of accent. He doesn't notice that Squiffy's not the genuine article. Too smashed most of the time to notice anything and, since the marquess's idea of a conversation is him rambling on and someone else listening, Squiffy doesn't get too much chance to give himself away.

Anyway, he's quite content to listen, thank you very much. The more he finds out about the Marquess of Gorsley's background, the happier he is. It all ties in with a sort of plan that's slowly emerging in his head.

Particularly he wants to know about the marquess's school-days. So, lots of warm, tropical evenings get whiled away over bottles of rum while the marquess drunkenly reminisces and Squiffy listens hard. It's really just an extension of how he started in the business, pretending to get plastered with the Hoorays. But this time he's after considerably more than the odd fifty.

The Marquess of Gorsley was, needless to say, at one of these really posh schools. Like his father before him, he had gone to Raspington in Wiltshire (near where your grandfather was arrested for the first time, Son). And as he listens, Squiffy learns all about it.

He learns that there was four houses, Thurrocks, Wilmington, Stuke and Fothergill. He learns that the marquess was in Stuke, that kids just starting in Stuke was called 'tads' and on their first night in the dorm they underwent 'scrogging'. He learns that prefects was called 'whisks', that in their common room, called 'the Treacle Tin', they was allowed to administer a punishment called 'spluggers'; that they could wear the top buttons of their jackets undone, and was the only members of the school allowed to walk on 'Straggler's Hump'.

He learns that the teachers was called 'dommies', that the sweet shop was called the 'Binn', that a cricket cap was a 'skiplid', that the bogs was called 'fruitbowls', that studies was called 'nitboxes', that lunch was called 'slops', and that a minor sports colours tie was called a 'slagnoose'.

He hears the marquess sing the school songs. After a time, he starts joining in with them. Eventually, he even gets a bit good at doing a solo on the School Cricket Song, traditionally sung in Big Hall on the evening after the Old Raspurian Match. It begins,

> Hark! the shout of a schoolboy at twilight
> Comes across from the far-distant pitch,
> Goads his team on to one final effort,
> 'Make a stand at the ultimate ditch!'
> Hark! the voice of the umpiring master
> Rises over the white-flannelled strife,
> Tells his charges that life is like cricket,
> Tells them also that cricket's like life . . .

Don't think you have that one at Eton, do you, Son?

I tell you, after two months in that prison, Squiffy Yoxborough knows as much about being at Raspington as the Marquess of Gorsley does himself. He stays on a couple more weeks, to check there's nothing more, but by now the marquess is just rambling and repeating himself, sinking deeper and deeper into an alcoholic coma. So Squiffy quickly organizes his own thousand quid release money, and scarpers back to England.

First thing he does when he gets back home, Squiffy forms a company. Well, he doesn't actually literally form a company, but he, like, gets all the papers forged so it looks like he's formed a company. He calls this company 'Only Real Granite House-Building Construction Techniques' (ORGHBCT) and he gets enough forged paperwork for him to be able to open a bank account in that name.

Next thing he gets his clothes together. Moves carefully here. Got to get the right gear or the whole thing falls apart.

Dark blue pinstripe suit. Donegal tweed suit. Beale and Inmans corduroy trousers. Cavalry twills. Turnbull and Asser striped shirts. Viyella Tattersall checked shirts. Church's Oxford shoes. Barbour jacket. Herbert Johnson trilby.

He steals or borrows this lot. Can't just buy them in the shops. Got to look old, you see.

Has trouble with the Old Raspurian tie. Doesn't know anyone who went there – except of course for the marquess, and he's rather a long way away.

So he has to buy a tie new and distress it a bit. Washes it so's it shrinks. Rubs in a bit of grease. Looks all right.

(You may be wondering, Son, how I come to know all this detail. Not my usual special subject, I agree. Don't worry, all will be revealed.)

Right, so having got the gear, he packs it all in a battered old leather suitcase, rents a Volvo estate and drives up to Scotland.

He's checked out where the Duke of Glammerton's estate is, he's checked that the old boy's actually in residence, and he just drives up to the front of Glammerton House. Leaves the Volvo on the gravel, goes up to the main door and pulls this great ring for the bell.

Door's opened by some flunkey.

'Hello,' says Squiffy, doing the right voice of course. 'I'm a chum of Alex's. Just happened to be in the area. Wondered if the old devil was about.'

'Alex?' says the flunkey, bit suspicious.

'Yes. The Marquess of Gorsley. I was at school with him.'

'Ah. I'm afraid the marquess is abroad.'

'Oh, really? What a swiz,' says Squiffy. 'Still, I travel a lot. Whereabouts is the old devil?'

Flunkey hesitates a bit, then says he'll go off and try to find out. Comes back with the butler. Butler confirms the marquess is abroad. Cannot be certain where.

'What, hasn't left a forwarding address? Always was bloody inefficient. Never mind, I'm sure some of my chums could give me a lead. Don't worry, I'll track him down.'

This makes the butler hesitate, too. 'If you'll excuse me, sir, I'll just go and see if his Grace is available. He might have more information about the marquess's whereabouts than I have.'

Few minutes later, Squiffy gets called into this big lounge-type room, you know, all deers' heads and gilt frames, and there's the Duke of Glammerton sitting over a tray of tea. Duke sees the tie straight away.

'Good Lord, are you an Old Raspurian?'

'Yes, your Grace,' says Squiffy.

'Which house?'

'Stuke.'

'So was I.'

'Well, of course, Duke, I knew you must have been. That's where I met Alex, you see. Members of the same family in the same house, what?'

Duke doesn't look so happy now he knows Squiffy's a friend of his son. No doubt the old boy's met a few unsuitable ones in his time, so Squiffy says quickly, 'Haven't seen Alex for yonks. Virtually since school.'

'Oh.' Duke looks relieved. 'As Moulton said, I'm afraid he's abroad.'

'Living there?'

'Yes. For the time being,' duke says carefully.

'Oh dear. You don't by any chance have an address, do you?'

'Erm . . . Not at the moment, no.'

Now all this is suiting Squiffy very nicely. The more the duke's determined to keep quiet about his son's real circumstances, the better.

'That's a nuisance,' says Squiffy. 'Wanted to sting the old devil for a bit of money.'

'Oh?' Duke looks careful again.

'Well, not for me, of course. For the old school.'

'Oh yes?' Duke looks interested.

'Absolutely.' (Squiffy knows he should say this every now and then instead of 'Yes'.) 'For my sins I've got involved in some fund-raising for the old place.'

'Again? What are they up to this time?'

'Building a new Great Hall to replace Big Hall.'

Duke's shocked by this. 'They're not going to knock Big Hall down?'

'Good Lord, no. No, Big Hall'll still be used. The Great Hall will be for school plays, that sort of thing.'

'Ah. Where are they going to build it?'

'Well, it'll be at right angles to Big Hall, sort of stretching past Thurrocks out towards "Straggler's Hump".'

'Really? Good Lord.' The old geezer grins. 'I remember walking along "Straggler's Hump" many a time.'

'You must've been a "whisk" then.'

He looks guilty. 'Never was, actually.'

'Doing it illegally, were you?'

Duke nods.

'But didn't that mean you got dragged into the "Treacle Tin" for "spluggers"?'

'Never caught.' Duke giggles naughtily. 'Remember, actually, I did it my second day as a "tad".'

'What, directly after you'd been "scrogged"?'

'Absolutely.'

'And none of the "dommies" saw you?'

Duke shakes his head, really chuffed at what an old devil he used to be. 'Tell me,' he says, 'where are you staying up here?'

'I was going to check into the . . . what is it in the village? The Glammerton Arms?'

'Well, don't do that, old boy. Stay here the night. I'll get Moulton to show you a room.'

Gets a good dinner, that night, Squiffy does. Pheasant, venison, vintage wines, all that. Just the two of them. Duchess had died a long time ago.

Get on really well, they do. Squiffy does his usual getting-plastered act, but, as usual, he's careful. Talks a lot about Raspington, doesn't talk too much about the marquess. But listens. And gets confirmation of his hunch that the duke never wants to see his son again. Also knows there's a very strong chance of this happening in the natural course of events. The amount of rum the marquess is putting away, his liver must be shrivelled down to like a dried pea.

Anyway, when they're giving the port and brandy and cigars a bash, the duke, who's a bit the worse for wear, says, 'What is all this about the old school? Trying to raise money, did you say?'

'Absolutely,' says Squiffy. 'Don't just want to raise money, though. Want to raise a monument.'

'What – a monument to all the chaps who died from eating "slops"?'

'Or the chaps who were poisoned in the "Binn"?'

'Or everyone who got "scrogged" in their own "nitbox"!'

'Yes, or all those who had a "down-the-loo-shampoo" in the "fruitbowls"!'

Duke finds this dead funny. Hasn't had such a good time for years.

'No, actually,' says Squiffy, all serious now, 'we want the new Great Hall to be a monument to a great Old Raspurian.'

'Ah.'

'So that every chap who walks into that hall will think of someone who was really a credit to the old school.'

'Oh. Got anyone in mind?' asks the duke.

'Absolutely,' says Squiffy. 'We thought of Alex.'

'WHAT!'

'Well, he's such a great chap.'

'Alex – great chap?'

'Yes. As I say, I've hardly seen him since school . . . nor have any of the other fellows on the fund-raising committee, actually, but we all thought he was such a terrific chap at school . . . I mean, I'm sure he's gone on to be just as success-ful in the outside world.'

'Well . . . er . . .'

'So you see, Duke, we all thought, what a great idea to have the place named after Alex – I mean he'd have to put up most of the money, but that's a detail – and then everyone who went into the hall would be reminded of what a great Old Raspurian he was. Give the "tads" something to aspire to, what?'

'Yes, yes.' The duke gets thoughtful. 'But are you sure that Alex is the right one?'

'Oh. Well, if there's any doubt about his suitability, per-haps we should investigate a bit further into what he's been up to since he left Raspington . . .'

'No, that won't be necessary,' says the duke, sharpish. 'What sort of sum of money are we talking about?'

'Oh . . .' Squiffy looks all casual like. 'I don't know. Five hundred thousand, something like that.'

'Five hundred thousand to ensure that Alex is always remembered as one of the greatest Old Raspurians . . . ?'

'I suppose you could think of it like that. Absolutely.'

A light comes into the old duke's eyes. He's had reports from the West Indies. He knows his son hasn't got long to go. And suddenly he's offered a way of . . . like *enshrining* the marquess's memory. With a great permanent monument at the old school, a little bit of adverse publicity in the past'll soon be forgotten. The Family Name will remain untarnished. Half a million's not much to pay for that.

He rings a bell and helps them both to some more pre-War port. Moulton comes in.

'My cheque book, please.'

The butler geezer delivers it and goes off again.

'Who should I make this payable to?' asks the duke.

'Well, in fact,' says Squiffy, 'the full name's the "Old Raspurian Great Hall Building Charitable Trust", but you'll never get all that on the cheque. Just the initials will do.'

With the cheque safely in his pocket, Squiffy starts humming the tune of the Raspington School Cricket Song.

'Great,' says the duke. 'Terrific. I always used to do the solo on the second verse. Do you know the descant?'

'Absolutely,' says Squiffy and together they sing,

> See the schoolboy a soldier in khaki,
> Changed his bat for the Gatling and Bren.
> How his officer's uniform suits him,
> How much better he speaks than his men.
> Thank the school for his noble demeanour,
> And his poise where vulgarity's rife,
> Knowing always that life is like cricket,
> Not forgetting that cricket's like life.

All right, Son. Obvious question is, how do I know all that? How do I know all that detail about Squiffy Yoxborough?

Answer is, he told me. And he'll tell me again every blooming night if he gets the chance.

Yes, he's inside here with me.

And why? Why did he get caught? Was it because the duke woke up next morning and immediately realized it was a transparent con? Realized that he'd been pissed the night before and that it really was a bit unusual to give a complete stranger a cheque for half a million quid?

No, duke's mind didn't work like that. So long as he thought he was dealing with a genuine Old Raspurian, he reckoned he'd got a good deal. OK, it'd cost him five hundred grand, but, as a price for covering up everything that his son'd done in the past, it was peanuts. The Family Name would remain untarnished – that was the important thing.

But, like I just said, that was only going to work *so long as he thought he was dealing with a genuine Old Raspurian.*

And something the butler told him the next morning stopped him thinking that he was.

So, when Squiffy goes to the bank to pay in his cheque to the 'Only Real Granite House-Building Construction Techniques' account, he's asked to wait for a minute, and suddenly the cops are all over the shop.

So what was it? He got the voice right, he got the clothes right, he got all the Old Raspurian stuff right, he used the right knives and forks at dinner, he said 'Absolutely' instead of 'Yes' . . . where'd he go wrong?

I'll tell you – when he got up the next morning he made his own bed.

Well, butler sussed him straight away. Poor old Squiffy'd shown up his upbringing. Never occur to the sort of person he was pretending to be to make a bed. There was always servants around to do that for you.

See, there's some things you can learn from outside, and some you got to know from inside. And that making the bed thing, it takes generations of treating peasants like dirt to understand that.

I hope I've made my point. Stick at it, Son. Both the work and the social bit. You're going to get right to the top, like I said. You're not going to be an old-fashioned villain, you're going to do it through the system. And if you're going to succeed, you can't afford the risk of being let down by the sort of mistake that shopped Squiffy Yoxborough. Got that?

Once again, sorry about the Fourth of June. (Mind you, someone else is going to be even sorrier.) I'll see to it you get better parents for the Eton and Harrow Match.

This letter, with the customary greasy oncers, will go out through Blue Phil, as per usual. Look after yourself, Son, and remember – keep a straight bat.

Your loving father,
Nobby Chesterfield

FALSE SCENT

The body of fifty-five-year-old Ralph Rudgwick was discovered by his wife, Jane, on the Sunday evening when she returned from a weekend water-colour painting course in the Lake District.

He was lying in a tangle of sheets in the overheated bedroom of their house near Henley, dressed only in a royal blue shirt, the front of which was plastered to his body with the brown blood that had spread from three bullet-holes in his chest.

His other clothes, Jane Rudgwick told Detective Inspector Bury, had been lying in an abandoned heap on the floor. She had hung up the trousers and aligned the shoes with his others in the wardrobe. The boxer shorts and socks she had placed in the dirty-clothes basket.

When the Inspector asked her why she had done this before contacting the police, she seemed at a loss. 'Well, I like to have everything tidy,' she had replied, puzzled by his question.

At first he had put the reaction down to shock. Discovering your husband murdered must be one of the most traumatic experiences in the life of any woman, and logical behaviour should perhaps not be expected at such a moment.

Anyway, at their first interview, it seemed incongruous to suspect anything sinister about Jane Rudgwick. She was a strange, vulnerable little woman, the wrong side of fifty, from whom all colour seemed slowly to have seeped away. Her face, and her flowered cotton dress, were as anaemically pastel as the decor of the obsessively neat sitting room in which they sat talking.

The eyes, blinking through transparent-framed glasses, were pink with crying, and she kept breaking down and rushing off to the bathroom to recover herself. From these sorties she would return with eyes redder than ever, and surrounded by a haze of cheap flowery perfume, as though she believed, pathetically, that that could cover up, or sanitize, or even dispel the ugliness that had invaded her life.

It was only when, the following morning, Detective Inspector Bury interviewed Jacob Keynes, Ralph Rudgwick's partner in the Keynes Rudgwick Gallery, that his suspicions began to move towards the dead man's wife.

The gallery was Cork Street smart, its narrow glass frontage dominated by a huge abstract oil in strident primary colours. The name of the painter, an unsolved anagram of Middle-European consonants, meant nothing to Detective Inspector Bury. But then he would never have claimed to know anything about art.

Jacob Keynes also favoured primary colours, a scarlet jacket of generous Italian cut over a yellow shirt and green trousers. His aftershave, an expensive, slightly sickly cologne, pervaded the atmosphere.

He seemed neither upset nor surprised by the news of his partner's murder.

'So the worm finally turned,' was his first comment.

'I'm sorry, Mr Keynes?' said Bury, urbanely unruffled, as his profession demanded. 'Could you amplify that remark a little?'

'Ah.' The gallery owner was struck by doubt. 'Well, perhaps I shouldn't . . .'

'I think, having gone that far, you *should*, Mr Keynes.'

'Yes . . . I'm obviously not making any accusation or anything like that—'

'Obviously not.'

'—but my first reaction to the news was, I'm afraid, to suspect Ralph's wife of killing him.'

'She being the worm you mentioned, the one who finally turned . . . ?'

'Yes.'

'Uh-huh. And do you have any reason for your suspicion – except for the obvious one that most murders prove to have domestic motivations?'

'I do have reasons, but I'm not sure that I should . . .'

'Once again, I think you absolutely *should*, Mr Keynes.'

'Right. Well, you'll find out soon enough from someone else if I don't tell you. Ralph was perhaps not the most faithful of husbands.'

'Ah. He had a lot of girlfriends?'

'Over the years there have been a few.'

'And do you think his wife knew about them?'

'I wouldn't know. Maybe not. None of them was very serious or lasted very long. However, recently . . .'

'Yes, Mr Keynes? Recently . . . ?' said Bury, deterring another attack of reticence.

'Recently Ralph had got into a more serious extramarital relationship.'

'Ah.'

'For the last – I don't know how long it's been – must be getting on for six months – he's had a mistress.'

'Really?'

'He has – *had* a flat in Covent Garden where he stayed two or three nights every week. When he's been in London over the last few months, he's spent most of his spare time with his mistress.'

'Could I have her name?'

'Gina. Gina Luccarini. She's Italian,' Jacob Keynes glossed unnecessarily. 'A painter. That's one of hers.'

The canvas he indicated was similar in style to the Middle-European anagram in the window. Bold swirls of bright colour. Angry. Slightly disturbing.

'Would you happen to know where Miss Luccarini lives?' asked the Inspector.

Jacob Keynes gave an address in Notting Hill. 'But you won't find her there at the moment.'

'Oh?'

'She's in Italy. Gone to visit her mother. Flew out at the weekend. Saturday, I think.'

'Hm. And, since Mr Rudgwick has been seeing Miss Luccarini, has he kept up with any of his other girlfriends? Or indeed picked up with any new ones?'

Jacob Keynes hooted with laughter. 'I can't see Gina tolerating that, Inspector. No, there's a rule with mistresses – particularly hot-blooded Italian mistresses – they can just about tolerate their man spending time with his wife – even, though this apparently wasn't the case with Ralph, making love to his wife – but if he starts anything else – anything extra-extramarital, as it were – then all hell's let loose. And Gina, I imagine, would be capable of letting loose quite a lot of hell.'

'Thank you, Mr Keynes,' said Detective Inspector Bury with a quiet smile. 'I'll bear that in mind. So . . . it is your belief that Ralph Rudgwick was very serious about Miss Luccarini?'

'Oh yes. He was in love with her, no doubt about it. And she with him. A very strong, passionate relationship. Ralph kept saying he would have moved in with her permanently – but for the fact that he was married.'

'Doesn't stop a lot of people these days, Mr Keynes. There is such a thing as divorce.'

'According to Ralph, Jane wouldn't hear of the idea. Anyway . . .' he gestured round the gallery, '. . . Jane's money bought most of this, and Ralph didn't want to put his nice cosy set-up here at risk.'

'Doesn't that mean that Mr Rudgwick's death puts you in financial difficulties, Mr Keynes?'

The gallery owner favoured him with a patronizing smile. 'No, Detective Inspector. Money has never been a problem for me. If I choose to replace Ralph, I will. And, if I don't . . .' he shrugged, '. . . I'll just run the place on my own.'

Bury looked thoughtful. 'So . . . To recap . . . It is your assumption that Mrs Rudgwick killed her husband because she could no longer stand the humiliation of his flaunting his mistress at her?'

'Something like that, yes.'

'Did you ever see him actually humiliate his wife in public by appearing with his mistress?'

'No. But then Jane was never there on such occasions.'

'Oh?'

'Jane hardly ever came to London. She stayed down in Henley. And tried to keep Ralph down there as much as possible too.'

'How do you mean exactly?'

'She kept being ill, so he had to go back home rather than stay in London. Well, at least she claimed she was ill . . .'

'Meaning you don't think she was?'

'I think it was just her way of demanding his attention. Since she didn't have any sexual power over him, she had to exert some other kind of control. Money was part of it, but her health was always there to fall back on. I mean, the whole of the last fortnight, for instance, Jane claimed to be ill. Poor

old Ralph was having to commute from Henley every day –
even stay down there some days. No opportunity to see Gina
for anything more than the odd meal – very frustrated he
was getting.'

'And you think Mrs Rudgwick's illness was pure fabri-
cation?'

'Well, the timing does seem a bit odd, doesn't it? She's so
ill for two weeks that hubby has to go back home every night,
but then when she wants to go off on her painting course –
and when she knows that hubby's mistress is about to go to
Italy for a fortnight – she suddenly gets better.'

'Hm.' The Inspector tapped his chin reflectively. 'And did
Ralph Rudgwick ever talk to you in detail about how unsatis-
factory his marriage was?'

'Well, no. Not in so many words. But, come on, I didn't
have to be Sherlock Holmes to deduce it from the circumstances, did I?'

'No,' said Detective Inspector Bury slowly. 'No, perhaps
not.'

In the pastel sitting room, Jane Rudgwick looked as puffy-
eyed as ever at their next encounter, which took place on the
Monday afternoon. Once again an invisible miasma of scent
floated around her.

'So you drove up to the Lake District for your painting
course, Mrs Rudgwick?'

'Yes.'

'Arriving there at ten o'clock in the evening.'

'Ah. You checked?'

'Yes, Mrs Rudgwick. Now, assuming Friday evening
traffic, and assuming you drove up the M5 and M6—'

'Oh, but I didn't.'

'What?'

'I hate driving on motorways. All that traffic, all going so fast. No, I drove up through Cheltenham, Worcester, Shrewsbury and so on . . . All the minor roads.'

Well, that's in character for this little mouse of a woman, thought the Inspector as he observed out loud, 'Must've taken you a lot longer.'

'Yes, but it put less of a strain on my nerves.'

'Of course. So what time did you leave the house on the Friday?'

'About three.'

'And was your husband here when you left?'

'Yes. He hadn't gone into the office that day.'

'Why not?'

'I don't know, Inspector.' The puffy eyes blinked ingenuously through the glasses.

'And you didn't have any argument before he left?'

'Argument?' Jane Rudgwick echoed the word, as if it was in a foreign language she didn't speak. 'Me and Ralph? No.'

'Are you suggesting that you never argued?'

'We didn't have anything to argue about.'

Detective Inspector Bury let that pass for the moment. 'So, Mrs Rudgwick, would you say yours was a happy marriage?'

'Oh yes,' she replied, 'yes,' as if she were surprised that he had even thought to ask the question.

He changed tack. 'According to our records, Mrs Rudgwick, your husband owned a pistol.'

'He did, yes. He used to be quite keen on target shooting. Hadn't done it for a year or two, but in the past he did. Was a member of a club, that kind of thing.'

'Mm. The gun that killed him was similar to the one he owned . . .'

'Ah.' A sob welled up in Jane Rudgwick's throat at this reminder of the reality of her husband's death.

'. . . but we haven't been able to find his gun anywhere in the house.'

'I think he used to keep it locked in one of the desk drawers in his study.'

'We've looked there. No sign of it. We've looked everywhere.'

'Oh.' She appeared genuinely puzzled by this information.

'On the other hand . . .' Detective Inspector Bury timed his *coup de théâtre* carefully '. . . we have found traces of gunshot residue particles on some tissues in a bag of rubbish.'

'What rubbish?'

'The rubbish that had been tied up in a plastic bag and placed in your dustbin, Mrs Rudgwick . . .'

'Oh.'

'. . . which would appear to have come from your bathroom.'

'Yes. Yes, it did. I emptied the waste-bin from the bathroom when I got in on Sunday.'

'After discovering your husband's body?'

'Yes.'

'And before contacting the police?'

She nodded again.

'Don't you think that's rather odd behaviour, Mrs Rudgwick?'

But again, the only reply she could give, in a wondering, almost childlike voice, was: 'Well, I like to have everything tidy.'

Detective Inspector Bury was silent in the car back to the station. He hadn't worked before with the Detective Sergeant who had been assigned to the case, and did not find the young man particularly congenial. Certainly not congenial enough to be elevated into any kind of Dr Watson confidant role.

How pleasant it would be, Bury thought wryly, always to work with the same sidekick, to have one of those sparky, joshing relationships between Inspector and Sergeant so beloved of crime novelists and television series. What a pity that real police duty rosters didn't work like that, and that only occasional coincidence would find him paired with the same assistant on two consecutive cases.

The thoughts that he kept to himself in the car ran on Jane Rudgwick. He had by now concluded that her naivety and the general pallor of her personality must be a front. Nobody could really be that wishy-washy.

But if she had killed her husband, she seemed to show little instinct for self-preservation. Bury had given her a good few opportunities to defend herself and she had taken none of them.

For example, he had pointed out that the soiled tissues from the dustbin did not correspond to any others found about the house. The boxes in her bathroom and bedroom contained plain white ones, while these had been coloured boutique tissues.

But Jane Rudgwick's reaction had not been to seize on this as proof that someone else had been in the house. All she said was that she hadn't looked closely at the contents of the bathroom waste-bin, just tidied it up automatically.

Again, when Detective Inspector Bury had reported that preliminary examination of her husband's corpse suggested he could have died any time on the Friday afternoon or evening, she had not hastened to assert an alibi about the time of her departure, nor offered specific details of the route she had taken for the Lake District.

And when he commented on the strangeness of her illness of the previous two weeks and the way it had suddenly got better on the Friday, her only response had been, 'Yes, that was odd, wasn't it?'

All these reactions were so unusual that Bury found himself unable to take them at face value. Nobody could be that naive. No wife could be so totally unaware of her own candidature as a murder suspect.

And, given what he had heard about the Rudgwicks' marriage from Jacob Keynes, Detective Inspector Bury felt sure that Jane Rudgwick was hiding something.

Back at the station, he managed to shake off his unwanted assistant by delegating some routine phone calls to the Detective Sergeant. When he reached his office, Bury discovered that there had been a call for him from Gina Luccarini. The number she had left was a London one, and his surmise that she had returned from Italy on the news of her lover's death was confirmed as soon as he got through to her.

'A friend told me. I came straight away. It is a tragedy!'

Her voice, heavily accented and operatic in its intensity, contained none of the crumbling weakness of Jane Rudgwick's grief. It was passionate and furious.

'She killed him! It is wicked. She is the – what you call – dog in the manger. Because she could not have him, she is determined no one else shall.'

As he had done with Jacob Keynes, Detective Inspector Bury made her spell out who she was talking about.

'His wife, of course. Jane.' Gina Luccarini spoke as to a child. 'She is a monster!'

This description seemed so at odds with the faded, blinking, red-eyed figure with whom he had spent the afternoon, that Bury could not help asking, 'Have you ever actually met Mrs Rudgwick, Miss Luccarini?'

'Well, no. I only heard about her from Ralph – and that was enough! From the start of their marriage, she allow him no sex-life at all. She use her money to have power over him. She treat him like garbage!'

Again, this behaviour seemed grotesquely inappropriate to the image Jane Rudgwick presented to the world, but Bury knew well the impossibility of imagining the inside of a marriage. And he found that the increasing incongruity of casting Ralph's widow in the role of murderer had the perverse effect of intensifying rather than weakening his suspicions of her.

'I think we ought to meet, Miss Luccarini.'

'Of course. Please.'

'Would it be all right if I were to come and see you this evening?'

'Yes.'

'What time would be convenient?'

'It does not matter. As late as you like. You think I will have any chance of sleeping after what has happened?'

Everything about Gina was as vibrantly colourful as everything about Jane was drab. It was not hard to sympathize with Ralph Rudgwick's choice.

The sitting room of her apartment in Notting Hill was painted deep red, the walls animated with her own explosive canvases. Bright printed fabrics drooped from the windows and were draped with random elegance across the furniture.

She was probably thirty-five, vivid in a dress of blood-red silk, which showed the full length of her black-stockinged legs. The red was picked up in heavy flamboyant earrings and on full lips. Her hair had the rich darkness of espresso coffee, and the same colour blazed with fury from her eyes.

Around her hung the musky sensuality of a perfume whose expense severely restricted the numbers of its users.

Just as Jane Rudgwick could be viewed almost as a parody of the boring, frigid, Anglo-Saxon wife, so Gina Luccarini was perfectly cast as the tempestuous, sexy, Latin mistress.

'When did you last see Ralph Rudgwick?' asked Detective Inspector Bury, after refusing offers of coffee or alcohol.

'We had lunch on Wednesday.'

'And – I hope you don't mind my asking – that was just lunch . . . ?'

'Yes. We had thought then that he would be coming here on Friday night – after his wife had gone off for her *water-colour course*.'

She deluged the last three words in contempt. 'Is not that typical of her – of Mrs Jane Rudgwick – that she should work on *water-colours*! And of course she had no talent. She is just a *weekend painter*. Pale, drab, useless – and she killed my lover!'

This reminder of the facts of the case which, in Jane Rudgwick, would have prompted sobbing, seemed only to make Gina Luccarini angrier. She was the type whose grief manifested itself in an active, rather than a passive way.

'You described Mrs Rudgwick as "pale", Miss Luccarini, but I thought you said you'd never seen her . . . ?'

'I have not. But I have heard a great deal about her from her husband. I feel I know her – know every cell of her pathetic, bloodless body!'

'Yes, yes, I see,' said Bury, not quite sure of the correct response to these arias. 'But, as it turned out, you did not see Ralph Rudgwick on the Friday night . . . ?'

'No,' Gina Luccarini replied. 'No, I did not.'

'He was probably already dead by then . . .' the Inspector mused, interested to see what reaction this deliberate insensitivity might provoke. 'Did he contact you on Friday?'

'No,' Gina replied through what, for the first time in their encounter, could have been a sob. She swept up a purple silk handkerchief from the arm of her chair and rubbed it brusquely against her face to cover the lapse.

'Presumably, Mr Rudgwick talked to you about his marriage?'

Gina Luccarini was once again fully combative as she

replied, 'He told enough for me to know that it was a marriage only in name – that there was no love, no passion.'

'But he didn't go into detail?'

'No. It was not an interesting subject – not one that we wished to talk about more than we had to. We had more interesting things to do with our time.'

'Yes. Of course. It is true, though, is it not, that Mr Rudgwick wanted to live with you, but his wife wouldn't give him a divorce?'

'That is true. That is what he told me, yes.' Another gust of anger swept through Gina. 'She was a dreadful woman! She gave him no freedom at all. Two months ago, Ralph he has to go to Paris for an auction. He is going to take me. We will have wonderful, romantic two days. Then suddenly his wife – Jane – she say she want to go. Right at the last minute. Once again she spoil our pleasure.'

'Do you think she did that deliberately?'

'I think so. Why else so suddenly? She could not make Ralph happy herself, and she was determined nobody else would do so. She is, as I say, a monster!'

'So you have no doubt that she knew about your relationship with her husband?'

'She must have known. Everyone knew. We make no secret. We go to restaurants, opera. We are a unit. I have keys to his flat, he has keys to my flat. Whenever Ralph is in London, we are together.'

'Of course, Mrs Rudgwick was very rarely in London.'

'No, but she still must know. She lives with the man. No woman can be so stupid and insensitive not to know.'

'Maybe not.' Bury was thoughtful for a moment. 'And how long had you and Mr Rudgwick been seeing each other?'

'We met at a private view. Five months ago. It was instant attraction, you know.'

'Yes. And, er, I hope you don't mind my asking this, Miss

Luccarini ... but do you know if Mr Rudgwick had had mistresses before you?'

After what Jacob Keynes had said on the subject, it had occurred to Bury that Gina might find this suggestion insulting, but the tornado of reaction it prompted left him in no doubt that she did.

'What are you suggesting: that I am just one in a long line of – what you call -- "totties"! That he just pick me up for a bit of sex! That it was not a serious relationship!'

'No, no, no.' The Inspector finally managed to calm her. 'I was just asking. I mean, he had been married for nearly twenty years. If his relationship with his wife was as unsuccessful as you've suggested, then it might not have been surprising if he'd looked elsewhere before he met you.'

'He did not!' she snapped. 'He met me, and for the first time he knew what it was to be in love – to be really, fully in love!'

'I see.' Bury hesitated. 'Well, your reaction to that makes me think perhaps I shouldn't ask the next question I had in mind ...'

'What was it?'

'I was going to ask whether you knew of any other girlfriends he was seeing while he was going around with you?'

Gina Luccarini's furious reaction proved that the Inspector's hesitancy about asking the question had been fully justified.

It was time, Detective Inspector Bury decided, for a bit of straight talking to Jane Rudgwick.

Her voice sounded strained when he rang her the next morning, but she was as co-operative as ever. No, she wasn't going out. Yes, he was welcome to come round whenever he wanted to.

Behind the spectacles, her eyes again looked very raw, as

if she had been crying all night. And the pervasive flowery aroma which surrounded her made a sharp contrast to the exclusive perfume of Gina Luccarini.

Now that he could contrast the mistress and the wife, Bury had no difficulty in sympathizing with – almost even condoning – Ralph Rudgwick's behaviour.

Vying with Jane's scent that morning, there was also a smell of furniture polish. He knew that the sitting room had not just been done for his benefit, but that its cleaning was part of an obsessive daily ritual.

'So, how're things going?' asked Jane Rudgwick, her small talk incongruous in the circumstances.

'Our investigations are proceeding,' replied Bury, all police-man. 'My Sergeant's making local house-to-house enquiries, to check whether anyone saw anything unusual. And forensic tests are continuing on various objects that were taken from the house, and, er . . . on your husband's body.'

'Oh. Oh.' A sob trembled through Jane Rudgwick. 'Excuse me . . .'

She rushed from the room. When she returned, her eyes were redder than ever, and it seemed as though she had drenched herself in scent.

'I'm sorry about that. It's still . . . a shock, you know . . . When you mention . . . you know . . .'

'Yes, of course . . .' Detective Inspector Bury soothed, lul-ling her into relaxation before his sudden change of approach.

'I want to talk about your husband's infidelity, Mrs Rudg-wick,' he announced firmly.

'Oh.' She looked totally crestfallen. 'You knew about that?'

Bury nodded, but before he could say anything, Jane Rudgwick continued, pleadingly, 'It was only the once, though.'

'What?'

'Once. Only once that Ralph was unfaithful to me. In Paris.'

'In Paris?' Bury was too stupefied to do more than echo the words.

'Yes. A couple of months ago. Ralph told me all about it. He met this girl in his hotel, and they had a few drinks, and got talking and ... well, one thing led to another. He was heartbroken about what had happened. He said he was completely in the wrong, and he swore it'd never happen again, and he said he'd fully understand if I turned him out, but ... our relationship wasn't like that ...'

'So what happened?' the Inspector asked dully.

'Well, I was hurt, obviously – it would be foolish for me to pretend otherwise – and my confidence was hit, but I think in some ways it turned out to be a good thing.'

'A good thing?'

'Yes, because it made us talk about our marriage. You know, if something works, you tend not to question it, you just let it tick over, and perhaps I had been getting to the stage of taking Ralph a bit for granted. I mean, the fact that he succumbed to the girl in Paris ... well, maybe it meant there was something he wasn't getting from being married to me. So, anyway, we talked about it – talked about things in a way we hadn't since the days when we were first engaged – and I think, though I'm sorry for what caused it, that in a strange way it made our relationship stronger.'

'Ah.' Bury realized he was almost literally gaping, and recovered himself sufficiently to ask, 'Wasn't there some thought of you going on that trip to Paris with your husband?'

She looked at him in innocent puzzlement. 'No. It would have involved flying. Ralph knew I hated flying. He would never even have suggested it.'

'Oh.' The Inspector tried once again. 'And you really do

believe that that was the only occasion in the course of your married life that your husband was unfaithful to you?'

'Of course,' she replied ingenuously. 'I was very lucky, because I know some men are dreadful when it comes to that kind of thing.'

'Yes,' said Bury slowly, 'yes. And – I hope you don't mind my asking – but your marriage, I mean the sexual side, was satisfactory . . . ?'

For the first time since he had met her, some colour came into Jane Rudgwick's cheeks. 'Well, it always seemed so to me,' she replied rather coyly.

'Ah,' said Detective Inspector Bury, 'ah, well . . .'

And he began to invert everything he had ever thought about the case. They always said the wife was the last one to know. Ralph Rudgwick had peppered his married life with infidelities, and his wife Jane had never known about any of them. Not even about the *grand amour* that had come to her husband at the age of fifty-five.

But, as he thought about it, Bury began to wonder just how *grand* the *amour* had been. He had Gina Luccarini's word for it – and indeed that had been supported by Jacob Keynes – but, given the kind of character that was beginning to form in the Inspector's mind for Ralph Rudgwick, they had perhaps both been deluded. A man who was capable of telling wholesale lies to his wife would have little compunction about doing the same to his mistress.

Before he could sort through all the ramifications of his changed thinking, the telephone rang. Jane Rudgwick answered it.

'Yes. Yes, he is.' She held the receiver across. 'For you.'

It was the young Detective Sergeant, bumptiously pleased with himself. 'I've got something. Old lady at the end of the road, apparently spends all her days snooping through the net curtains at everyone's comings and goings.'

'What about her?' Bury asked, a little testily.

'Early Friday evening, she saw a red Golf GTi arrive at the Rudgwicks' house.'

'How long did it stay?'

'She doesn't know. It was getting dark and she left her vantage point soon after to cook her supper. But she definitely saw it arrive about half-past seven.'

'Hm. Well, that could be very useful information . . . *if* we happened to know someone who owns a red Golf GTi.'

'We do.' The Detective Sergeant was now downright crowing. 'Gina Luccarini owns a red Golf GTi.'

'Ah,' said Bury. 'Does she?'

'But this is ridiculous!' Gina Luccarini protested. 'What makes you think that I would kill the one person I have ever really loved?'

'I'm not yet saying you did,' Detective Inspector Bury replied evenly. 'I'm just asking you to answer some questions which might clarify a few points.'

'Clarify a few points!' She threw her arms in the air. 'All right – ask me what you want to ask.'

She was dressed on this occasion in black trousers and a buttercup-yellow silk blouse. Huge yellow kite-shapes dangled from her ears. Her perfume was heady, almost soporific, in the enclosed space of the flat.

Bury clicked the answerphone once again, rewound the tape and replayed it. A cultured, male voice oozed charm from the machine.

'Love, it's me. Look, for reasons that are too complicated to go into, I can't make it to your place tonight. But I've got to see you before you go to Rome – got to! So please come down here, as soon as you can. I'll be alone after seven, and I'll explain everything then – promise. I can't

wait to see you. I love you and I want to kiss you all over. See you very soon. Bye.'

Bury switched the answerphone off and again asked, 'Why didn't you tell me about that? Why didn't you tell me you went down to Henley on Friday evening?'

Gina looked sulky as she reiterated, 'I just thought it'd make things more complicated. I thought, since I didn't see Ralph, it would be simpler to pretend I hadn't been there.'

'But you must realize that it makes your behaviour look extremely suspicious.'

'Yes, now I realize that, but at the time . . . I am a person of passion, Inspector – if an Englishman can understand such a concept! Often I act before I think. When you ask me about Friday, I make a decision on – what you call – the spur of the moment, and now I can see it was the wrong decision.'

'I think I would agree with you there, Miss Luccarini.'

He let the silence hang between them. Small sounds came from the other parts of the flat, where the young Detective Sergeant and two uniformed constables were going through the artist's belongings. She had given permission for the search, but then refusing it would only have increased their suspicions.

A detail came back to the Inspector, of how, the night before, Gina had covered her confusion with a handkerchief when asked directly if she'd heard from Ralph on the Friday. Slowly, the case against her was falling into place.

'The trouble is,' he went on, 'that wrong decision you made means that you lied to me about Mr Rudgwick contacting you on the Friday. And if you lied to me about that "minor detail", it does make me wonder whether you were lying to me about anything else . . . ?'

'No! I was not! Everything else it is the truth!'

'So you're sticking to your story that you drove all the way down to Henley and didn't see him.'

'Yes. I get there. I knock on the door – there is no reply. I try the back door. Nothing.'

'Miss Luccarini, as I said, the forensic tests on the rubbish left in the Rudgwicks' bathroom found some boutique tissues of the kind that you use which show traces both of gunshot residue particles and of your rather distinctive perfume.'

'She must have planted them! Jane Rudgwick planted them. I have never been inside the house in Henley. I have keys for the flat in Covent Garden, but not for the house. I tell you, when I go there Friday at seven-thirty, I don't go inside. There is no reply from the house. Jane has already killed him!' she concluded on a spurt of anger.

'But why would she want to do that?'

'How many times do I have to answer the same questions! She did not want our happiness! She wanted to destroy it!'

'Miss Luccarini, I don't think Mrs Rudgwick even had any idea that you knew her husband.'

'But she must have done.'

'I think she thought she had a very happy marriage.'

'But how could she think that? After the things Ralph said to me about their marriage—'

'Yes, but he had reasons to say those things to you.'

'What kind of reasons?'

'Well, initially, to get you into bed with him.'

Her eyes blazed and she tensed forward. For a moment Bury thought she was actually going to slap him, but she managed to control herself.

'That is not true. Ours was a real relationship. Ralph and I loved each other.'

'I think you'd find Mrs Rudgwick would use exactly the same words.'

'But she was ... she had ...' Gina Luccarini's hands clenched and unclenched as articulacy deserted her. Then she shook her head and said softly, 'I come back to the same thing – why would I want to kill a man I love?'

'Perhaps if he'd betrayed you ... ?' Bury hazarded casually.

'But he did not betray me.'

'When he went to Paris two months ago, he went to bed with another woman.'

'What, with his wife? All right, maybe the hotel only had double beds. But, even in your peculiar, anaemic language, "going to bed with" does not mean the same as "making love to"!'

'Ralph Rudgwick *made love to* a woman he met in the hotel.'

For the first time, Gina Luccarini looked pale, paler even than the translucent Jane Rudgwick. 'I don't believe you. His wife was there, for God's sake!'

Bury shook his head. 'His wife was not there. He told you his wife would be with him, but there was never any question of her going.'

'But it was supposed to be our wonderful, romantic time together. You are talking nonsense. Why would he tell me his wife was going with him and so I could not go?'

'Perhaps because he had already made arrangements to meet this other woman in the hotel ... ?'

It took a moment for the implications of this to sink in, before the fury seized her. Her hands clawed at the bright print artfully draped over the arm of her chair, tearing through the thin fabric.

'No,' she moaned. 'No ...'

Detective Inspector Bury pressed home his advantage. 'And I think – in spite of this wonderful acting performance you're giving me at the moment – you knew that. I think that's why you killed him. Ralph Rudgwick was very vain, proud of his conquests. And he made the mistake of telling you about the latest one. That's what signed his death warrant.'

He found himself echoing Jacob Keynes' words. 'You could cope with the idea of him with his wife, but the thought of Ralph Rudgwick cheating on you with another woman – that you couldn't tolerate. It reduced you to the level of just another in a sequence of purely physical relationships, another pick-up, another easy lay. And your pride wouldn't allow him to get away with that.'

She shook her head in a terrified, mesmerized way. Her full lips still shaped the word 'No', but no sound emerged from them.

At that moment the Detective Sergeant appeared, beaming and cocky, in the doorway. In his hand was a dripping polythene bag, whose contents could be clearly seen.

'Taped on to the inside of the lavatory cistern, Inspector,' he announced. 'Oldest trick in the book.'

Gina Luccarini looked at the pistol and continued to mouth silently and helplessly. She no longer looked beautiful or sexy. She looked like a beached fish.

And the sweat of terror had soured the aroma of her expensive perfume.

Jane Rudgwick stood in the pale pink bathroom of the house in Henley and looked at herself in the mirror. She had taken off her glasses and her pale blue eyes looked clear and sparkling. The previous day they had been puffy and red, but a long night's sleep had healed them.

She found, after all the traumas of the previous weeks, she was finally beginning to relax.

The knowledge that Gina Luccarini was in prison, awaiting trial for the murder of Ralph Rudgwick, contributed significantly to Jane's feeling of security.

It hadn't really been so hard. All marriages are unknowable – that was the single fact that had made the whole thing possible.

The man who tells his mistress that his home life is terrible, that his wife is frigid and refuses to give him a divorce, is a stereotype of modern life.

As is the devoted wife at home, blithely unquestioning of her husband's fidelity, the little woman who is, in obedience to tradition, 'the last to know.'

All Jane Rudgwick had had to do was to play variations on those stereotypes.

The outline of her plan had been formed from the moment she found out about Ralph and Gina's relationship.

She had known about the other women, of course, but they had not worried her. Ralph had only gone with them for sex, an activity for which Jane had no feeling except a mild revulsion. The other women had at least deterred him from attempts to offload his restless libido on to her (though pretty early into their marriage he had given up any attempts in that direction). And the squalor of his furtive couplings had given Jane further ammunition with which to vilify her husband when she felt the need.

Because, of course, she had always been in control. Her money, and the threat of her withdrawing it from the Keynes Rudgwick Gallery, had always ensured that.

At one stage, when Ralph had been fulminating particularly violently against the trap in which she had incarcerated him, she had briefly worried that he might resort to murder to resolve the situation.

But she soon realized that he never would. Ralph Rudgwick didn't have that kind of strength in him.

Unlike his wife.

From the moment Gina Luccarini appeared on her husband's scene, Jane Rudgwick knew that she was different from the other women. This time there was more than sex involved.

And, instead of his customary shabby duplicities, this time he made no attempt to keep the relationship a secret from Jane. He told her everything about it, calmly announced that he wanted a divorce and, when she refused him that option, spoke seriously of getting out of the Keynes Rudgwick Gallery and trying something else.

It was this that had made Jane determined to teach him a lesson. Sexual jealousy was an alien concept to her, but she did deeply resent the idea of her husband finding happiness with someone else.

She decided that it was not just Ralph who should be taught a lesson. The woman who had had the effrontery to engage her husband's love should share in the punishment that Jane was preparing for him.

The idea of killing Ralph and having Gina convicted for the crime was so blissfully tidy that Jane Rudgwick hugged herself for days after she had thought of it.

The details were simple. It was really round the time of the Paris trip that the plan had crystallized. Jane knew her husband was intending to take his mistress on the jaunt, and she just had to choose her moment to announce that she herself wished to go. Ralph had remonstrated, but knew too well how Jane could make his proposed idyll a misery, so quickly caved in and put Gina off.

Jane had waited till they were actually at the airport before changing her mind. She knew by then it was too late for Ralph to salvage his previous arrangement with Gina.

Borrowing her husband's keys and getting Gina's copied had presented no problem. Nor had a trip to Notting Hill Gate on a day when she knew Gina to be out of town. A search of the flat had quickly revealed Miss Luccarini's tastes in tissues and perfume, as well as allowing Jane to reconnoitre a suitable hiding place for the pistol when the appropriate moment came.

All that was required then was a fortnight of bullying, blackmail and generally bad behaviour in the run-up to Gina's departure for Rome. The only risk at that stage had been that Jane really would frighten her husband off, make him act on his oft-spoken intention to cut loose and move in with his mistress.

But Jane Rudgwick knew the man's fundamental weakness, and her judgement of his character had proved to be correct. He had fretted and whinged, but stayed around.

Getting him to invite Gina to Henley had been a potential problem, but in the event easily negotiated. It was the threat of Jane not going on her water-colour course and thus preventing him from seeing his mistress at all before her departure for Rome that had clinched it.

Suddenly, mid-afternoon on the Friday, Jane had announced that yes, she felt better and she *was* going on the course, but she was worried about what Ralph might get up to in her absence, so she would stop every hour or so to phone and check up on him.

A man with any real character would have ignored this, but Ralph was very weak. He still hoped to find some solution to his situation that would combine having Gina with retaining his position in the Keynes Rudgwick Gallery set-up. For that reason he wanted to keep Jane sweet (or at least as sweet as she ever got).

So his only way out had been to do as he had done for most of his married life, and go along with what his wife said.

Jane had timed the announcement that she really was going to the Lake District very carefully. Her rival, she knew, tended to go out to a gym every afternoon between half-past three and five. By choosing quarter-past three as the moment to unleash her decision, Jane was certain that Ralph would try to contact Gina as soon as possible to let her know the change of plan.

She had waited outside his study door until she heard him leave the inevitable message.

Then all she had to do was to tell him to go upstairs to fetch her bag and, once he was in the bedroom, shoot him with his own gun.

That was the bit she had really enjoyed. Three wonderfully satisfying tugs at the trigger. And, on her husband's face, a very rewarding expression of surprise giving way, first to terror, and then to oblivion.

She had wiped the gun on some of Gina's tissues, already impregnated with the artist's perfume, and thrown them into the bathroom waste-bin.

She had turned up the thermostat in the bedroom, having read somewhere that an overheated environment could make it more difficult to establish the exact time of a corpse's death.

Then she had driven up to Notting Hill Gate. She had time. The difference between the journey to the Lake District by the back routes she said she was using and the motorways she really intended to use was considerable.

She watched her rival leave the apartment block on the abortive journey to Henley, slipped inside the flat, planted the murder weapon in the cistern, and then set off in her car for the motorways leading north.

A pleasant weekend's water-colouring, and back to Henley on the Sunday evening.

Yes, thought Jane Rudgwick, it really has all been very satisfactory.

Soon I'll be able to relax completely. But not quite yet. Still have to keep up the appearance of the grieving widow. You never know who might be watching.

So Jane Rudgwick picked up her atomizer of cheap scent and, bracing herself for the pain, once again sprayed it into her open eyes.

THE BATTERED CHERUB

I didn't invite her to the office. When your office is your bedroom you play these things a bit tactfully. Last thing you want to do is frighten a client off and, though I'm not one of them, there are a lot of funny people about. I don't know that there are actually more of them in Brighton than anywhere else, but it often seems that way. Maybe it's an occupational hazard. My line of work means, almost by definition, the only ones I meet are the misfits. The lonely. The sad. And loneliness and sadness can so quickly sour into something nastier.

Or maybe I am drawn to them on the old 'birds of a feather' principle. My former wife certainly said as much towards the end, as our marriage spiralled down into insult and recrimination. She said a lot more, too, in those last sick days when every statement of hers was a loaded grenade from which every response of mine seemed to take out the pin.

Anyway, she's long gone and I'm still in Brighton, still no doubt demonstrating all those negative attributes she catalogued with such relish. Mooching around what the estate agent called a 'studio flat', but what ten years ago would have been called a 'bedsitter', and what I now have the nerve to call an 'office'. When there are no jobs you're qualified for, why not stick a shingle on the door and set up on your own?

Perhaps I disqualified myself from other work. Getting

busted for drugs didn't help. I started on that after my wife walked out. Stupid, stupid, I know, but at least I did manage to crack it in the end. Not before the police had found the stuff on me, unfortunately. And prison records aren't exactly assets in these days of mass unemployment.

I sometimes think, having got off the drugs, I could get off the vodka too. I will, one day. But I don't feel quite strong enough yet.

So, anyway, as I say, I had to set up on my own. Can't lose, really. Even if you don't get any business at all, you're no worse off than you were.

Anyway, I do get occasional business. Sad people who think a little information will at least explain their sadness. Frightened people who feel reassured by the illusion of protection. Cowardly or fastidious people who want someone else to perform unpalatable services. Even dying people who think they've still got time to tie up the loose ends.

Some I can help. Some know even when they contact me that they're beyond help. I close my mind to their circumstances and send bills to all of them. They all pay, except for the one or two who don't survive. I disapprove of sending bills to the recently bereaved.

And the trickle of money that comes in helps to keep me in the manner to which I have accustomed myself: 'the office', with its bed, its table, its two chairs, the clothes chest, the vodka-bottle cupboard, the shower, the sink, the microwave and – its one good feature – the long window that ignores the terracing of roofs beneath it and looks straight out to the shifting edge of the gunmetal sea.

I don't actually have a shingle on the door. People tend to come to me by word of mouth. I'm not in *Yellow Pages*, either. But I suppose, if I were, my name, B. Cotter, would be listed under 'Detective Agencies'.

*   *   *

She edged into the pub, as tentative as a kitten testing a duvet for landmines. My first impression was that she was attractive. She recognized me from the description I'd given her, but with some surprise.

'I didn't really believe it when you said your hair was bleached.' She perched a neat but cautious buttock on the chair opposite me.

'Why not?'

'Well, for a detective . . . I mean, I'd have thought a detective should melt into the background. Bleached hair does kind of stand out.'

'You mean I don't look like your idea of a detective?'

'No. Not at all.'

'Seems to answer your objection. Doesn't matter how much I stand out, so long as no one thinks I look like a detective.'

'I suppose not,' she agreed uncertainly.

The bleached hair was another of the personal attributes my former wife had taken against. That and the black clothes. She saw it as a fashion thing. 'Why do you go round looking like a punk when punks are dead?' She couldn't understand it was more habit, more self, than fashion. After she'd gone I stayed the same out of defiance, some kind of ineffectual revenge maybe.

'Can I get you a drink?'

She asked for a dry white wine. I had a Perrier with ice and lemon in front of me. Didn't say it was Perrier. Sometimes helped to pretend I was on the vodka and tonic. All depended, really. Wary moments, meeting a client for the first time. Always required a bit of ritual circling, rationing out information, assessing the moment to feed out each new fact.

As I walked back to her, my first impression was reinforced. She was more than attractive. Kind of face a randy Florentine painter might have sneaked into the crowd at a Crucifixion, following some carnal deal with the model. A battered cherub. Brown hair, quite stiff and thick, fringing fanlike over unsettling blue eyes. They were unsettling partly because everything else in her colouring predicated brown eyes; partly because they held, together with innocence, a knowingness which belied that innocence; and partly because they were beautiful. She had owned the dark grey leather coat long enough for it to take on her imprint, its soft curves ghosting her own. For someone like me, she was trouble.

I gave her the drink and returned to my maybe Perrier. 'Right, what's the problem, Mrs McCullough?'

'Call me Stephanie. I don't like even being reminded that I've got that bastard's surname.'

I didn't respond to this, but noted the over-reaction. Premature, I thought. She, like me, should still be at the circling stage of our encounter, and she was feeding out too much information too soon. Had to be a reason for that.

'All right. Then you'd better call me Bram.' I got in before she could say it. 'And I don't think there are any Dracula jokes I haven't heard. And in fact it is only short for Abraham. And no, I don't know why my parents chose it.'

As usual, the speech had the right effect. All she said was, 'Ah.'

'So . . . what do you want me to do for you, Stephanie?'

She moved closer. Her pupils dilated. When they did that, the black almost eclipsed the blue, and the eyes' innocence had the same effect on their knowingness. She looked like something small and fluffy that'd just fallen out of a nest and never heard of pussycats.

'It's my husband,' she murmured.

'What is he? Unfaithful? Violent? Criminal? Gay? Missing? I may as well tell you now – if it's infidelity, I tend to think that's just between the two of you.'

'It's not infidelity. Well, I mean, obviously he's unfaithful,' she added dismissively, 'but that's not why I need your help . . .'

I let her get there in her own time.

'The fact is . . . Stuart – that's my husband – is . . . well, I think he's involved in something . . .'

Still let her ride it out.

'Something criminal. I mean, he is basically a crook. But this time I think he may have got a bit out of his depth . . .'

The eyes appealed, but got no help from me.

'Look, all right, normally when Stuart's on a job, I turn a blind eye – I'm not that interested in what he does these days, anyway – but I can always tell there's something up because he's, I don't know, kind of cocky. This time's different. This time he's frightened.'

She petered out. Finally, my cue came.

'What kind of crime is your husband likely to be involved in?'

'Robbery. Always is, he's not bright enough for anything more elaborate. Isolated country houses. Used to all be in Sussex, but the M25 has widened his range a bit.'

'Just breaking and entering or are we talking robbery with violence?'

'He's never looked for violence. Usually tries to do jobs when the owners are away, but, well, occasionally his information isn't all that hot, so there's someone there and . . .' she shrugged, '. . . someone gets hurt. But the violence is incidental. Means to an end.'

'And you reckon he's just done a job?'

She nodded, her face still disconcertingly close. 'No question. He's flush. Just ordered himself a new BMW. Even bought me something.' She shook a Rolex Oyster out from the shadow of her sleeve. 'Real thing, not a Hong Kong cheapo.'

'But you say he's frightened?'

'Yes. Jumpy when the phone rings. Not sleeping. I find empty bottles of Scotch in the sitting room in the mornings. He's certainly scared of something.'

'Police? Maybe he's got the wink they're on to him?'

She shook her head firmly. 'That wouldn't frighten Stuart. Always rather relishes a set-to with the cops. Reckons he can run circles round them.'

'And can he?'

'Has done so far.' She looked pensive. When she did that, her top teeth chewed a little on her lower lip. The movement was at least as unsettling as the eyes. I tried not to watch. 'No, he's shit-scared of something.'

'You don't think he's ill? Imagining things?'

She let out a little bitter laugh. 'No way. Stuart wouldn't know what imagination was if it came up and punched him on the nose.'

'I see.' I sipped the Perrier, deciding that the next drink would definitely be a vodka. 'And you want me to find out what it is that he's scared of?'

'No, it's not that. It's . . .'

'What?'

'Look, I've a feeling I do know what it is that he's scared of.' Once again, she got no prompts and had to flounder on. 'I think the last place he hit, big mansion up at Ditchling . . . well, he got a lot of stuff there, but I think the stuff was already nicked.'

'He cleaned out another villain's place?'

'Yes.'

'What makes you think that?'

'Look, it was a big job, no question, fifty grand's worth at least – I know because of the time he's spent on the phone trying to offload the stuff – but there hasn't been a murmur in the press about it.'

'Ah.'

'Papers, TV, radio – nothing. Suggests to me that whoever was hit had reasons not to make it public.'

'I'll buy that.'

'Doesn't want a public investigation, with the police involved . . .'

'But will probably be organizing a private investigation with a lot of muscle involved.'

'Exactly.'

'Which would explain why your husband's worried.'

She nodded and drew back, satisfied that her point had been made. The pupils contracted and cunning returned to her eyes.

'And you don't think he knows who it was he robbed by mistake?'

'No, I'm sure he doesn't, but the size of the house and the size of the haul suggest it could be someone pretty big.'

'Right. And you don't think the . . . aggrieved party has actually fingered your husband yet?'

'I think we'll know pretty quickly when they do identify him.'

'Yes. Which, given the way news travels in that kind of world, is not going to take too long, is it?'

'No.'

I drained the Perrier and grimaced, still maintaining the fiction that it might be vodka. 'What do you want me to do about it, then?'

'I want you to find out who it was who got robbed and do a deal with them.'

'To let Stuart off the hook?'

'Right.'

'Is that all?'

'Yes.' She grinned her louche cherubic grin. 'That's all.'

* * *

Considering how quickly I obtained the relevant information, Stuart McCullough was living on borrowed time. It cost me two visits to the right pubs, a couple of rounds of drinks, a couple more rounds of 'drinks' in folded form, and I knew the names of the other members of his gang, as well as the identity of the villain they had so incautiously robbed.

If they had been looking for massive contusions and internal bleeding, they could hardly have chosen a quicker route to the supplier. The Ditchling mansion they had so breezily cleaned out belonged to Harry Day, a major London villain, nicknamed 'Flag' Day because of the number of charges the law had tried to pin on him. He was a canny operator, though, who, by employing the right solicitors and bunging the right amounts into the right palms at the Yard, had never actually been inside. But his CV was generally agreed to include robbery with violence, protection rackets with violence, a fairly definite couple of murders with violence and – by way of weekend recreation – violence with violence. Not the kind of big boy a little boy like Stuart McCullough ought to be challenging to a game of conkers.

The only surprise about the situation was that Stephanie's husband wasn't already a mass of multiple fractures. If an outsider like me could get the information that easily, a man with 'Flag' Day's connections should have been on the ball seconds after the kickoff. But apparently he wasn't; or, if he did know the score, he was taking his time to devise appropriately cruel and unnatural punishments for the perpetrator of this professional insult.

I think actually what was keeping Stuart McCullough out of intensive care was the absence of his accomplices. He'd done the job with two Brighton small-timers who'd taken their cut the next morning and gone straight off to Tenerife with a couple of tarts. If they'd been around, 'Flag' Day's network would have soon been on to them. Stuart on his own was a marginally better security risk. He had every reason to keep quiet about the set-up, and I felt pretty certain I was the only person in whom Stephanie had confided.

I tried not to think about her. When I did, my thoughts kept spreading like cancer cells into bits of me I didn't want reinfected.

I concentrated on her husband. The thoughts he inspired weren't pretty ones, but they were more the kind I could cope with.

Clearly, if Stuart McCullough was going to evade the attentions of Harry Day in any long-term sense, something had to happen quickly. Day might not be on to him yet, but it was only a matter of time. Brighton suddenly becomes a very small place when a villain starts buying new BMWs and Rolexes.

I had an arrangement with Stephanie that she'd ring me daily for progress reports and that, if I had to phone her home and got through to her, she wouldn't recognize me. I needn't have worried. Stuart snatched up the phone on the first ring as if he were defusing it.

'Mr McCullough?' I always use my own voice on this kind of conversation. For one thing, I'm no good at disguising it and, for another, it's a myth that anyone's going to recognize a person they've never met by the voice heard on a telephone.

'Yes?' I could almost hear the sweat popping on his brow.

'Mr McCullough, I have information that you acquired certain property last Tuesday night . . .'

He didn't deny it.

'Now that property belongs to my employer . . .'

'Oh?'

'And he's far from happy about the situation.' There was a crackle on the line, or it could have been the clearing of a

terminally dry throat. 'My employer's name is Harry Day.'
This time the crackle was definitely human. 'Now,' I lied,
'Mr Day's not a vindictive man . . .'

'Really?' Stuart McCullough didn't sound convinced by
that either.

'No. And he also is not the sort of man to want a fuss
made about something like this . . . I mean, we don't want
the police brought in, do we?'

'No.'

'All Mr Day *does* want is the return of his property . . .'

'Is that really all he wants?' the dry voice croaked. 'He
doesn't want any . . . reprisals?'

'Oh, come on, Mr McCullough, everyone makes mistakes,
don't they? And it's not as if we aren't all in the same business,
is it?'

He sounded encouraged by this. A trickle of saliva lubri-
cated his voice. 'Exactly. Right. Look, I regret it as much as
. . . you know, I mean . . . but got to stick together, haven't
we?'

'Sure,' I soothed, and bit my lip to stop myself saying,
'Honour among thieves.'

'Good. Good.'

'So . . . Mr McCullough, if we can make some arrangement
whereby the property is returned intact, can I assume you
would not be averse to that?'

'Certainly. No, you tell Mr Day it was just a silly mistake
on my part and . . .'

'Of course,' I purred.

'Look, er, could I ask who I'm talking to? Or where I can
give you a bell if—?'

'I'll contact you,' I said, and put the phone down.

That was the easy bit. I didn't approach the next phone
call with quite the same relish.

*   *   *

'Could I speak to Mr Day, please?'

'Mr Day doesn't take calls. If he wants to speak to people, he rings them.'

'Well, could I give him a number and could he call me?' It wouldn't be my own number. I've got various public phones round Brighton I use for that kind of thing. On this part of the job I was going to keep strictly incognito.

'I should think that's very unlikely,' the voice replied, silkily insolent. 'Why should Mr Day want to speak to you?'

'I have some information about some property of his. Property that was stolen from his house last Tuesday.'

'Oh yes?' The tone was still cool, but I could hear an edge of interest.

'Yes, and in fact the person responsible for taking the property does regret what he did very much.'

'You don't surprise me.'

'In fact, all he wants to do is get the property back to its rightful owner.'

'I see.'

'Do you think Mr Day would be agreeable to that kind of deal?'

'Hmm . . .'

'I mean, he does want the property back, doesn't he?'

'Yes.' The voice made a decision. 'Call again in an hour.' The line went dead.

When Stephanie rang in for her daily report, I'd got the meeting set up. 'Crown and Anchor on the seafront. Neutral ground. I've told Stuart. He sounded relieved.'

'Yes. The sooner he can offload that gear, the sooner he can start breathing again.'

'Hm. I know some of the stuff's already been fenced, but Stuart said he could raise cash to cover it, and Day's man's happy with that.'

'I know,' she said ruefully. 'He came and asked for my Rolex back. And he's cancelled the order on the BMW.'

'So, Stephanie, in a couple of days – with a bit of luck – your husband'll be off the hook . . .'

'Mm.'

'And,' I went on, not knowing why I was saying it, 'you can settle back into being a nice cosy little domestic couple again.'

'It's not like that,' she said. 'I thought I made it clear that our marriage is over.'

'Then why're you going to all this trouble to save him?'

'The fact that you've stopped loving someone doesn't mean you want to see him beaten to pulp.'

'No. True.'

'But once this is sorted out, I'm leaving him. There's nothing happening there. I want to get out, find a real man.'

'Ah,' I said, meaning a lot more than 'Ah'. I could picture the pupils swelling to block out the blue in her eyes. It wasn't a picture I wanted in my mind's private gallery.

But it stayed, damn it.

She phoned me again a couple of hours before the meeting. 'Stuart's just gone out. I need to see you.'

Not for the first time, I knew the words should have been 'Sorry, can't make it' and I heard my voice saying, 'OK. Where?'

'Under the pier. By the rock stall.'

The rock stall was boarded up that time of year. The sea sucked through the shingle like an old man drawing in his breath against the cold. The weather seemed to have frightened off the junkies – or maybe it was too early in the evening for them – but it couldn't freeze the lust of the few couples twined against the encrusted steel pillars, their hands finding inevitable ways through swags of clothing.

They didn't help my concentration. Nor did the fact that, as soon as Stephanie saw me, she rushed straight up and nestled into my arms. She wore leather again, a black thigh-length coat, quilted, but not so quilted that I couldn't feel her outline pressing against mine. She stayed there longer than the strict protocol of a casual greeting demanded. The top of her head fitted neatly into the hollow of my shoulder. I had forgotten the sheer softness of women, and felt a pang when she drew back and trained those huge black pupils on me.

'I had to see you, Bram. This meeting . . .'

'Yes?'

'Stuart had a gun with him when he left.'

'Stupid idiot! I told him not to.'

'He's not going to meet someone like Day unarmed.'

'He's not meeting Day. Only a sidekick.'

'Doesn't make a lot of difference, so far as the danger's concerned.'

'Look, if he carries a gun, he's only going to—'

Something hard and cold was thrust into my hand. 'Bram, I want you to take this.'

I looked down at it. Watery moonlight pencilled a pale line along the barrel.

'I don't like carrying guns. I can usually deal with anything that—'

'Stuart's got a gun. I'll lay any money Day's man's got one too. You're meant to be refereeing this contest. You've got to be at least as well-armed as they are.'

Maybe she had a point. I shoved the gun into my coat pocket.

'I must go, Bram. I've got things to do.'

But the way she came back into my arms to say goodbye, and the length of time she stayed there, suggested that the 'things' weren't that urgent.

* * *

173

It's remarkable how civilized three people carrying guns can be. The meeting in the Crown and Anchor was conducted with all the decorum of a Buckingham Palace garden party. Day's man was thin, balding, tweed-jacketed, wouldn't have looked out of place behind the counter of a bank; only the deadness in his eyes suggested that his interest rates might be prohibitive. Stuart McCullough was big, fit gone to fat, his features almost babyishly small as the face around them had spread. He wore a leather jacket like a chesterfield, pale grey trousers, poncy little white leather shoes with tassels, heavy gold rings and bracelets – too like a stage villain to be taken seriously as a real one. With my bleached hair and draped black coat, our table must've looked like something from a television series whose casting director was having a nervous breakdown.

But, as I say, the conversation was extremely decorous. Day's man, who incidentally never mentioned Harry Day by name, confirmed that all his boss wanted was the return of his property and cash to make up for any of it that had been irreclaimably sold. Stuart said he was happy with this arrangement (and I could see from his face just how happy he was). All that remained was the transfer of the goods. Day's man said he had a van outside. Sooner it was done, the better.

The deal had only taken one round of drinks. I should have had Perrier but had gone straight for the vodka because I was cold and twitchy. After the easy conclusion of the agreement, I felt like a second one to celebrate, but the others wanted to sort out the handover as soon as possible.

So we left the pub. The sea was dull and flat in the darkness, no light twinkling on its surface, only the half-heard growl over pebbles reminding of its presence. I was to drive with Stuart. Day's man would follow us to the stash.

*   *   *

We went in my old yellow 2CV. Neither of the others wanted McCullough's car spotted by the police. Seemed reasonable enough. He was on their lists for any number of robberies, proved and suspected; my one lapse had been in a different area altogether. His car had been parked outside a lot of places where it shouldn't have been; mine had never done worse than double-yellow lines.

The smell of aftershave in the car suggested that he'd marinated himself in the stuff overnight.

He was surprisingly incurious as we drove along. I don't know whether Stephanie had said anything to him or not, but he didn't ask any questions about my rôle in the proceedings. Maybe he thought I was just more of Day's hired help. Or maybe the lack of imagination she had mentioned was so total that it never occurred to him to ask anything.

He didn't say much at all, just gave me directions. The stuff was stowed in a beach-hut at Lancing. Pretty risky hiding place, I'd have thought, but he didn't seem worried. Only temporary, he said, and no one was likely to break in that time of year. I wasn't sure whether his confidence demonstrated canniness or incompetence.

He seemed a lot more relaxed now the deal was on. Yes, he'd made a mistake tangling with Day, but now that mistake was being rectified, there would be no reprisals, and in future he'd check his information a bit more carefully. To Stuart McCullough, it seemed, that was all there was to it.

Me, I wasn't so sure. I've said I hate guns, but, driving along, I was reassured by the heaviness on my thigh.

I glanced across at him as a streetlight outlined his pudgy face in sudden gold, and asked myself once again how something as fragile and delicate as Stephanie could end up with this slab of corned beef. Fruitless speculation, of course. Which could only lead to painful follow-up questions.

To get my mind off those, I tried to draw him out on the

Ditchling job, but didn't get far. 'How come you didn't know you were doing over "Flag" Day's place?' I asked.

'I was given the wrong info, wasn't I?' he replied grumpily. 'I always get the places checked out. Usually the detail's spot-on. Only do houses when I know they're empty and know they don't belong to anyone who's going to cause aggravation. This is the first time the info's been wonky.'

That didn't tie in with what Stephanie had said, but I let it pass. 'Do you always use the same person to check the houses out for you?'

'No point in changing a winning team, is there?' As he calmed down, I could hear the cockiness his wife had mentioned coming back into his voice.

'Can I ask who you get your information from?'

He was sufficiently relaxed now to chuckle. 'You can ask. You won't get no answer. Some things better just kept in the family.'

'OK. One thing I did want to—'

'Here. Pull over by the kerb. There – between the streetlights.'

I brought the 2CV to a halt. The following van indicated punctiliously and drew in behind us, dousing its lights as soon as it came to a standstill. The beach-huts, regular as crenellations, backed on to the road. Between them came the odd dull flash of the tarnished sea. Once again we could hear it grudging against the pebbles. I looked cautiously up and down the road. A few uninterested cars went past, but there was no sign of any pedestrians.

'Don't worry,' said McCullough. 'Only people you get along here are pensioners with their pooches, and they'll all be safely back in their baskets by now.'

We heard the door of the van behind open. Day's man emerged, pulling on leather gloves, casual as a weekend driver looking for a picnic spot.

'Right, let's get this sorted.' Stuart McCullough got out of the car. I switched off the headlights and, patting the heavy lump against my thigh, followed him.

'Which one is it?' asked Day's man.

McCullough pointed, reaching into his pocket for keys.

We moved down on to the beach, our shoes rasping on the shingle. Day's man brought out a pencil torch, which scanned the hut. It was small, little more than a garden shed, and had been painted a colour that might once have been dark blue. Didn't look a very secure hiding place for fifty thousand pounds' worth of stolen goods, though maybe, as McCullough had implied, any hiding place is safe so long as no one's looking there.

'Shall I open it?' he asked.

The balding head shook. 'No. He can.'

'Big one for the Yale, little for the padlock.'

I took the proffered keys. The Yale clicked home easily, but I couldn't get the smaller key into the padlock. 'Could you shine the torch over here, please?'

I heard the crunch of shoes behind me, but no light came. Instead, I was aware of a sudden, shattering impact across the back of my neck, before the plugs were pulled on me and all my circuits went dead.

It was the splash of rain that woke me. I felt the cold and damp before I felt the pain. Icy wet pebbles pressing into my face. It was when I tried to raise my head that the pain struck. I think I screamed and lay as still as I could.

But now I was awake, the pain stayed, whether I moved or not. I tried to reassemble my brain into something that could do more than register how much my head hurt.

It was still night, but the note of the sea had changed to a swish of water on sand. The tide had gone out some way.

I dared to flex my frozen hands and in one felt the icy outline of a gun.

Slowly, agonizingly, I forced my back to arch and eased myself up on to hands and knees. The pain across the back of my neck winded me, obliterating everything else.

Clutching at my face, I inched my reluctant body upright.

Through the network of my fingers, I saw the outline of Stuart McCullough, lying on the shingle beside me. He was still and silent.

I shambled across to him on hands and knees, then tried to raise myself. My arm gave way under me and I reached forward to save myself from falling. My hand landed on his chest, and slid on the stickiness there.

Seized with a horror greater than the pain, I rose to my feet. The meagre light from distant streetlamps was enough to identify the dark liquid on my hand. I stumbled away and was violently sick.

Then, staggering, scuttering on pebbles, I found my way down to the sea's edge. I was still holding the gun. I dropped it, fell to my knees and grubbed in the sand, scraping off the foul witness from my hands. Then I dug the gun down and rubbed its surfaces with more sand.

I somehow got to my feet and, finding the strength from God knew where, hurled the weapon out into the sea.

Then I managed to get back to the 2CV and drive my trembling way home.

The needling of a hot shower was a necessary agony. I tried to crane round and check the damage in the mirror, but my neck hurt too much, so I rigged up a second mirror behind me. I saw an ugly swollen line, red and getting redder by the minute, but the skin wasn't broken. I dressed painfully, pulling on a black roll-neck sweater. Didn't want to advertise my injury. Didn't want to advertise anything that might connect me with the body on the beach.

The vodka bottle was calling out plaintively, but virtue triumphed; I made do with black coffee and a handful of Nurofen. I lay on the bed and tried to piece together my situation.

Didn't do too well. Vital links in my brain's reasoning circuitry hadn't been reconnected yet. All it could cope with was the blindingly obvious.

And it was blindingly obvious that I had been set up. It was also blindingly obvious that, if the rain hadn't woken me and some pensioner taking his pooch for an early morning stroll had found Bram Cotter with a gun in his hand beside McCullough's body, the set-up would have looked very ugly indeed.

That was all the intellectual effort I was capable of. I slipped into a sleep so deep that concussion must have played a part in it.

The buzzing of the entryphone woke me. I staggered across the room and released the door downstairs before the pain had time to hit me. And before I had time to register that the voice crackling in my ear had said, 'Police.'

There were two of them, neat, unassuming men, both in sheepskin jackets. They were hard, efficient and didn't waste compassion on people with records of drug offences. The smaller one did the talking. The bigger one just watched.

'Bram Cotter?'

I made the mistake of nodding, and winced.

'You look pretty bad.'

'A few too many drinks last night,' I mumbled.

'Sure it was just drinks?'

'Yes. I don't do drugs any more.'

'No.' The monosyllable was poised between scepticism and downright disbelief.

'Search the place if you like. You won't find anything. But presumably that's why you've come.'

'It isn't, as it happens. We've come about a murder.'

'Oh?'

'Man called Stuart McCullough has been found shot dead on Lancing Beach.'

Had to be very careful now. Find out how much they knew before I gave them anything. But my brain wasn't in ideal condition for fine-tuned pussyfooting. I kept quiet and let them do the talking.

'Now you may well ask what reason we have for connecting you with what's happened . . .'

I didn't ask. I could think of too many reasons. But the one they came up with wasn't on my list.

'Fact is, we had an anonymous call at the station linking you with the killing.'

'Me?'

'Mm. Could be a crank, of course. Someone's idea of revenge. You got a lot of enemies, Mr Cotter?'

I shrugged. Not a good thing to do when you've just been slugged across the back of the neck. 'Some,' I said.

'You knew Stuart McCullough?'

I reckoned a half-truth might be safer than a whole lie. 'Heard of him. Small-time crook, wasn't he?'

The detective nodded. 'He'd been shot near a beach-hut full of stolen property.'

'Oh.'

'Where were you last night, Mr Cotter?'

Time for whole lies now. I didn't know how much they knew. My car might have been spotted in Lancing. I might have been spotted in Lancing. But I wasn't going to give in without a fight. 'As I say, had a few drinks. A few too many drinks.'

'Where?'

'Round Brighton.'

'With friends?'

'Mostly on my own.'

'Sounds a bit sad, drinking on your own . . .'

I didn't risk another shrug, but I hope my expression did it for me.

'Would you be able to put us in touch with people who might have seen you last night?'

'Maybe. I'd have to think about it. All a bit hazy, I'm afraid.'

'Mm.' He let a silence establish itself. I was aware of the bigger detective looking round the room. 'We have to take tip-offs seriously, Mr Cotter,' the smaller one went on.

'Of course.'

The bigger detective picked up the trainers I'd been wearing the night before, turned them over, and spoke for the first time. 'Sand on the soles of these. And a bit of tar.'

'Yes,' I said innocently. 'I go for a walk on the beach most days.'

The smaller one nodded, assimilating and assessing this information. 'You said you knew Stuart McCullough . . . ?'

Had I been that stupid? 'Knew *of* him,' I qualified.

'Assuming – and as yet we have no reason to assume otherwise – that you had nothing to do with Mr McCullough's death, can you think of anyone who might have had a reason to murder him?'

If my brain had been in better nick, I might have been more cautious. As it was, I said, 'I have heard that he'd recently fallen foul of someone called Harry Day.'

The name had an instant effect on both of them. 'I'd be careful what you say about Harry Day, Mr Cotter.'

'Oh?'

'There are laws about slander and defamation in this country, you know.'

'All I said was—'

'Trying to stain the reputation of Mr Day could be a very bad move, Mr Cotter.'

The detectives exchanged glances; some private cue passed between them. When the smaller one next spoke, his words had an air of conclusion about them. 'There are a lot more lines of enquiry we have to follow up, of course. We'll probably need to ask you further questions, Mr Cotter, at a later date.' He handed me a card. 'I'd be grateful if you could ring me on this number if you're likely to be leaving Brighton over the next few days.'

'OK.'

'Thank you for your time, Mr Cotter.'

And they went. Leaving me totally bemused. Why on earth had the whole tone of the interview suddenly changed? It had to be my mention of Harry Day. Up until then they had been looming, aggressive, trying to nail me. But the moment Harry Day's name came up they had folded, given in, surrendered.

My head still hurt like hell, but my brain was repairing itself quickly. I rang through to a contact I had in the West Sussex Constabulary, and he made the situation a bit clearer.

A big operation had been mounted over the last year to nail Harry Day. West Sussex had been working with the Yard on it, following a sequence of robberies in London and tracking the goods through a series of stashes till they were taken to the house in Ditchling. A raid was planned, the raid that was finally going to catch the big operator red-handed, finally pin something on 'Flag' Day.

The raid had happened. A day after Stuart McCullough had cleaned the house out. Nothing was found that wasn't strictly kosher.

The boys in blue were left with egg all over their faces and dripping down on to their uniforms. And Harry Day was mustering his cohorts of expensive lawyers to make the police extremely sorry for the slanderous mistake they had made. In future they were going to be unbelievably cautious and sure of all their facts before they made any further allegations against Mr Harry Day.

I tried phoning Stephanie, but there was no reply. I found out where her house was and went along there. No one answered. The second time I tried, there was a 'For Sale' notice fixed to the gatepost. My battered cherub had vanished as if she'd never existed.

Three days after their visit I had a phone call from the police. The smaller detective apologized for troubling me on the previous occasion, but reiterated that they did have to check everything. Anyway, he could now put my mind at rest, I had been eliminated from their enquiries. He wanted to leave it at that, but I demanded to know if they did have any leads on the murder. He told me that it was thought Stuart McCullough had been killed in a dispute over the division of profits from various robberies he had perpetrated in London. The murderer was probably one of his accomplices. 'A gangland killing', he called it, dismissively, as if the phrase precluded further enquiries.

Clearly Harry Day was still bunging the right amounts to the right people.

I pieced it together as I drove up over the moonless Downs. I wasn't the only one who had been set up. Stuart McCullough, too. He had been very convenient. As soon as 'Flag' Day's information service got wind of the planned police raid, McCullough had been told of an ideal target for his next robbery. That way the London robberies would be attributed to McCullough and Harry Day would remain as Mr Clean. But, of course, for the scheme to work, Stuart McCullough couldn't be around to answer questions when the goods were finally discovered. He needed to be dead. Killed by some irrelevant small-time crook, someone with a police record. Which was where I came in.

These conclusions raised other questions. Who had tipped McCullough off about the stuff in Day's house? Why hadn't Day taken reprisals straight away? Whose idea had it been to bring me in? Was McCullough's death convenient for other reasons than just keeping him quiet about the robberies?

The answers to all these questions were glaringly obvious, but I tried to evade them, tried to find other explanations. Until I had proof.

I soon had proof. It winded me and made me nauseous like a blow to the stomach. I had crept over the perimeter fence of Day's estate, a dark balaclava masking my bleached hair. I had edged myself through the trees, and dashed across the shadows of the lawn to the house, drawn mothlike to its leaded mock-Gothic windows. Perched on an upturned wheelbarrow, craning like a Bisto kid towards a slit between curtains, I saw them.

Harry Day was as big as Stuart McCullough, white hair, black eyebrows over mean eyes. She sat on his lap. A burgundy leather dress this time, tight, hugging. Champagne glasses in their hands, and on their faces the confidence of their immunity from prosecution. Her vulnerability and innocence had been erased completely. There was nothing cherubic about that hard, hard face. Except its beauty.

I felt the wheelbarrow shift and slid down, clattering on to the patio. I heard a door open, a rough male shout, dogs barking.

I ran.

*   *   *

I had a couple of stiff drinks and fell asleep round one. I woke again before two, feeling, as amputees are supposed to, pain in a part of me that had been cut off. I got out of bed. I hadn't closed the curtains, so didn't have to open them to look out over the blackness of the sea.

The vodka bottle and I sat there, sharing each other's solitude, until dawn first speckled, then linked up the shifting waves in the embroidery of another day's light.

WAYS TO KILL A CAT

'There are more ways to kill a cat than choking it with cream.'
Old Proverb

1. Putting the Cat Among the Pigeons

Seraphina Fellowes felt very pleased with herself. This was not an unusual state of affairs. Seraphina Fellowes usually felt very pleased with herself. This hadn't always been the case, but her literary success over the previous decade had raised her self-esteem to a level that was now almost unassailable.

Only twelve years before, she had been no more than a dissatisfied mousy haired housewife, married to a Catholic writer, George Fellowes, whose fondness for 'trying ideas out' rather than writing for commercial markets, coupled with an increasingly close relationship with the bottle, was threatening both his career and their marriage.

Seraphina clearly remembered the evening that had changed everything. Changed everything for her, that is. It hadn't affected George's fortunes so much, even though the original life-changing idea had been his. This detail was one of many that Seraphina tended to gloss over in media interviews about her success. George may have given her a little help in the early days, but he had long since ceased to have any relevance, either in her career or her personal life.

When the idea first came up, Seraphina hadn't even been Seraphina. She had then just been Sally, but 'Sally Fellowes' was no name for a successful author, so that was the first of many details that were changed as she created her new persona.

Like an increasing number of evenings at that stage of the Fellowes' marriage, the pivotal evening had begun with a row. Sally, as she then was, had crossed from the house to the garden shed in which her husband worked, and found George sprawled across his desk, fast asleep. Cuddled up against his head had been Mr Whiffles, their tabby cat. Well, the cat was technically 'theirs', but really he was George's. George was responsible for all the relevant feeding and nurturing. Sally didn't like cats very much.

It was only half-past six in the evening, but already in George's waste-paper basket lay the cause of his stupor, an empty half-bottle of vodka. That had been sufficient incentive for Sally to shake him rudely awake and pull one of the common triggers of their rows, an attack on his drinking. George's subsequent picking up and stroking of the disturbed Mr Whiffles had moved Sally on to another of her regular criticisms: 'You care more about that cat than you do about me.'

George had come back, predictably enough, with: 'Well, this cat shows me a lot more affection than you do,' which had moved the altercation inevitably on to the subject of their sex-life – George's desire for more sex and more enthusiastic sex, his conviction that having children would solve many of their problems, and Sally's recurrent assertion that he was disgusting and never thought about anything else.

Once that particular storm had blown itself out, Sally had moved the attack on to George's professional life. Why did he persist in writing 'arty-farty literary novels' that nobody wanted to publish? Why didn't he go in for something like crime fiction, a genre that large numbers of the public might actually want to *read*?

'Oh yes?' George had responded sarcastically. 'What, should I write mimsy-pimsy little whodunnits in which all the blood is neatly swept under the carpet and the investigation is in the hands of some heart-warmingly eccentric and totally unrealistic sleuth? Or,' he had continued, warming to his theme and stroking Mr Whiffles ever more vigorously, 'why don't I make a cat the detective? Why don't I write a whole series of mysteries which are solved by lovable Mr Whiffles?'

The instant he made the suggestion, Sally Fellowes' anger evaporated. She knew that something cataclysmic had happened. From that moment she saw her way forward.

At the time, though the cat mystery was already a burgeoning sub-genre in American crime fiction, it had not taken much of a hold in England. Cat picture books, cat calendars, cat quotation selections and cat greetings cards all sold well – particularly at Christmas – but there didn't exist a successful home-grown series of cat mysteries.

Sally Fellowes – or rather Seraphina Fellowes, for the name came to her simultaneously with the idea – determined to change all that.

George had helped her a lot initially – though that was another little detail she tended not to mention when talking to the media. She rationalized this on marketing grounds. The product she was selling was 'a Mr Whiffles mystery, written by Seraphina Fellowes'. To mention the existence of a collaborating author would only have confused potential purchasers.

And George didn't seem to mind. He still regarded the Mr Whiffles books as a kind of game, a diversion he took about as seriously as trying to complete the crossword. Seraphina would summon him by intercom buzzer from his shed when she got stuck, and he, with a couple of airy, nonchalant sentences, would redirect her into the next phase of the mystery. George was still, in theory, working on his 'literary' novels, and regarded devising whodunnit plots as a kind of mental chewing gum.

Seraphina proved to be a quick learner and an assiduous researcher. She negotiated her way around library catalogues; she established good relations with her local police for help on procedure; she even bought a gun, which ever thereafter she kept in her desk drawer, so that she could make her descriptions of firearms authentic.

As the Mr Whiffles mysteries began to roll off the production line, the summonings of George from his shed grew less and less frequent. While Seraphina was struggling with the first book, the intercom buzzer sounded every ten minutes, and her husband spent most of his life traversing the garden between shed and house. With the second, however, the calls were down to about one a day, and for the third – except to unravel a couple of vital plot points – Seraphina's husband was hardly disturbed at all.

The reason for this was that George had made the first book such an ingenious template, writing the rest was merely a matter of doing a bit of research and applying the same formula to some new setting. Seraphina, needless to say, would never have admitted this, and had indeed by the third book convinced herself that the entire creative process was hers alone.

As George became marginalized from his wife's professional life, so she moved him further away from her personal life. As soon as the international royalties for the Mr Whiffles books started to roll in, Seraphina organized the demolition of George's working shed in the garden, and its replacement with a brand-new self-contained bungalow.

There her husband was at liberty to lead his own life. Whether that life involved further experimentation with the novel form or a quicker descent into alcoholic befuddlement, Seraphina Fellowes neither knew nor cared.

She didn't divorce George, though. His Catholicism put him against the idea, but also Seraphina needed him around to see that Mr Whiffles got fed during her increasingly frequent absences on promotional tours or at foreign mystery conventions. Then again, there was always the distant possibility that she might get stuck again on one of the books and need George to sort out the plot for her.

Besides, having a shadowy husband figure in the background had other uses. When asked about him in interviews, she always implied that he was ill and that she unobtrusively devoted her life to his care. This did her image no harm at all. He was also very useful when over-sexed crime writers or critics came on to her at mystery conventions. Her assertion, accompanied by a martyred expression of divided loyalties, that 'it wouldn't be fair to George' was a much better excuse than the truth that she didn't in fact like sex.

As the royalties mounted, Seraphina had both herself and her house made over. Her mousy hair became a jet-black helmet assiduously maintained by costly hairdressing; her face was an unchanging mask of expertly applied make-up; and she patronized ever more expensive couturiers for her clothes. The house was extended and interior designed; the garden elegantly landscaped to include a fishpond with elaborate fountain and cascade features.

And Seraphina always had the latest computer technology on which to write her money-spinning books. After taking delivery of each new state-of-the-art machine, her first ritual action was to programme the 'M' key to print on the screen 'Mr Whiffles'.

So, twelve years on from the momentous evening that

changed her life, Seraphina Fellowes had good cause to feel very pleased with herself. The previous day she had achieved a lifetime ambition. She had rung through an order for the latest model Ferrari. There was a year-and-a-half's waiting list for delivery, but it had given Seraphina enormous satisfaction to write a cheque for the full purchase price without batting an eyelid.

She looked complacently around the large study she had had built on to the house. It was decorated in pastel pinks and greens, flowery wallpapers and hanging swathes of curtain. The walls were covered with framed Mr Whiffles memorabilia: book jackets, publicity photographs of the author cuddling her hero's namesake, newspaper best-sellers listings, mystery organizations' citations and awards. On her mantelpiece, amongst lesser plaques and figurines, stood her proudest possession – the highest accolade so far accorded to the Mr Whiffles industry: an Edgar statuette from the Mystery Writers of America. Yes, Seraphina Fellowes did feel very pleased with herself.

But even as she had this thought, a sliver of unease was driven into her mind. She heard once again the ominous sound that increasingly threatened her wellbeing and complacency. It was the clatter of a letterbox and the solid thud of her elastic-band-wrapped mail landing on the doormat. She went through into the hall with some trepidation to see what new threat the postman had brought that day.

Seraphina divided the letters into two piles on her desk. The left-hand pile comprised those addressed to 'Seraphina Fellowes, Author of the Mr Whiffles Books'; the right-hand one was made up of letters addressed to 'Mr Whiffles' himself. A lot of those, she knew, would be whimsically written by their owners as if they came from other cats. In fact, that morning over half of Mr Whiffles' letters had paw-prints on the back of the envelopes.

But that wasn't what worried Seraphina Fellowes. What really disturbed her – no, more than disturbed – what really twisted the icy dagger of jealousy in her heart was the fact that the right-hand pile was much higher than the left-hand one. This was the worst incident yet, and it confirmed an appalling trend that had been building for the last couple of years.

Mr Whiffles was getting more fan mail than she was!

The object of her jealousy, with the instinct for timing which had so far preserved intact all nine of his lives, chose that moment to enter Seraphina Fellowes' study. He wasn't, strictly speaking, welcome in her house – he spent most of his time over in George's bungalow – but Seraphina had had cat-flaps inserted in all her doors to demonstrate her house's cat-friendliness when journalists came to interview her, and Mr Whiffles did put in the occasional appearance. To get to the study he'd had to negotiate four cat-flaps: from the garden into a passage, from the passage into the kitchen, kitchen to hall and hall to study.

He looked up at his mistress with that insolence cats don't just reserve for kings, and Seraphina Fellowes felt another twist of the dagger in her heart. She stared dispassionately down at the animal. He'd never been very beautiful, just a tabby neutered tom like a million others. Seraphina looked up at one of the publicity shots on the wall and compared the cat photographed five years previously with the current reality.

Time hadn't been kind. Mr Whiffles really was looking in bad shape. He was fourteen, after all. He was thinner, his coat more scruffy, he was a bit scummy round the mouth, and he might even have a patch of mange at the base of his tail.

'You poor old boy,' Seraphina Fellowes cooed. 'You're no spring chicken any more, are you? I'm rather afraid it's time for you and me to pay a visit to the vet.'

And she went off to fetch the cat-basket.

* * *

At the surgery, everyone made a great fuss of Mr Whiffles. Though he'd enjoyed generally good health, there had been occasional visits to the vet for all the usual minor feline ailments and, as the fame of the books grew, he was treated there increasingly like a minor royal.

Seraphina didn't take much notice of the attention he was getting. She was preoccupied with planning the press conference at which the sad news of Mr Whiffles' demise would be communicated to the media. She would employ the pained expression she had perfected for speaking about her invalid husband. And yes, the line 'It was a terrible wrench, but I felt the time had come to prevent him further suffering' must come in somewhere.

'How incontinent?' asked the vet, once they were inside the surgery and Mr Whiffles was standing on the bench to be examined.

'Oh, I'm afraid it's getting worse and worse,' said Seraphina mournfully. 'I mean, at first I didn't worry about it, thought it was only a phase, but there's no way we can ignore the situation any longer. It's causing poor Mr Whiffles so much pain, apart from anything else.'

'If it's causing him pain, then it's probably just some kind of urinary infection,' said the vet unhelpfully.

'I'm afraid it's worse than that.' Seraphina Fellowes choked back a little sob. 'It's a terrible decision to make, but I'm afraid he'll have to be put down.'

The vet's reaction to this was even worse. He burst out laughing. 'Good heavens, we're not at that stage.' He stroked Mr Whiffles, who reached up appealingly and rubbed his whiskers against the vet's face. 'No, this old boy's got another good five years in him, I'd say.'

'Really?' Seraphina realized she'd let too much pique show in that one, and repeated a softer, more relieved, more tentative, 'Really?'

'Oh yes. I'll put him on antibiotics, and that'll sort out the urinary infection in no time.' The vet looked at her with concern. 'But you shouldn't be letting worries about him prey on your mind like this. You mustn't get things out of proportion, you know.'

'I am not getting things out of proportion!' Seraphina Fellowes snapped with considerable asperity.

'Maybe you should go and see your doctor,' the vet suggested gently. 'It might be something to do with your age.'

Seraphina was still seething at that last remark as she drove back home. Her mood was not improved by the way Mr Whiffles looked up at her through the grille of the cat-basket. His expression seemed almost triumphant.

Seraphina Fellowes set her mouth in a hard line. The situation wasn't irreversible. There were more ways to kill a cat than enlisting the help of the vet.

2. Fighting Like Cats and Dogs

'Are you sure you don't mind my bringing Ghengis, Seraphina?'

'No, no.'

'But I thought, what with you being a cat person, you wouldn't want a great big dog tramping all over your house.'

A great big dog Ghengis certainly was. He must have weighed about the same as the average nightclub bouncer, and the similarities didn't stop there. His teeth appeared too big for his mouth, with the result that he was incapable of any expression other than slavering.

'It's no problem,' Seraphina Fellowes reassured her guest.

'But he doesn't like cats.' Seraphina knew this; it was the sole reason for her guest's invitation. 'I'd hate to think of him doing any harm to the famous Mr Whiffles,' her guest continued.

'Don't worry. Mr Whiffles is safely ensconced with George.' The mastiff growled the low growl of a flesh addict whose fix is overdue. 'Maybe Ghengis would like to have a run around the garden . . . to let off some steam?'

As she opened the back door and Ghengis rocketed out, Seraphina looked with complacency towards the tree under which a cat lay serenely asleep. 'No, no!' her guest screamed. 'There's Mr Whiffles!'

'Oh dear,' said Seraphina Fellowes with minimal sincerity. Then she closed the back door and went through the passage into the kitchen to watch the unequal contest through a window.

The huge slavering jaws were nearly around the cat before Mr Whiffles suddenly became aware and jumped sideways. The chase thereafter was furious, but there was no doubt who was calling the shots. Mr Whiffles didn't chose the easy option of flying up a tree out of Ghengis's reach. Instead, he played on his greater mobility, weaved and curvetted across the grass, driving the thundering mastiff to ever more frenzied pitches of frustration.

Finally, Mr Whiffles seemed to tire. He slowed, gave up evasive action and started to move in a defeated straight line towards the house. Ghengis pounded greedily after him, slavering more than ever.

Mr Whiffles put on a sudden burst of acceleration. Ghengis did likewise, and he had the more powerful engine. He ate up the ground that separated them.

At the second when it seemed nothing could stop the jaws from closing around his thin body, Mr Whiffles took off through the air and threaded himself neatly through the outer cat-flap into the passage, and the next one into the kitchen.

Seraphina Fellowes just had time to look down at the cat on the tiled floor before she heard the splintering crunch of Ghengis hitting the outside door at full speed.

Mr Whiffles looked up at his mistress with an expression which seemed to say, 'You'll have to do better than that, sweetie.'

As Seraphina Fellowes was seeing her guest and bloody-faced dog off on their way to the vet's, the postman arrived with the day's second post. The usual thick rubber-banded wodge of letters.

That day two-thirds of the envelopes had paw-prints on the back.

3. Letting the Cat Out of the Bag

It was sad that George's mother died. Sad for George, that is. Seraphina had never cared for the old woman.

And it did mean that George would have to go to Ireland for the funeral. What with seeing solicitors, tidying his mother's house prior to putting it on the market, and other family duties, he would be away a whole week.

How awkward that this coincided with Seraphina's recollection that she needed to go to New York for a meeting with her American agent. Awkward because it meant for a whole week neither of them would be able to feed Mr Whiffles.

Not to worry, Seraphina had reassured George, there's a local girl who'll come in and put food down for him morning and evening. Not a very bright local girl, thought Seraphina gleefully, though she didn't mention that detail to George.

'Now, Mr Whiffles is a very fussy eater,' she explained when she was briefing the local girl, 'and sometimes he's just not interested in his food. But don't you worry about that. If he hasn't touched one plateful, just throw it away and put down a fresh one – OK?'

Seraphina waited until the cab taking George to the station was out of sight. Then she picked up a somewhat suspicious

Mr Whiffles with a cooing, 'Who's a lovely boy then?' and opened the trap door to the cellar.

She placed the confused cat on the second step, and while Mr Whiffles was uneasily sniffing out his new environment, slammed the trap down and bolted it.

Then she got into her BMW – she couldn't wait till it was a Ferrari – and drove to the executive parking near Heathrow which she always used when she Concorded to the States.

Seraphina made herself characteristically difficult with her agent in New York. Lots of little niggling demands were put forward to irritate her publisher. She was just flexing her muscles. She knew the sales of the Mr Whiffles books were too important to the publisher, and ten per cent of the royalties on them too important to her agent, for either party to argue.

She also aired an idea that she had been nurturing for some time – that she might soon start another series of mysteries. Oh yes, still cat mysteries, but with a new, female protagonist.

Her agent and publisher were both wary of the suggestion. Their general view seemed to be 'If it ain't broke, don't mend it'. An insatiable demand was still out there for the existing Mr Whiffles product. Why put that guaranteed success at risk by starting something new?

Seraphina characteristically made it clear that the opinions of her agent and publisher held no interest for her at all.

On the Concorde back to London, she practised and honed the phrases she would use at the press conference which announced Mr Whiffles' sad death from starvation in her cellar. How she would excoriate the stupid local girl who had unwittingly locked him down there in the first place, and then not been bright enough to notice that he wasn't appearing to eat his food. Surely anyone with even the most basic intelligence could have put two and two together and realized that the cat had gone missing?

There was indeed a press conference when Seraphina got back. The story even made its way on to the main evening television news – as one of those heart-warming end pieces which allow the newsreader to practise his chuckle.

But the headlines weren't the ones Seraphina had had in mind. 'PLUCKY SUPERCAT SUMMONS HELP FROM CELLAR PRISON.' 'MR WHIFFLES CALLS FIRE BRIGADE TO SAVE HIM FROM LINGERING DEATH.' 'BRILLIANT MR WHIFFLES USES ONE OF HIS NINE LIVES AND WILL LIVE ON TO SOLVE MANY MORE CASES.'

To compound Seraphina's annoyance, she then had to submit to many interviews in which she expressed her massive relief for the cat's survival, and to many photographic sessions in which she had to hug the mangy old tabby with apparent delight.

Prompted by all the publicity, the volume of mail arriving at Seraphina Fellowes' house rocketed. And now almost all the letters were addressed to 'Mr Whiffles'. Seraphina thought if she saw another paw-print on the back of an envelope, she'd throw up.

4. Playing Cat and Mouse

In July 1985, in a speech to the American Bar Association in London, Margaret Thatcher said: 'We must try to find ways to starve the terrorist and the hijacker of the oxygen of publicity on which they depend.'

Seraphina Fellowes, a woman not dissimilar in character to Margaret Thatcher, determined to apply these tactics in her continuing campaign against Mr Whiffles. His miraculous escape from the cellar had had saturation coverage. The public was, for the time being, slightly bored with the subject of Mr Whiffles. Now was the moment to present them with a new publicity sensation.

She was called Gigi, and she was everything Mr Whiffles wasn't. A white Persian with deep blue eyes, she had a pedigree that made the Apostolic Succession look like the invention of parvenus. Whereas Mr Whiffles had the credentials of a streetfighter, Gigi was the unchallenged queen of all she surveyed.

And, Seraphina Fellowes announced at the press conference she had called to share the news, Gigi's fictional counterpart was about to become the heroine of a new series of cat mysteries. Stroking her new cat, Seraphina informed the media that she had just started the first book, *Gigi and the Dead Fishmonger*. Now that 'dear old Mr Whiffles' was approaching retirement, it was time to think of the future. And the future belonged to a new feisty, beautiful, young cat detective called Gigi.

The announcement didn't actually get much attention. It came too soon after the blanket media coverage accorded to Mr Whiffles' escape and, though from Seraphina's point of view there couldn't have been more difference between the two, for the press it was 'just another cat story'.

The only effect the announcement did have was to increase yet further the volume of mail arriving at Seraphina Fellowes' house. At first she was encouraged to see that the majority of these letters were addressed to her rather than to her old cat. But when she found them all to be condemnations of her decision to sideline Mr Whiffles, she was less pleased.

Seraphina, however, was philosophical. Just wait till the book comes out, she thought. That's when we'll get a really major publicity offensive. And by ceasing to write the Mr Whiffles books, she would condemn the cat who gave them their name to public apathy and ultimate oblivion. She was turning the stopcock on the cylinder that contained his oxygen of publicity.

So Seraphina Fellowes programmed the letter 'G' as the shorthand for 'Gigi' into her computer, and settled down to write the new book. It was hard, because she was canny enough to know that she couldn't reproduce the Mr Whiffles formula verbatim. A white Persian aristocrat like Gigi demanded a different kind of plot from the streetwise tabby. And Seraphina certainly had no intention of enlisting George's help again.

So she struggled on. She knew she'd get there in time. And once the book was finished, even if the first of the series wasn't quite up to the standard of a Mr Whiffles mystery, it would still sell in huge numbers on the strength of Seraphina Fellowes' name alone.

While she was writing, the presence – the existence – of Mr Whiffles did not become any less irksome to her.

She made a half-hearted attempt to get rid of him by means of a plate of catfood laced with warfarin, but the tabby ignored the bait with all the contempt it deserved. And Seraphina was only just in time to snatch the plate away when she saw Gigi approaching it greedily.

Mr Whiffles took to spending a lot of time in the middle of the study carpet, washing himself unhurriedly, and every now and then fixing his green eyes on the struggling author with an expression of derisive pity.

Seraphina Fellowes gritted her teeth and, as she wrote, allowed the back burner of her mind to devise ever more painful and satisfying revenges.

5. *The Cat's Pyjamas*

'I've done it! I've finished it!' Seraphina Fellowes shouted to no one in particular as she rushed into the kitchen, the passive Gigi clasped in her arms. The author was wearing a brand-new designer silk blouse. Mr Whiffles, dozing on a pile of dirty washing in the utility room, opened one lazy eye to observe the proceedings. He watched Seraphina hurry to the fridge and extract a perfectly chilled bottle of Dom Perignon.

It was a ritual. In the euphoria of completing the first Mr Whiffles mystery, Seraphina and George had cracked open a bottle of Spanish fizz and, even more surprisingly, ended the evening by making love. Since then the ritual had changed. The love-making had certainly never been repeated. The quality of the fizz had improved, but after the second celebration, when he got inappropriately drunk, George had no longer been included in the festivities. Now, when Seraphina Fellowes finished a book, she would dress herself in a new garment bought specially for the occasion, then sit down alone at the kitchen table and work her way steadily through a bottle of very good champagne. It was her ideal form of celebration – unalloyed pampering in the company she liked best in the world.

When her mistress sat down, Gigi, demonstrating her customary lack of character, had immediately curled up on the table and gone to sleep. So the new mystery star didn't hear the rambling monologue that the exhausted author embarked on as she drank.

Mr Whiffles, cradled in his nest of dirty blouses, underwear and silk pyjamas, could hear it. Not being blessed with the kind of anthropomorphic sensibilities enjoyed by his fictional counterpart, he couldn't of course understand a word. But from the tone of voice he didn't have much problem in getting the gist. Continued vigilance on his part was clearly called for.

Seraphina Fellowes drained the dregs of the last glass and rose, a little unsteadily, to her feet. As she did so, she caught sight of Mr Whiffles through the open utility-room door. She stared dumbly at him for a moment; then an idea took hold.

Seraphina moved with surprising swiftness for one who'd just consumed a bottle of champagne, and was beside Mr Whiffles before he'd had time to react. She swept up the arms of the silk pyjama top beneath the cat and wrapped them tightly round him. Then she tucked the bundle firmly under her right arm. 'You're getting to be a very dirty cat in your old age,' she hissed. 'Time you had a really good wash.'

She was remarkably deft for someone who'd had a woman to come in and do all her washing for the previous ten years. Mr Whiffles struggled to get free, but the tight silk tied his legs like a straitjacket. Though he strained and miaowed ferociously, it was to no avail. Seraphina's arm clinched him like a vice, and he couldn't get his claws to work through the cloth.

With her spare hand, she shovelled the rest of the dirty washing into the machine, finally pitching in the unruly bundle of pyjamas. She pushed the door to with her knee, then turned to fill the plastic soap bubble.

Claws snagging on the sleek fabric, Mr Whiffles struggled desperately to free himself. Somehow he knew that she had to open the machine's door once more, and somehow he knew that that would be his only chance.

The right amount of soap powder had been decanted. Seraphina bent down to open the door and throw the bubble in. With the sudden change of position, the champagne caught up with her. She swayed for a second, put a hand to her forehead and shook her head to clear it.

'Quietened down a bit, have you?' she crowed to the tangled bundle of garments, then slammed the door shut. 'Won't you be a nice clean boy now?' She punctuated the words with her actions, switching the dial round to the maximum number of rinses, then vindictively pulling out the knob to start the fatal cycle.

* * *

Seraphina Fellowes was a bit hung-over when she woke the following morning. And the first thing that greeted her pained eyes when she opened them was a ghost.

Mr Whiffles sat at the end of her bed, nonchalantly licking clean an upraised back leg.

Seraphina screamed and he scampered lazily out of the bedroom.

She was far too muzzy and confused to deduce that Mr Whiffles must have jumped out of the washing machine during the few seconds when the alcohol had caught up with her. She was too muzzy and confused for most things, really.

Her bleared gaze moved across to the chair, over which in the fuddlement of the night before she'd hung her new designer shirt.

The rich silk had been shredded into a maypole of tatters by avenging claws.

6. *Cat on Hot Bricks*

It was nine months later. A perfect summer day, drawing to its close.

On such occasions a finely tuned heat-seeking instrument like a cat will always know where the last of the day's warmth lingers. Mr Whiffles had many years before found out that the brick driveway in front of the house caught the final rays of sunlight and held that warmth long after the surrounding grass and flowerbeds had turned chilly. So, as daylight faded, he could always be found lying on the path, letting the stored heat of the bricks flow deliciously through his body.

Seraphina Fellowes felt very pleased with herself. Her self-esteem had taken something of a buffeting through the last months, but now she was back on course. She was on the verge of greater success than she'd ever experienced. And, to make her feel even better, she had taken delivery that morning of her new Ferrari.

Seraphina was driving the wonderful red beast back from the launch of *Gigi and the Dead Fishmonger*, and she felt powerful. The party had been full of literati and reviewers; the speech by her publisher's managing director had left no doubt about how much they valued their top-selling author; and everyone seemed agreed that the new series of books was destined to outperform even the success of the Mr Whiffles mysteries.

Oh yes, it might take a while for the new series to build up momentum, but there was no doubt that Mr Whiffles would quickly be eclipsed for ever.

Seraphina looked fondly down at Gigi, beautiful as ever, deeply asleep on the passenger seat. The cat had been characteristically docile at the launch, and the pair of them had been exhaustively photographed. Gigi was much more of a fashion accessory than Mr Whiffles could ever have been, and Seraphina had even begun to buy herself clothes with the cat's colouring in mind. Together one day, she reckoned, they could make the cover of *Vogue*.

She leant across to give Gigi a stroke of gratitude, but her movement made the Ferrari swerve. She righted it with an easy flick of the steering wheel, and reminded herself to be careful. In the euphoria of the launch, she'd probably had more to drink than she should have done. Not the only occasion recently she'd overindulged. Must watch it. George was the one with the drink problem, not her.

The thought drove a little wedge of unease into her serenity. It was compounded by the recollection of a conversation she'd had at the launch with a major book reviewer. He'd expressed the heresy that he thought she'd never top the Mr Whiffles books. Those were the ones for him; no other cat detective could begin to replace Mr Whiffles in the public's affections.

The wedge of unease was now wide enough to split Seraphina's mind into segments of pure fury. That wretched, mangy old cat was still getting more fan mail than she was! Bloody paw-prints over bloody everything!

Her anger was at its height as she turned the Ferrari into her drive. And there, lying fast asleep on the warm bricks, lay as tempting a target as Seraphina Fellowes would ever see in her entire life.

There was no thought process involved. She just slammed her foot down on the accelerator and was jolted back as the huge power of the engine took command.

Needless to say, Mr Whiffles, alerted by some sixth or seventh sense, shot out of the way of the huge tyres just in time.

The Ferrari smashed into a brick pillar at the side of the garage. Seraphina Fellowes needed five stitches in a head wound. Gigi, who'd been catapulted forward by the impact, hit her face against the dashboard and was left with an unsightly permanent scar across her nose. For future publicity, the publishers would have to use the photographs taken at the launch; all subsequent ones would be marred by her disfigurement.

And the Ferrari, needless to say, was a write-off.

7. Shooting the Cat

One morning a few weeks later, along with the rubber-banded brick of fan mail – almost all with bloody paw-prints on the back – came an envelope from the publicity department of Seraphina Fellowes' publishers. She tore it open and, reading the impersonal note on the 'With Compliments' slip – 'These are all the reviews received to date' – decided she might need a quick swig of vodka to see her through the next few moments.

It wasn't actually that morning's first swig of vodka, but, Seraphina rationalized to herself, she had been under a lot of stress over the previous weeks. Once she got properly into the second Gigi book, she'd cut back.

Through the vodka bottle, as she raised it to drink, Seraphina caught sight of Mr Whiffles, perched on her mantelpiece. The refraction of the glass distorted the features of his face, but the sneering curl to his lips was still there when she lowered the bottle.

Seraphina Fellowes firmly turned her swivel chair to face away from the fireplace, took a deep breath and started to read the reviews of *Gigi and the Dead Fishmonger*.

She had had inklings from her publisher over the previous few weeks that the reaction hadn't been great, but still was not prepared for the blast of universal condemnation the cuttings contained. Setting aside the clever quips and snide aphorisms, the general message was: 'This book is rubbish. Gigi is an entirely unbelievable and uninteresting feline sleuth. Get back to writing about Mr Whiffles – he's great!'

As she put the bundle of clippings down on her desk, Seraphina Fellowes caught sight once again of the tabby on the mantelpiece. She would have sworn that the sneer on his face had now become a smirk of Cheshire-cat proportions.

Seized by unreasoning fury, Seraphina snatched open her desk drawer and pulled out the gun she had bought all those years ago when researching the first book. Her wavering hand steadied to take aim at the cat on the mantelpiece. As she pulled the trigger, she felt as if she was lancing a boil.

Whether her aim was faulty, or whether another of Mr Whiffles' extra senses preserved him, it was hard to judge. What was undoubtedly true, though, was that the bullet missed, and before the echo of the shot died down, it had been joined by the panicked clattering of a cat-flap.

Mr Whiffles had escaped once again.

Seraphina Fellowes' Edgar, however, the precious ceramic statuette awarded to her by the Mystery Writers of America, had been shattered into a thousand pieces.

8. All Cats are Grey in the Dark

What had started as a niggle and developed into a continuing irritation, was by now a full-grown obsession. Seraphina couldn't settle to anything – certainly not to getting on with the second Gigi mystery. The critical panning of the first had left her battered and embittered. It was a very long time since Seraphina Fellowes had felt even mildly pleased with herself.

She now spent her days lolling in the swivel chair in front of her state-of-the-art computer, gazing at the eternally renewed moving pattern of its screensaver, or drifting aimlessly around the house. She ceased to notice what clothes she put on in the mornings – or, as her sleep patterns got more erratic, afternoons. More and more white showed at the roots of her hair, but the effort of lifting the phone to make an appointment at her hairdressers seemed insuperable. The vodka bottle was never far away.

And, with increasing certainty, Seraphina Fellowes knew that only one event could restore the self-esteem and success that were hers by right.

She could only be saved by the death of Mr Whiffles.

One day she finally decided there would be no more pussy-footing. He was just a cat, after all. And if one believed in the proverbial nine lives, his stock of those was running very low. Seraphina decided that she really would kill him that day.

Bolstered by frequent swigs from the vodka bottle, she sat and planned.

George was away for the day, on one of his rare visits to hear his agent apologize for her inability to find a buyer for the latest George Fellowes 'literary novel'. So Seraphina went down to the bungalow, checked carefully that Mr Whiffles wasn't inside, and locked the cat-flaps shut.

Then she looked in her house for Gigi. That didn't take long. The characterless, but now scar-faced, white Persian was, as ever, asleep on her mistress's bed. Seraphina firmly locked the bedroom door and the cat-flap set into it. The little fanlight window was still open, but Gigi would never overcome her lethargy sufficiently to leap up and climb through a fanlight.

Seraphina went down to the kitchen and prepared a tooth-some plate of turkey breast, larded with a few peeled prawns. Then she sat down by the cat-flap, and waited.

In one hand she held the vodka bottle. In the other, the means that would finally bring about Mr Whiffles' quietus.

After lengthy consideration of more exotic options, Sera-phina had homed in on the traditional. From time immem-orial, it had been the preferred way of removing unwanted kittens, and she saw no reason why it shouldn't also be suit-able for an ageing tabby like Mr Whiffles.

She must've dozed off. It was dark in the kitchen when she heard the clatter of the outer cat-flap.

But Seraphina was instantly alert, and she knew exactly what she had to do.

It seemed an age while her quarry lingered in the little passage from the garden. But finally a tentative paw was poked through the cat-flap into the kitchen.

Seraphina Fellowes held her breath. She wasn't going to put her carefully devised plan at risk by a moment of impetu-ousness.

She waited as the metal flap slowly creaked open. And she waited until the entire cat outline, tail and all, was inside the room, before she pounced.

The furry body kicked and twisted, but the contest was brief. In seconds, the cat had joined the three bricks inside, and Seraphina had tied the string firmly round the sack's neck.

She didn't pause for a second. She allowed no space for even the finest needle of conscience to insert itself. Seraphina Fellowes just rushed out into the garden, and hurled the miaowing sack right into the middle of the fishpond.

It made a very satisfying splash. A few bubbles, then silence.

The next morning, Seraphina woke with a glow of well-being. For the first time in weeks, her immediate instinct was not to reach for the vodka bottle. Instead, she snuggled luxuriously under her duvet, feeling the comforting weight of Gigi across her shins, and planned the day ahead.

She would go up to London, for the first time in months. The morning she would devote to having her hair done. Then she'd visit a few of her favourite stores and buy some morale-boostingly expensive clothes. She wouldn't have a drink all day, but come back late afternoon and at five o'clock, which she'd often found to be one of her most creative times, she'd start writing the first chapter of *Gigi and the Murdered Milkman*. Yes, it'd be a good day.

Seraphina Fellowes stretched languidly, then sat up and looked down at the end of the bed.

There, licking unhurriedly at his patchy fur, his insolent green eyes locked on hers, sat Mr Whiffles.

9. Cat's Cradle

After that, Seraphina Fellowes really did go to pieces. She forgot to change her clothes, falling asleep and waking in the same garments, in a vodka-hazed world where time became elastic and meaningless. Her hair hung, lank and unwashed, now more white than black.

And the thought that drove all others from her unhinged brain was the imperative destruction of Mr Whiffles.

Now that Gigi wasn't around – yes, a sad, white, bedraggled lump had indeed been pulled out of the sack in the fishpond – there was no longer any limitation on the means by which that destruction could be achieved. There was no longer any risk of catching the wrong victim by mistake.

Mr Whiffles, apparently aware of the murderous campaign against him, went into hiding. Seraphina cut off his obvious escape route by telling George the cat had died, and organizing a carpenter to board over the cat-flaps into the bungalow. George was very upset by the news, but Seraphina, as ever, didn't give a damn about her husband's feelings.

All through her own house, meanwhile, she established an elaborate network of booby traps. 'Network' was the operative word. Seraphina set up a series of wire snares around every one of the many cat-flaps. She turned the floors into a minefield of wire nooses, which, when tightened, would release counterweights on pulleys to yank their catch up to the ceiling. Designer-decorated walls were gouged out to accommodate hooks and rings, gleaming woodwork peppered with screws and cleats. The increasingly demented woman lived in a cat's cradle of tangled and intersecting wires. She ceased to eat, and lived on vodka alone.

And she waited. One day, she knew, Mr Whiffles would come back into the deathtrap that had been her home.

And one day – or rather one evening – he did.

The end was very quick. Mr Whiffles managed to negotiate the snares on the two cat-flaps into the house. He skipped nimbly over the waiting booby traps on the kitchen floor. But, entering the hall, he landed right in the middle of a noose, which, as he jumped away, tightened inexorably around one of his rear legs. He tried to pull himself free, but the wire only cut more deeply into his flesh. He let out a yowl of dismay.

At that moment, Seraphina, who had been waiting on the landing, snapped the light on, and shouted an exultant 'Gotcha!' Mr Whiffles, frozen by the shock of the sudden apparition, looked up at her.

Had Seraphina Fellowes by then been capable of pity, she might have noticed how thin and neglected the cat looked. But her mind no longer had room in it for such thoughts – no room in fact for any thoughts other than felicidal ones. She reached across in triumph to free the jammed counterweight which would send her captive slamming fatally up against the ceiling.

But as she moved, she stumbled, caught her foot in a stretched low-level wire, and tumbled headfirst down the staircase.

Seraphina Fellowes broke her neck and died instantly.

Mr Whiffles, jumping out of the way of the descending body, had moved closer to the anchor of the noose around his leg. Its tension relaxed, the springy wire loosened, and he was able to step neatly out of the metal loop.

And he started on his next set of nine lives.

10. *The Cat Who Got the Cream*

George Fellowes was initially very shocked by his wife's death. But when the shock receded, he had to confess to himself that he didn't really mind that much. And that her absence did bring with it certain positive advantages.

For a start, he no longer had the feeling of permanent brooding disapproval from the house at the other side of the garden. He also inherited her state-of-the-art computer. At first he was a bit sniffy about this, but as he started to play with it, he quickly became converted to its many conveniences.

Then there was the money. In the press coverage of Seraphina Fellowes' death, her recent doomed attempt to start a new series of cat mysteries had been quickly forgotten. But interest in Mr Whiffles grew and grew. All the titles were reissued in paperback, and the idea of a Hollywood movie using computer animation, which had been around for ages, suddenly got hot again. The agents of various megastars contacted the production company, discreetly offering their client's services for the year's plum job – voicing Mr Whiffles.

So, like a tidal wave, the money started to roll in. And, because his wife had never divorced him, George Fellowes got the lot.

More important than all of this, Seraphina's death freed her Catholic husband to remarry. And there was someone George had had in mind for years for just such an eventuality.

The evening of Seraphina's funeral, George was sprawled across his desk, asleep in front of the ever-moving screensaver on his late wife's computer, so he didn't hear the rattle of the reopened cat-flap. He wasn't aware of Mr Whiffles' entrance, even when the old cat landed quietly on his desk top, but a nuzzling furry nose in his ear soon woke him.

'How're you, old boy?' asked George, reaching up with his left hand to scratch Mr Whiffles in a favourite place, just behind the ear. At the same time, George's right hand reached out instinctively to the nearly full litre of vodka that stood on the edge of his desk.

Mr Whiffles, however, had other ideas. Speeding across the surface, he deliberately knocked the bottle over. It lay sideways at the edge of the desk, its contents glugging steadily away into the waste-paper basket.

George Fellowes looked at his cat in amazement, as Mr Whiffles moved across to the computer. One front paw was placed firmly on the mouse. (That bit was easy; for centuries cats have been instinctively placing their front paws on mice.) But, as the screensaver gave way to a white screen ready for writing, Mr Whiffles did something else, something much more remarkable.

He placed his other front paw on the keyboard. Not just anywhere on the keyboard, but on one specific key. The 'M'.

Obedient to the computer's programming, two words appeared on the screen: 'Mr Whiffles'.

George Fellowes felt the challenge in the old green eyes that were turned to look at him. For a moment he was undecided. Then, out loud, he said, 'What the hell? I'm certainly not getting anywhere with my so-called "literary" novels.'

And his fingers reached forward to the keyboard to complete the title: *Mr Whiffles and the Murdered Mystery Writer.*

A GOOD THING

Generally speaking, it has to be said I'm quite good with money. I mean, I think about it; I don't just rush out and do daft things; I'm careful about whose advice I listen to. I can always spot a good thing.

Obviously, having been born to it helps. I mean, I have got this kind of genetic aptitude. You know, some ancestor of mine back in the seventeenth century or whenever caught on to the idea that there was money to be made in this new slave-trade business, and he went for it. Then subsequent generations chose their moment to go into coffee, or rubber, or railways, or armaments, or whatever it happened to be and, generally speaking, they got it right. Money breeds money, as the saying goes, though my view is more that breeding breeds money.

And it has to be said, we Foulkeses have got the breeding. Obviously we didn't have it when we started, but then who did? Mind you, once one of my distant ancestors had saved up enough to buy a peerage from James I of England – and VI of Scotland, don't let us forget – well, we were up and away.

And haven't really looked back since. Entrepreneurial we've always been – that's the word – entrepreneurial. We haven't just let our money sit and vegetate – good heavens, no – we've been out there watching it work for us. I mean,

214

I've got a lot of chums who caught nasty colds over the Lloyds insurance debacle, and though I feel sorry as hell for the poor buggers – and particularly for their wives – I have to say they had it coming to them.

I'd never get involved in something like that – just salting the money away and sitting quietly at home, waiting for the divvies to come in. No, I invest in things I can see. And let me tell you, I'm pretty damned sharp about recognizing the kind of guy who's going to point me in the direction of the right sort of investments. I'm an extremely good judge of character. I know a good thing when I see it.

Which is why I was so delighted when I first met Roland Puissant.

It was in my club, actually. Blake's. The Foulkeses have been members there virtually since the place started, back in the – what? – 1830s, some time round then. Roland himself isn't a member – came as the guest of a friend. He told me frankly when we met at the bar that Blake's wasn't really his scene. Didn't like the idea of being anywhere where he had to wear a suit and tie. Wasn't that he hadn't *got* suits and ties – he was wearing a very nice pinstriped number and the old Harrovian colours that day, actually – but he didn't like being *forced* to conform by club regulations. Said he thought it was an infringement of the rights of the individual.

And I respected him for that. Respected him for coming out with his opinion right there, at the bar in Blake's, surrounded by all those crusty old members. As I discovered later, there's never any pretence about Roland. If he thinks something, he says it. Would rather run the risk of offending someone than compromising his opinions and values.

Good thing, so far as I'm concerned. There are so many bullshitters around these days, who'll contort themselves into knots agreeing with everything you say to them, that a direct approach like Roland's is very refreshing.

Anyway, we got talking at the bar. His friend had nipped off to make a phone call – though Roland secretly suspected that the phone call would quickly lead to a nearby hotel where the friend had set up an assignation with a rather dishy little thing from a public relations company. Roland had a nasty feeling that he was being used simply as an alibi for the chap's wife.

Well, the bloke I was meant to be meeting hadn't shown, either. Can't say I was too disappointed. Some fellow I'd apparently known from Eton, though the name didn't ring a bell. Phoned up saying he'd been out of the country for some years and was dead keen to meet up with old chums like Nicky Foulkes. This already made me a bit leery; so many times that sort of introduction leads to someone trying to sell you insurance. Even been known for people in that world to lie about having been at school with you. Buy a tie and invent some rigmarole about having been three years below you in a different house and always looking up to you, soften you up a bit, then wham, in with the 'I don't know if you've ever stopped to consider what your family would stand to receive if – and heaven forbid – but *if* something were to happen to you . . .'

So, basically, I was standing at the bar wondering why the hell I'd agreed to meet this bloke, and getting chirpier with every passing minute that he didn't show up. I was beginning to feel confident that the danger had passed, reconciling myself quite cheerfully to an evening's drinking, assuming I could find someone congenial to drink with . . . when – lo and behold – Roland Puissant turned up.

Answer to a maiden's prayer, eh? The other members I was surrounded with in the bar were of the crotchety nothing's-been-the-same-since-we-lost-the-Empire persuasion, so it was a relief simply to see someone round my own age, apart from anything else.

And, once we got talking, it pretty soon became clear that Roland hadn't just got age going for him. Oh no, he was very definitely an all-round good bloke.

Could put back the sauce too. I'm no mean performer in the tincture stakes, but he was more than matching me glass for glass. We were on the malt. Lagavulin from Islay's my favourite. Turned out Roland loved the stuff too. Clearly a man of taste.

Well, after an hour or so on the blessed nectar, I suggested eating something by way of blotting paper. And since the food at Blake's is indistinguishable from blotting paper, I said we should eat in the club dining room. Roland said fine, so long as it was his treat – he insisted on that. I said, your treat next time, old lad. Non-members aren't allowed to pay at Blake's.

At first he wasn't keen on being in my debt, but he came round graciously enough. So we got stuck into the club claret. Long experience has taught me that the only way to deal with Blake's food is to anaesthetize the old tastebuds with alcohol. Always works for me – I can never remember what I've ordered and don't notice what it is while I'm eating the stuff. Perfect.

We were into the second bottle before we got talking about money. Roland just let something slip by mistake. He tried to cover it up, but I'm pretty Lagavulin- and claret-resistant, so I leapt on it straight away.

All he actually said was '. . . and you know that wonderful feeling of confidence when you're on to an absolute copper-bottomed cert of a good thing.'

He could have been talking in purely general terms, but the way he hastily moved the conversation on told me he was dealing with specifics. I'm pretty sharp about that kind of stuff. Something of an amateur psychologist, actually. Well, you need to be in the kind of circles I move in. Stuffed full of shysters trying to put one over on you – particularly if you happen to have a bit of the old inherited.

So I pounced. '"Good thing," Roland?' I said. 'And what particular "good thing" are you talking about at the moment?'

'Oh, nothing.'

But I stuck at it. 'Horse?'

'No, not a horse in this instance.'

I was rather pleased with myself: my line of questioning had made him admit that he was talking about something specific rather than general.

'Investment opportunity?' I pressed on.

He was embarrassed that I'd seen through him so quickly, but nodded.

'Tell me more,' I said. 'Always like to hear the details of any investment opportunity. We Foulkeses have traditionally had a nose for this kind of thing.'

Still Roland prevaricated. 'Oh, I don't think it'd interest you.'

'Let me be the judge of that. Go on, tell me – unless of course you've got the whole thing sewn up yourself and don't want to let anyone else in on it.'

'No, for heaven's sake,' he protested. 'I wouldn't do that. It's just I do hate giving tips to friends. It's like selling them a car – hellish embarrassing if the thing breaks down.'

'Listen,' I said. 'I'm a grown-up. I'm quite capable of making my own decisions. I don't get taken in by anything iffy. Don't forget, my surname's Foulkes, and we Foulkeses have had quite a reputation over the years for making some pretty damned good business decisions. Come on, Roland, you bloody well tell me what this is all about!'

That little barrage broke down his resistance. He sighed, shrugged, and told me what it was all about.

Basically, like most financial projects, it was buying and selling. Buying cheap and selling expensive – the principle on which the British Empire was built. And the principle by which the Foulkeses had done so well out of the British Empire.

Like the slave trade on which the family fortune had been built, Roland's investment scheme was not illegal. Some people might perhaps go a bit wobbly about its ethics, but it was undoubtedly within the law. Sounded just the sort of 'good thing' a member of the Foulkes family should get involved in.

In fact the project's parallels with the slave trade didn't stop at its legality. The commodities being bought and sold were domestic servants. Men and women from the Caribbean were offered a complete service – flight to London, job found, work permit sorted out. The investment required was to pay for these services. The profit came from the fee the clients paid to the agency which handled their cases.

When Roland mentioned this, I shrewdly asked whether the word 'fee' was appropriate. Wasn't 'bribe' nearer the mark? He just gave me a charming grin and said we didn't want to get bogged down in semantics.

But wasn't it hellish difficult to arrange work permits for foreigners? was my next question. Roland agreed it was. 'This is the beauty of the scheme, though,' he went on. 'My contact has an "in" with the Home Office.'

It was the first time he'd mentioned a 'contact'. Felicia Rushworth, she was called. She had had the idea for the business and needed capital. Roland Puissant had backed her to the tune of fifty grand six months before. The return on his stake had quadrupled since then. People from the Caribbean definitely did want to get jobs in England.

I didn't ask how much the 'fee' they paid for this privilege was. Nor did I ask the rates they were paid once they started working in London. When you're investing in something, there are some details you just don't need to know about.

By the end of the evening – rather late, as it happened, because we'd moved on to a little drinking club I know round the back of Bond Street – Roland had agreed that the next week he'd introduce me to Felicia Rushworth.

It has to be said – she was bloody stunning. I mean, I've known a lot of girls, but Felicia Rushworth definitely took the Best of Show rosette. Generally speaking, I keep girls at arm's length. Of course I go around with a good few – everyone needs sex – but I don't let them get close. Always have to be on the lookout if you've come into a bit – lots of voracious females out there with their beady eyes fixed solely on the old inherited. So I've never even got near marriage. Never wanted to. Mind you, the sight of a creation like Felicia Rushworth could go a long way towards making a chap change his mind about that kind of thing.

She had this long blonde hair that looked natural. I don't know much about that stuff, but if it wasn't natural it was damned cleverly done. Come to that, if it *was* natural, it was damned cleverly done.

Shrewd blue eyes. Intelligent. Normally, I don't look for that in a girl, but then what I'm looking for in most of them isn't a business partnership. Anyway, in Felicia's case, the intelligence in the eyes wasn't so overpowering they stopped being pretty.

And beautifully tanned skin. I suppose that's one of the perks of doing business with the Caribbean. Slender brown arms and endless brown legs, of whose unseen presence beneath the table I was aware right through that lunch at Nico at Ninety.

I'd suggested the venue. One of my regular bread-and-watering holes. Sort of place that can impress clients when they need impressing. Mind you, Felicia Rushworth looked cool enough to take anything in her stride.

Roland was kind of formal with her. Don't know why I thought that odd. I'd probably assumed he knew her better than he did. After all, she was just someone he was doing business with. He was done up to the nines again, old Harrovian tie neatly in place. I think he was probably trying to impress her.

Felicia had a no-nonsense approach to the reason for our meeting. 'Let's get the serious bit out of the way first,' she said firmly. 'Then we can enjoy the rest of our lunch.'

And she spelled it all out to me. The more she said, the better I felt about the whole picture. That old Foulkes nose for a 'good thing' was twitching like a ruddy dowsing rod. Felicia's long-term plan was to run the business completely on her own with her own savings, but in the short term she needed start-up capital. The experimental six months with Roland's fifty grand had worked so well that now she wanted to expand the operation – set up offices in London and Kingston, Jamaica, take on staff, put the whole affair on a more permanent footing.

'One thing I should ask at this point . . .' I said, 'is about the legality of what's going on. Roland's told me it's kosher, and obviously I believe him, but in my experience you don't get the kind of profits we're talking about here without the odd rule being ever so slightly bent.'

Felicia turned the full beam of those shrewd blue eyes on me. 'You're not stupid, are you, Mr Foulkes?'

I gave her a lazy grin back. 'No. And please call me Nicky. Everybody does.'

'All right, Nicky. Well, you've probably worked out that the area where the rules are being bent a little is round the work permits.' I nodded, confirming her assumption that I was way ahead of her. 'And yes, people involved in that area of the business are running risks. They're being well paid to run risks, but I suppose in a worst-case scenario they might get found out. In that eventuality, no blame could possibly be attached to the investors in the company ... although, of course, trouble of that sort could cut down the kind of returns they'd get.' Once again she fixed those unnerving blue eyes on mine. 'But I'm looking for the kind of investor who likes risks.'

'I like risks.' Then I added, 'In all areas of my life.'

She didn't give me anything so rude as a wink, but I could see she'd salted the message away. There was now a kind of private bond between us, something that excluded Roland.

I moved briskly on. 'So what size of investment are you looking for at the moment?'

'Over the next year I need a quarter of a million,' she replied coolly. 'Immediately a hundred thousand. Roland's supplying most of that, so I'm just looking for top-up funds at the moment.'

'Top-up to the tune of how much?'

'Ten grand.'

'What, Roland, you're already committed for the ninety?'

He nodded. 'Seeing the return I got on fifty, can you blame me?'

'No.' I was silent for a moment. 'Pity I came in so late on the deal, isn't it?'

'What do you mean?'

'Well, ten grand's not much of a stake for a real *risk-taker*, is it?' As I said the word, I fixed Felicia with my eye. She gave an almost imperceptible acknowledgement of the secret between us.

'There'll be more opportunities,' she said soothingly. 'Better for you to start small. See how it goes. I mean, the next six months may not go as well as the first. I don't want you to be out of pocket.'

'Not much danger of that, is there?'

She shook her head firmly and, with a little smile, said, 'No.'

'So are you going in for the ten grand, Nicky?' asked Roland.

'You try and stop me.' I took a sip of wine. 'You sure I can't go in for more, Felicia?'

'Absolutely positive.'

'But look, if you're after a quarter of a million over the next year, surely I could—'

The blue eyes turned to steel. 'Mr Foulkes, I am offering you a stake of ten thousand pounds in my business. That is the offer. Ten grand – no more. Take it or leave it.'

Felicia Rushworth was quite daunting in that mode. I left it there for the rest of the lunch. But I was a bit miffed. She'd opened up this glowing prospect to me, and then severely limited my access to it. Ten grand's nothing to an entrepreneur like me. I knew this was a really good thing, and I wanted to be into it a lot deeper than that.

Still, we didn't talk about it further, just enjoyed Nico Ladenis's cooking. Bloody good. Makes you realize just how bad the garbage is you get dished up at places like Blake's. We got through a couple of rather decent bottles of Pouilly Fumé too.

Which inevitably led to Roland and me needing an excursion to the Gents. It was there that I moved on to the next stage of the plan I'd been forming during the lunch.

'Any chance of my getting in for more, do you reckon?' I asked casually.

'Mm?' Roland was preoccupied with his zip.

'More than ten grand ... in Felicia's little scheme ... I mean, ten grand's nothing ... I want to be a serious player.'

Roland grimaced. 'Hm ... Felicia's a strong-willed lady. She says she'll let you in for ten grand, that's what she means.

Probably just protecting herself. I mean, she doesn't know much about you – only what I've told her. I know you're the genuine article, but you can't blame her for being cautious. There're a lot of villains about, you know.'

'You don't need to tell me that. Do you think it's worth my having another go – asking Felicia straight out if I can invest more?'

He jutted out a dubious lower lip. 'Like I say, when she's decided something . . .' He turned thoughtfully to wash his hands in the basin. 'Tell you what,' he said after a moment, '. . . I could cut you in on a bit of mine.'

'How do you mean?'

'Well, so long as I give Felicia the ninety grand, she's not going to know where it comes from. If you give me another ten, your stake goes up to twenty, doesn't it?'

'Yes, but that's cutting down your profits, isn't it?'

Roland Puissant shrugged. 'I did all right first time round. Got a few other good things I could divert the spare into.'

'What are they?'

'Hm?' He shook the water off his hands and reached for a towel.

'The other good things?'

He grinned at me and shook his head. 'Have to keep some secrets, you know, Nicky.'

'OK. Point taken.' I straightened my old Etonian tie in the mirror. 'You wouldn't consider letting me in for more than another ten . . . ?'

We haggled a bit, but basically I got what I was after. I'd pay ten grand to Felicia and forty to Roland. She'd get the promised ninety from him, and not know that I'd contributed nearly half of it. Then Roland would account the profits back to me.

I felt pretty pleased with my day's work. Though I say it myself, I'm a bloody good negotiator. And I had achieved a fifty-grand stake in one of the most lucrative little projects I'd ever heard of: lunch for three at Nico at Ninety was a small price to pay.

Struck me as I was walking down Park Lane from the restaurant that in fact I was almost going into the family business. The Foulkes fortune had been built up by ferrying Africans across the Atlantic. What I was now involved in was ferrying them back the other way. Rather neat, I thought.

'I just feel so dreadful about this.'

Roland Puissant looked pretty dreadful too. We were at dell'Ugo, noisy as ever but smashing nosh. 'Tell me about it,' I said.

'I'm almost embarrassed to.'

'Come on, you don't have to be embarrassed with me. I'm unembarrassable. Anyway, I'm a mate, aren't I? Not to mention a business partner. You, me and Felicia, eh?'

'That's it. Felicia,' he said glumly.

'Come on, me old kipper. Pour it all out.'

And he did. It was bad.

Basically we'd been had. Felicia Rushworth had calmly taken our money and gone off to Jamaica with it. Whether there actually was any employment agency business seemed doubtful. Whether there was some useful contact at the Home Office who could fix work permits for Caribbean visitors seemed even more doubtful. Roland and I had fallen for the oldest ploy in the book – a pretty girl with a convincing line of patter.

'And I just feel so guilty towards you,' Roland concluded. 'I should never have mentioned the project to you.'

'Oh, now come on. I have to take my share of the blame too. You never volunteered anything. You never wanted to talk about it. Every detail I got out of you was like drawing a tooth.'

'Yes, but I shouldn't have got you involved. Or I should have seen to it that your stake stayed at ten grand.'

'Well, you didn't. You were bloody generous to me about that, Roland. At the time you were taking a considerable potential loss just to give me a chance.'

'A chance I bet you wish now you hadn't taken.'

'Look, it's done. I did it. Maybe I was bloody stupid but I did it. If you take risks, some of them are going to pay off and some aren't. Anyway we're in the same boat – both of us fifty grand to the bad . . .' My words trailed off at the sight of his face. 'You mean more than fifty . . . ?'

Roland Puissant nodded wretchedly. 'Practically cleaned me out, I'm afraid.'

'But I thought you said you'd got a lot of other good things going?'

'Yes, I did. Trouble is, all of those were recommended by Felicia. She generously took care of those investments too.'

'Oh. So she's walked off with the whole caboodle?'

'About one point two million in all,' he confessed.

I whistled. 'Bloody hell. That is a lot.'

'Yes. God, I'm stupid. I suppose . . . someone who looks like that . . . someone who's as intelligent as that . . . it just never occurs to you that they'd . . . I was putty in her hands. Is there anything more ridiculous than a man of my age playing the fool because of a pretty face? Some of us just never learn, eh?'

I didn't tell him how closely I identified with what he was saying. Instead, I moved the conversation on. 'Question is . . . what're we going to do about it?'

'Bloody well get revenge!' Roland spat the words out. I'd never seen him so angry.

'How?'

'I don't know.' He shook his head hopelessly. 'No idea. Mind you, if I was out in Jamaica, I could do something . . .'

'Like what?'

'I know people out there. People who could put pressure on Felicia. Reckon they could persuade her to return our money.'

'Are you talking about criminals?'

He shrugged. 'Often hard to say where legitimate business practice stops and criminality starts, wouldn't you say? But yes, this lot's means of persuasion are perhaps more direct than traditional negotiations.'

'Would she get hurt?' The words came out instinctively. Whatever Felicia might have done to us, the idea of injury to that fragile beauty was appalling.

'She's a shrewd cookie. I think she'd assess the options and come across with the goods before they started hurting her.'

'So you think we'd get the money back?'

'Oh yes. I mean, obviously we'd have to pay something for the . . . er, hired help . . . so we wouldn't get everything back . . . but we wouldn't be that much out of pocket.'

'Well, then, for God's sake, let's do it.'

Roland Puissant gave me a lacklustre look. 'Yeah, great. How? I told you, she's cleaned me out.'

'Couldn't I go to Jamaica and organize it?'

'Wish you could.' He shook his head slowly. 'Unfortunately, the people whose help we need are a bit wary of strangers. They know me, they've dealt with me before. But the last unfamiliar bloke who tried to make contact with them . . . ended up with his throat cut.'

'Ah.'

'No, I'm sorry. It'd have to be me or no one. But . . .' He spread his hands despairingly wide. '. . . I don't currently have the means to fly to Jamaica – let alone bribe the local villains. At the moment I'd be pushed to raise the bus fare to Piccadilly Circus.'

'Well, look, let me sub you, Roland.'

'Now don't be ridiculous, Nicky. You're already down fifty grand. I absolutely refuse to let you lose any more.'

'Look, it's an investment for me. It's my only chance of getting my fifty grand back.'

He still looked dubious. 'I don't like the idea of you . . .'

'Roland', I said, 'I insist.'

It was nearly a month later when Roland next rang me. He was calling from Heathrow. 'I wanted to get through to you as soon as possible. I've had one hell of a time over in Jamaica, I'm afraid.'

'Any success?'

'Not immediately, no. I was just beginning to get somewhere, but then the money ran out and—'

'You got through the whole ten grand I subbed you?'

'Yes. As I said, the kind of help I was enlisting doesn't come cheap.'

'But why didn't they come up with the goods? I thought you said they'd just put the frighteners on Felicia and she'd stump up the cash.'

'That's how it should have worked, yes. But she was a step ahead of us.'

'In what way?'

'She'd hired some muscle of her own. I'm afraid what I got into was like full-scale gang warfare. Bloody nasty at times, let me tell you. This time last week I didn't reckon I'd ever see Heathrow again.'

'Really? What, you mean your life was at—'

'You don't want to hear all this, Nicky. It's not very interesting. Main point is, I've let you down. I said I'd go over there and get your money back and I haven't. And I've spent your extra ten grand. In fact, you're now sixty grand down, thanks to me.'

'Listen, Roland, I walked into it quite knowingly. If you

want to blame anyone, blame me. Blame my judgement.'

'That's very sporting of you to put it like that, but I can't buy it, I'm afraid. You're out of pocket and it's my fault. But don't worry, I'll see you get your money back.'

'How? You've lost one point two million.'

'I know, but there's stuff I can do. There's something I'm trying to set up right now, actually. And if that doesn't work out, I'll take another mortgage on the house. Anything to stop this awful guilt. I can't stand going round with the permanent feeling that I've let an old chum down.'

'Roland, you're getting things out of proportion. I won't hear of you mortgaging your house just for my sake. We can sort this thing out. Best thing you can do is get a good night's sleep and we'll meet up in the morning. See where we stand then, eh?'

'Well, if you . . .'

'I insist.'

'Where're we going to meet?'

'Roland, you don't by any chance play Real Tennis, do you?'

Don't know if you know the Harbour Club. Chelsea, right on the river. Converted old power station, actually, but they've done it bloody well. Very high spec. Pricey, of course, but then you have to pay for class. And the clientele is, it has to be said, pretty damn classy.

Anyway, I try to play Real Tennis down there at least once a week. Enjoy the game, and it stops the body seizing up totally. Good way of sweating out a hangover too, so I tend to go for a morning court.

I thought it'd be just the thing to sort out old Roland. He'd sounded frankly a bit stressed on the phone, but I reckoned a quick canter round the court might be just the thing to sort him out. I was glad to hear he knew the game – not many people do – but surprised when he said he'd played it for the school. I didn't know Harrow had a Real Tennis court. Still, Roland was at the place and I wasn't, so I guess he knew what he was talking about.

I said we should play the game first, to kind of flush out the old system, and then talk over a drink. Roland wasn't so keen on this – his guilt hadn't gone away and he wanted to get straight down to the schemes he had for replacing my money – but I insisted and won the day. I can be quite forceful when I need to be.

I must say his game was pretty rusty. He said he hadn't played since school but in the interim he seemed to have forgotten most of the rules. I mean, granted they are pretty complicated – if you don't know them, I haven't got time to explain all about penthouses and galleries and tambours and grilles and things now – but I thought for anyone who had played a bit, they'd come back pretty quickly. Not to poor old Roland Puissant, though. Acted like he'd never been on a Real Tennis court in his life.

Still, I suppose he was preoccupied with money worries. Though, bless his heart, he seemed to be much more concerned about my sixty grand than his own one point two million. I think he was just an old-fashioned gentleman who hated the idea of being in debt to anyone – particularly a friend of long standing. The idea really gnawed away at him.

The game seemed to come back to him a bit more by the end of the booking and, when our time was up, we'd got into quite a decent knock-up. Enough to work up a good sweat, anyway, and dictate that we had showers before we got stuck into the sauce.

It was when Roland was stripped off that I noticed how tanned he was. Except for the dead white strip where his swimming shorts had been, he was a deep, even brown all over.

'I say,' I joked as he moved into the shower, 'you been spending all my money lying about sunbathing, have you, Roland?'

He turned on me a look of surprising intensity. 'Damn, I didn't want you to see that,' he hissed.

'Why? My suggestion true then, is it?' I still maintained the joshing tone, but for the first time a little trickle of suspicion seeped into my mind.

'No, of course not,' Roland replied impatiently. 'This happened when I got captured.'

'You got captured? You didn't tell me.'

'No, well, I . . . No point in your knowing, really – nothing you could do about it now. And I . . . well, I'd rather not think about it.' He looked genuinely upset now. I'd stirred up some deeply unpleasant memories.

'What did they do to you, Roland?' I asked gently.

'Oh, they . . . Well, they stripped me off down to my boxer shorts and left me strapped out in the sun for three days.'

'Good God.'

He gave me a brave, wry grin. 'One way to get a suntan, eh? Though there are more comfortable ones.'

'But if you were strapped down . . .' I began logically '. . . wouldn't you just be tanned on your front *or* your back? . . . Unless of course your captors came and turned you over every few hours.' I chuckled.

Roland's eyes glowed painfully with the memory as he hissed, 'Yes, they did. That's exactly what they did. So that I'd have to have the pressure of my body bearing down on my sunburnt skin.'

'Good heavens! And those scratches on your back – were they part of the torture too?'

'Scratches?'

I pointed to a few scrapes that looked as if they might have been made by clutching fingernails.

'Oh yes,' said Roland. 'Yes, that was when they . . .' He coloured and shook his head. 'I'm sorry, I'd really rather not talk about it.'

'I fully understand, old man.' I patted him on the shoulder. 'Still, you escaped with your life.'

'Yes.' He gritted his teeth. 'Touch and go on a few occasions, but I escaped with my life . . .' He sighed mournfully. 'Though sadly not with your money.'

'Don't worry. We'll have another go. We'll get our revenge on Felicia Rushworth one way or the other.'

'Hope so,' said Roland ruefully as he ducked in under the spray of his shower.

At that moment his mobile phone rang. It was in the clothes locker he had just opened. 'Shall I get it?' I asked.

'Well, perhaps I should—'

I pressed the button to establish contact. The caller spoke immediately. It was a voice I recognized.

I held the receiver across to Roland, who had emerged from the shower rubbing his eyes with a towel. 'Felicia Rushworth,' I said.

He looked shocked as he took the phone. He held his hand over the receiver. 'Probably better if I handle this privately,' he said, and moved swiftly from the changing room area to the corridor outside.

I sat down on the wooden bench, deep in thought. The words Felicia Rushworth spoke before she realized the wrong person had answered had been: 'Roland, is the idiot still buying the story?'

Now, I'm a pretty shrewd guy, and I smelled a rat. For a start, Felicia's tone of voice had sounded intimate, like she and Roland were on the same side rather than ferocious adversaries. Also, if one was looking round for someone to cast in the role of the 'idiot' who was hopefully 'buying the story' . . . well, there weren't that many candidates.

Roland's wallet was in the back pocket of his trousers, hanging in the locker. Normally I wouldn't pry into a chap's private possessions, but, if the ugly scenario slowly taking shape in my brain was true, then these weren't normal circumstances.

Nothing in the wallet had the name 'Roland Puissant' on it. All the credit cards were imprinted with 'R. J. D. Rushworth.' In the jacket pocket I found a book of matches from the Sunshine Strand Luxury Hotel, Montego Bay, Jamaica.

I heard the door to the changing room clatter closed and looked up. 'Roland' was holding the phone, and had a towel wrapped round his waist.

'God, she's got a nerve, that woman – bloody ringing me up to taunt me about what she's done.'

'Oh yes?'

He must've caught something in my tone, because he looked at me sharply. 'What's up, old man?'

'The game, I would say, "Roland Puissant."'

He looked genuinely puzzled. 'Look, I'm sorry. I told you I haven't played for a while, bit rusty on the old—'

'Not that game. You know exactly what I mean.'

'Do I?'

I hadn't moved from the bench. I'd curbed my anger, not even raised my voice while I assessed how I was going to play the scene.

I still didn't raise my voice as I said, 'I've just looked in your wallet. All your credit cards are in the name of "R. J. D. Rushworth."'

'Yes,' he replied in a matter-of-fact way. 'I only got back last night. I haven't got round to changing them yet.'

'What do you mean? Aren't you R. J. D. Rushworth?'

He looked at me incredulously. 'Of course I'm not, Nicky. For God's sake – you know I'm Roland Puissant, don't you? But you surely never thought I was going to travel to Jamaica

233

under my own name, did you? I didn't want to advertise to Felicia what I was up to.'

For a second I was almost convinced, until another discordant detail struck me. 'But why, of all the names in the world, did you choose her name – "Rushworth"?'

'Well, I had to get to see her, didn't I? Felicia's got her security pretty well sorted out. I had to pretend to be her husband, so that they'd let me through *to* her.'

'But the minute she saw you, your cover'd be blown.'

'That was a risk I was prepared to take.' He winced. 'An ill-advised one, as it turned out.'

'What do you mean?'

'I'd been hoping that I'd get to see her on her own, but a couple of her heavies took me in. Well, I had no chance then, had I?'

'That's when the torturing started?'

He nodded, then shook his head. 'I'd rather not talk about it, if you don't mind.'

My heart went out to him. Poor bugger, not only had he lost all his money and been tortured by Caribbean thugs, now one of his best friends was suspecting him of . . .

Just a minute. Just a minute, I said to myself, hold your horses there, old man. The way he'd accounted for the credit cards was maybe feasible, but it didn't explain the words with which Felicia had opened her telephone call.

'When I answered your phone,' I began coolly, 'Felicia, presumably thinking she'd got through to you, said: "Roland, is the idiot still buying the story?" . . .'

'Yes,' he agreed, totally unfazed.

'Well, would you like to explain to me what she meant by that, because I'm not much enjoying the only explanation my mind's offering.'

Roland looked torn. At last he sighed and said, 'Well, all right. I suppose I'll have to tell you. I wanted to keep it a secret, but . . .' He sighed again. 'Nicky, you've heard of Jeffrey Archer?'

'Hm? Yes, of course I have, but what the hell's he got to do with what we're talking about?'

'Well, you may know that he lost a lot of money in an investment that went wrong . . .'

'Yes. I've heard the story.'

'. . . and then he fixed the situation by writing his way out of it.'

'Mm.'

'He sold books and ideas for books and made another huge fortune from that.'

'Yes, I still don't see—'

'That's what I've been trying to do, Nicky. I've felt so absolutely lousy about the way you've lost money over this – and all because of me – that I've been trying to sell a book idea so that I can pay you back.'

'Really?'

'Yes. I've worked out a synopsis for this story about a conman and – touch wood – it's looking good. There's a publisher who's expressing interest – strong interest. Trouble is, I was stupid enough to mention this to Felicia when I was in Jamaica, and now of course she'll never let me hear the end of it. She's tickled to death that she's driven me to try and make money as a writer.'

'So what she said . . . ?'

'Exactly. She was talking about this publisher . . . for whom she doesn't have a lot of respect. That's why she said, "Roland, is the idiot still buying the story?"'

I couldn't think of anything to say.

'And the answer,' Roland went on, 'is – please God – yes. Because if the idiot *does* buy the story, then I have a chance of paying back at least some of the money that my foolish advice has cost one of my best mates – Nicky Foulkes.'

I felt very humbled, you know, by the way Roland was taking my troubles on himself in this way. And to think of the suspicions I'd been within an ace of voicing about him. Well, thank God some instinct stopped me from putting them into words.

Even a nature as generous and loyal as Roland Puissant's might have found that kind of accusation a bit hard to take. Sort of thing that could ruin a really good friendship.

Roland's back in the country again. Called me a couple of days ago. He's been having a dreadful time. Well, we'd both agreed after Felicia managed to escape him in Jamaica, he should have another go to try and retrieve our money. He went on again about mortgaging his house, but I said, don't be daft, we're in this together, and stumped up a bit of ante for his expenses.

Trouble was, when he got to Jamaica, he found Felicia'd moved on. To Acapulco. So he's had to spend the last month down there trying to find her and put the pressure on. Poor bugger, rather him than me, I must say. But one can't but admire his dedication. I'm lucky to have someone like him out there rooting away on my behalf.

Anyway, we've fixed to get together next week. Roland's a bit busy at the moment. But he's making time to meet up with me. Letting me take him out for dinner at Bibendum. Expensive, I know, but it'll be a small price to pay. Roland never stops, you know. Always grafting away on some new scheme or other. He's got a whole lot of new investment opportunities he's going to put my way. If I play my cards right, you know, I think I could be on to another good thing.